UPDATES FROM THE FANTASTIQUE...

enter the world of hidden forces psychologically, rather than materialistically. This aspect of occultism most applies to the contents of issue #32 of *Dark Discoveries*.

The writers in this issue have set out to transcend the boundaries of the natural and supernatural, the magical and mundane, visible and invisible, to explore what happens when somebody (fictional or historical) crosses those boundaries, or even manipulates them. The image of Alice phasing through the looking-glass is appropriate here. Whether it's the characters in this issue's fiction, or the famous authors who dabbled in the occult (which feature prominently in this issue's essays), the idea of the influence of a hidden, supernatural world is brought to the fore.

It is my distinct pleasure to bring readers of DD a brand new full-length interview I carried out with international bestselling author Graham Hancock, in which we discuss his fictional *War God* series as well as his new nonfiction book *Magicians of the Gods*, sequel to his 1995 blockbuster *Fingerprints of the Gods*; an excerpt from Hancock's *War God* novel is also included. Author and critic of esoteric and weird fiction Mark Valentine, also editor of *Wormwood: Writings about fantasy, supernatural and decadent literature*, gives us his unique, visionary tale; New York Times

bestselling author Rebecca Cantrell offers a chilling glimpse into the inner realms of pregnancy; Jonathan L. Howard and Ronald Malfi each offer their take on the relationship between books or texts and the occult, both arriving at different, yet equally terrifying conclusions; and finally, Damien Angelica Walters spins a haunting story of magic, heartbreak, and the feminine divine.

For our nonfiction, we have an interesting article by Donald Tyson chronicling the use of the occult in dark fiction throughout modern literature; myself and Mark Valentine complement Tyson's explorations with pieces on Arthur Machen and Charles Williams. K. H. Vaughan discusses the life and legacy of author C. M. Eddy, Jr., including an interview with a living relative of this largely obscured weird fictionist. Finally, the issue's theme is tackled by our usual stable of columnists, including a very good interview with game designer and professor Jeff Howard.

But enough of my prattle. In the pages that follow you'll find pathways that are not of this world, and harken I say, for I warn you to be careful—here be dragons…

—Aaron J. French
Editor-in-Chief

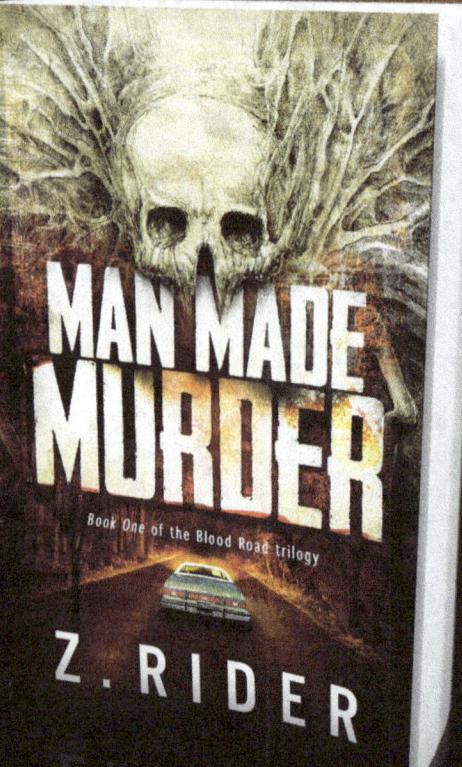

DARK DISCOVERIES

Summer 2015, Issue Number 32, www.DarkDiscoveries.com

Publisher
JournalStone Publishing, LLC

Editor-in-Chief and Art Director
Aaron J. French

Contributing Editor
K. H. Vaughan

Assistant Editors
Russ Thompson (Senior Submissions Editor)
Stuart Conover (Assistant Reviews Editor)

Layout and Design
Paul Fry

Contributors

Graham Hancock
Santha Faiia
Mark Valentine
Damien Angelica Walters
Rebecca Cantrell
Ronald Malfi
Jonathan L. Howard
Jim Dyer
Aaron J. French
K. H. Vaughan
Robert Morrish

Bari Wood
Yvonne Navarro
Richard Dansky
Jeff Howard
Michael R. Collings
Donald Tyson
Catherine Bader
Duncan Ralston
James Newman
Denise Daniel

Founding Publisher and Editor
James R. Beach

Special Thanks
Graham Hancock
Jim Dyer
Santha Faiia
Jeff Howard
Bari Wood

Contributing Artists/Photographers
Santha Faiia (Photographer)
Denise Daniel
Steve Santiago (pg 19 & 43)
Greg Chapman (pg 31, 57 & 69)
Luke Spooner (pg 46 & 80)

DARK DISCOVERIES
(ISSN 1548-6842) is published (Qtrly) by
JournalStone Publications
439 Gateway Dr., #83, Pacifica, CA 94044

Christopher C. Payne
JournalStone Publications
439 Gateway Dr., #83, Pacifica, CA 94044, U.S.A.
christophercpayne@journalstone.com.

Please make check or money order payable to:
JournalStone Publishing and send to the address above.
Credit/Debit cards via Paypal at:
christophercpayne@journalstone.com. Advertising
rates available. Discounts for bulk and standing retail
orders.

FICTION

War God: Nights of the Witch (an extract) by Graham Hancock   19
These Things, They Linger Still by Damien Angelica Walters   31
The Wine of the Serpent by Mark Valentine   43
Caulbearer by Rebecca Cantrell   57
Pembroke by Ronald Malfi   69
The Commission of The Philosophical Alembic by Jonathan L. Howard   80

FEATURES

Explorations in the Unknown: An Interview with Graham Hancock
by Aaron J. French   5
Weird Fictionist & Esotericist Arthur Machen by Mark Valentine   40
The Legacy of C. M. Eddy, Jr. by K. H. Vaughan   48
Magic and the Outré: A Discussion on C. M. Eddy, Jr. by K. H. Vaughan   52
Charles Williams and A.E. Waite: A Magical Relationship by Aaron J. French   66
Horror in a Hundred Stories   76

COLUMNS

Murmurs from the Dark: "Occultists and Occult Fiction" by Donald Tyson   25
Double X Chromosome: "The Occult Around Us" by Yvonne Navarro   37
"On Occultism in F. Paul Wilson's The Keep" by Michael R. Collings   63
"What the Hell Ever Happened to…Bari Wood" by Robert Morrish   77
"The Occult in Video Games: An Interview with Jeff Howard"
by Richard Dansky   88

REVIEWS

Hellnotes/Horror World Reviews   91
Film Reviews   101

EDITORIAL

Hello again, and welcome to the newest issue of *Dark Discoveries*. Our present theme is The Occult in Dark Fiction, in which we explore the use and effect of employing elements of occultism in dark fiction, both horror and dark fantasy. Occultism is a tricky word to define; literally, of course, it means "hidden," that is to say something kept out of sight. Most horror might be thought of as representative of hidden forces: ideas, emotions, evils. Monsters, ghosts, and so forth, in any well-crafted horror tale, keep largely to the outskirts of the narrative, only arriving on scene in the final conclusion, commonly in a confrontation between good and evil; or, just as well—and certainly this seems to be the case with much contemporary horror—the ending evokes a feeling of total hopelessness and despair, in which nothing is going to be the same ever, ever again (we have Lovecraft to thank for this); or—and, again, just as well—everyone in the story winds up dead, devoured by the universal hatred of an uncaring world.

But is this what we mean when we speak of The Occult in Dark Fiction? No, not exclusively. The above indeed represents one side of the picture, but another angle, the opposite side of the mirror, is what interests us in this issue more specifically—that is, magic, or the magical worldview.

The term "occult" in the theme of this issue refers to hidden phenomena, such as monsters and emotions and the like, but also the hidden forces which remain at play in our daily lives, and of which we are most commonly unaware. The magician, in the occult sense, is one who extends his knowledge about these hidden forces and learns to both evoke and manipulate them to bring about world events. We tend to think of events in life and history happening at random, or at best as the product of some cause and effect mechanism that is the universe as a machine, clunking and grinding along through vast, unknown regions of space. Not so with the occult, for we here refer to the concept of worldly occurrences being the *product* of hidden nonmaterial forces and even beings, whose very actions determine what takes place in physical reality.

For instance, gravity. Gravity is an invisible force that, though invisible, determines the outcome of, say, when I drop a rock off of a cliff. Thanks to gravity, something nonmaterial, the rock is sure to plummet. But is it possible to *control* gravity, to commune with it? Scientifically and technologically, sure. I've ridden The Gravitron at the county fair. However, the magicians of the occult seek to

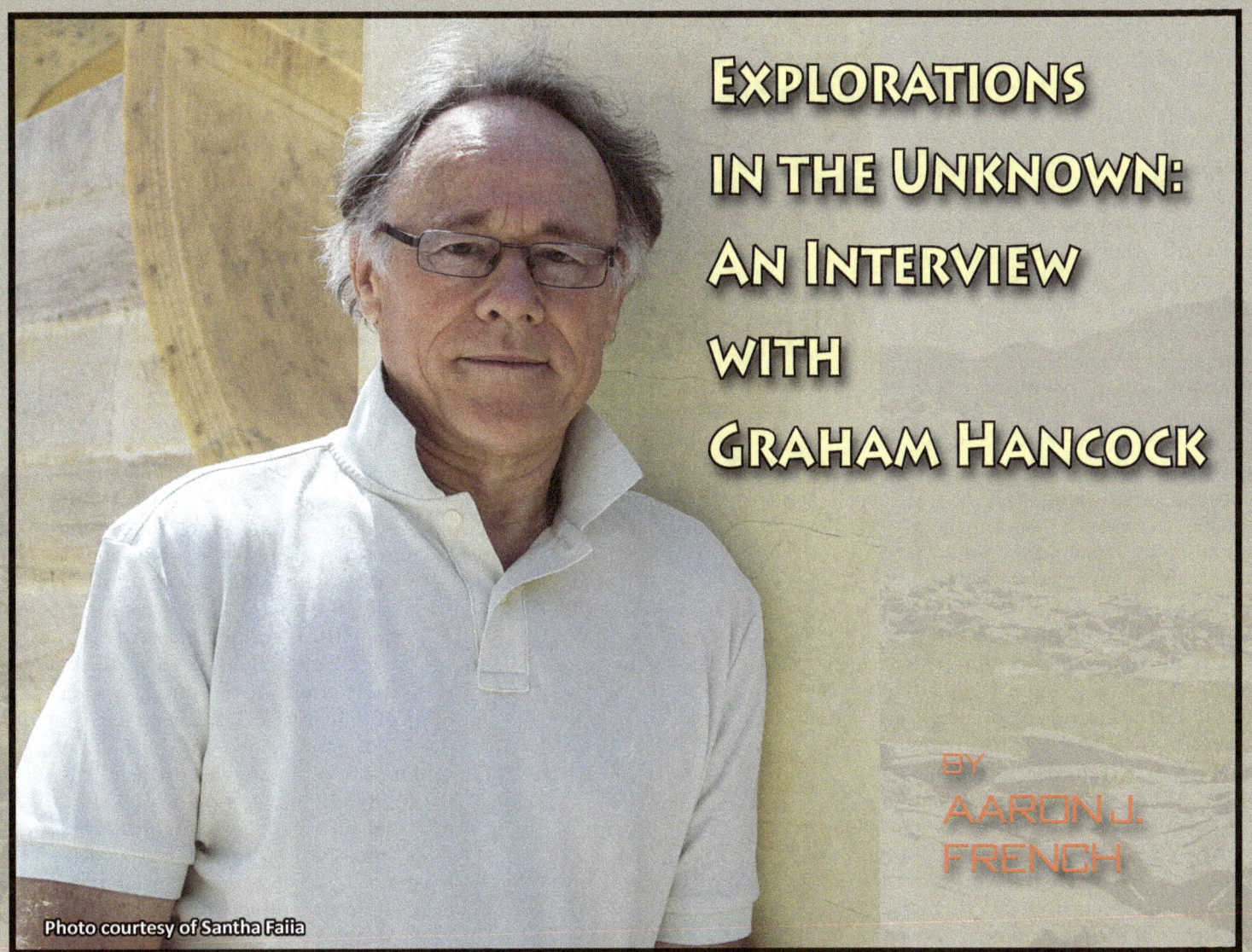

EXPLORATIONS IN THE UNKNOWN: AN INTERVIEW WITH GRAHAM HANCOCK

BY AARON J. FRENCH

Photo courtesy of Santha Faiia

ARON J. FRENCH: I was hoping you could begin by telling us a little about how you made the transition to writing fiction after so many years of writing successful nonfiction, also the role that Ayahuasca and altered states of consciousness played in making that transition, and how all this culminated in your first novel, *Entangled*?

Graham Hancock: I've always regarded myself first and foremost as a writer, rather than a researcher or somebody working in the field of archeology, consciousness, or anything like that. My self-identification is that of a writer, and I have felt that way since I was about ten years old. My writing career took me in the direction of journalism in the early 1970s, and then in the direction of nonfiction books—but nonfiction books about current affairs issues. I was still very much plugged into the journalist paradigm. And I was writing nonfiction books and doing journalism because that's what I could get paid for doing, but what I actually liked doing was writing stories and writing fiction, and I always hoped that a time would come when I could do some work on a novel or on a series of novels. Sure enough, since the nonfiction did well and gave me some space in my life to explore other avenues of creativity—quite late in life, around the year 2006 or 2007—I got to a place where I

could take time off completely from writing nonfiction and try my hand at writing what became my first novel, *Entangled*.

I mean it's interesting, there are definite differences between writing fiction and nonfiction. With nonfiction, particularly in the controversial areas in which I operate, I'm presenting an argument, and that argument goes against the mainstream view; it goes against the view that historians and archeologists give us. So if I'm presenting an argument I've got to thoroughly nail it down; I've got to take account of what my critics might say, and how they might attack me—and boy do they attack alternative ideas!—and as far as possible to bulletproof my argument against them. In the case of some books, this involves as many as 2000 footnotes. Whereas with fiction, all of that goes away. There are no furious critics who are going to attack me because they claim I haven't represented the facts correctly. That's a tremendous liberation and there's an immediate feeling of freedom as a writer when you step from one genre into the other. This doesn't stop me from exploring extraordinary or difficult ideas in my novels; I'm just doing so in a different way. I think the central narrative skill that makes a nonfiction book work can also make a novel work. But there's something else in fiction which doesn't happen in nonfiction, and that is characters. If you don't create characters who are believable and who readers identify with, then you're dead in the water. And that's not a skill with which one is necessarily equipped from writing nonfiction books, and that is something I've had to learn. For instance, how best to handle dialogue. Some fiction authors are absolutely brilliant at dialogue, and I wonder how much of that is the result of years and years of hard work and carefully listening to how people speak to one another, and how much it's a born gift. In my case, I've had to work on that, but I think I'm learning as I go along.

So it wasn't so much a transition for me, it was something that I always wanted to do and finally got space in my life to do, where I could take time out and really explore this different genre. But the second part of your question concerning Ayahuasca is interesting. I did begin drinking Ayahuasca, which is the sacred medicine of the Amazon jungle, the sacred vine. It's actually a mixture of plants, one of which contains Dimethyltryptamine, the most powerful hallucinogen known to man. It's been used by shamans in the Amazon for thousands of years and it affects their creativity enormously. There is a huge body of art which is created by Amazonian shamans, and there's also a huge body of art that's created by Western artists who have worked with Ayahuasca. It was because of this that I first considered the idea of going down to the Amazon to drink Ayahuasca. I was writing a nonfiction book that became *Supernatural: Meetings with the Ancient Teachers of Mankind*, which concerned cave art containing many of the elements of Ayahuasca visionary art. I realized in order to research that book properly, I needed to have the kinds of experiences we thought ancient shamans in Upper Paleolithic times were having, and I could do that by going and drinking this powerful visionary brew with shamans in the Amazon. So initially it was a research project for a nonfiction book, but the effects of Ayahuasca were so transformative and so nourishing to my imagination and my spirit—also so difficult and so challenging. It's like an initiation, it's incredibly hard work, and it's very demanding psychically.

Once I'd finished the book *Supernatural*, I realized I wanted to carry on drinking Ayahuasca. Now people can mistake that because they'll think, "Oh, Ayahuasca's a drug, the man is addicted to a drug," but it's impossible to get addicted to Ayahuasca. You have to brace yourself every time you drink it: it tastes ghastly, it makes you

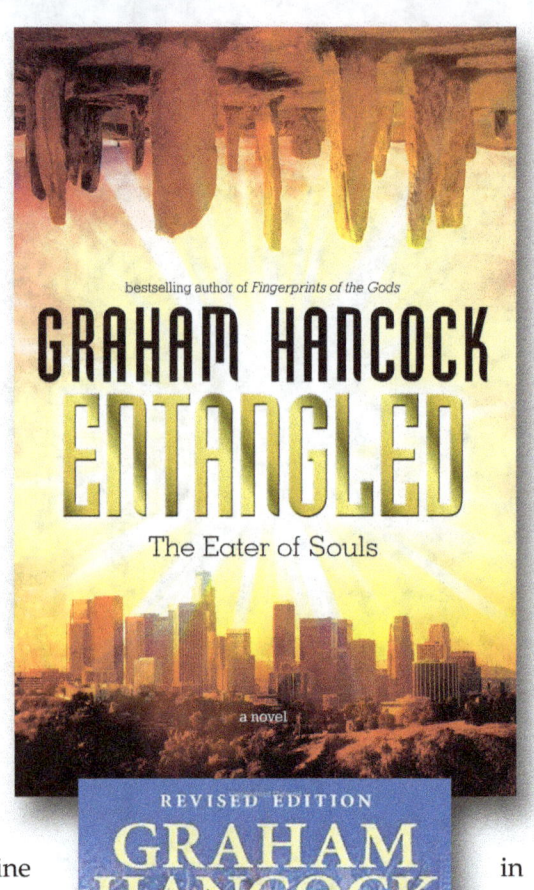

vomit. I mean, nobody's doing this for fun. It's the deep personal work the vine unleashes which is of great value. And I decided I had more work to do with Ayahuasca.

Now I was aware that friends of mine like Martina Hoffmann and Alex Grey, the great visionary artists, had both had their art dramatically affected by their encounters with Ayahuasca, and I wondered if I went into a series of sessions with the deliberate intent to see what Ayahuasca could teach me about the possibility of writing fiction, whether something useful would come out of it. And sure enough, in a series of sessions around 2007, I was given a very intense teaching, which basically told me that I had to write the book that became *Entangled*.

It gave me the scenario that there were two young women, one living 24,000 years ago in the Stone Age, and one living in modern Los Angeles, whose fates were literally entangled across time, and that time is not a straight line that goes from past to future, but that it's a tangle, a series of knots, and that it is possible to intervene in time. So this gave me the basic plot for what became my first novel. And I even saw scenes, I actually envisaged scenes, and I learned something about the Neanderthals who feature in my novel. When I had written about the Neanderthals previously in my nonfiction book *Supernatural*, I portrayed them as dull and ignorant savages, knuckle-draggers, the typical stereotype of Neanderthals, but what Ayahuasca showed me was they weren't that way, they were filled with love and light and they communicated telepathically and we've completely misunderstood them. And so I felt compelled to put that aspect into the story. Ayahuasca gave me a launching pad, it gave me the framework and inspiration, but of course it didn't take away from the hard work. I still had to sit down and write the novel. But I am certain that I would never have written it had I not had those Ayahuasca sessions, which I approached with the intention of seeing what I could do in the realm of fiction.

AJF: I know a lot of fiction writers often have dreams and try to incorporate those dreams into their stories. You can't really do that with nonfiction, but with fiction you can translate a visionary experience into words a little more easily.

GH: Absolutely. This whole process of creativity is really intriguing. It's one of the reasons I don't prepare an outline when I'm writing a novel. I don't want to be bound by something I've made when I wasn't in the creative flow. I'd rather begin with the germ of an idea, start putting words down on paper, and then see what comes up. There's a huge realm of the unconscious that is at play in writing fiction. I think the more we allow that unconscious, un-thought-through aspect of our creativity to emerge—the more we set that free—the better result we're going to end up with.

And dreams are part of that. I've often made the point that our society is one that despises dreams. If we want to insult someone, we call them "a dreamer." In fact, that's what my teachers use to call me when I was in school (much to the annoyance of my parents when they received the termly reports),

Photo courtesy of Santha Faiia

I recently reread *The Stand*, the most recent version, and it's a masterpiece. I had no sense that I was reading a 1200 page book, I just raced through it and loved every minute, and was annoyed when I had to be taken away from it. So that's a great writer at work. Okay, so he writes in the horror genre, so what? Why does the horror genre have to be regarded in any way as inferior? We have great writers in the past who have written incredible horror, and Stephen King is doing that with depth and with style, in a way that nobody else can really match.

Of course, J.R.R. Tolkien. There are definite elements of horror in what he investigates and explores. And I really enjoy George R.R. Martin and the whole *Game of Thrones* series. I read those as novels before I watched them on TV—and I think they've done a reasonable job with

that "Hancock is a dreamer." But of course in ancient times, dreaming was regarded as a very valuable form of knowledge. It was regarded as a means to gain access to truth. Not every dream, but within the network of dreams that one experiences there are certain ones that are true tellings. And I believe it was in the *Odyssey* where a distinction was made between dreams that come through the Gate of Horn, and dreams that come through the Gate of Ivory.[1] The dreams that come through the Gate of Ivory are just fantastical creations of your mind, but the dreams that come through the Gate of Horn are true tellings. The trick is to learn the difference between the two and pay attention to the true tellings.

AJF: Are there any fiction authors you like who have inspired your fiction, particularly horror authors?

GH: Hey, I love Stephen King. There's a man who reaches deep into the unconscious and every time comes up with the goods, with incredible professionalism and productivity.

the TV show actually. And then a British writer called Joe Abercrombie, who is a fantasy adventure writer, and again elements of his work definitely cross over into horror. Joe is a very powerful, very engaging, and very convincing writer. These are some of the modern writers I like.

AJF: You mentioned characters earlier. Stephen King is very good at creating characters that feel alive.

GH: There I think we're looking at a gifted individual. Let's face it, human beings have different gifts, and some people have the storytelling gift. But his storytelling gift is accompanied by great professionalism and is done with rigor and care, and no doubt he works extremely fast. He's been exercising those muscles for so long that the result is almost always effective. I can think of few modern writers who have the same feeling for dialogue he has. The way he does the American voices—because he does the different regions and dialects—is brilliant.

AJF: You often highlight the supernatural (including supernatural abilities) in your fiction, and indeed the fiction model allows for more freedom in this regard over nonfiction, as we've discussed. So to what extent do you actually believe in the existence of these forces?

GH: I think the area of reality that we call the supernatural is very real. I don't think it's a fantasy. I don't think it's

---

1 *Odyssey*, Book 19, lines 560-569: "Stranger, dreams verily are baffling and unclear of meaning, and in no wise do they find fulfilment in all things for men. For two are the gates of shadowy dreams, and one is fashioned of *horn* and one of *ivory*. Those dreams that pass through the gate of sawn *ivory deceive* men, bringing words that find no *fulfilment*. But those that come forth through the gate of polished *horn bring* true issues to *pass,* when any mortal sees them. But in my case it was not from thence, me-thinks, that my strange dream came."

something people have made up either out of superstition or wish fulfillment. Reality is very complicated and mysterious. We are physical beings, we live in a physical, material realm, we have five physical senses, and most of the time we are tuned in to material reality. And our laws of physics and explanations of how the world works are based on that physical reality. But there are certain things that happen which can't be explained by the laws of physics, and those are defined as supernatural.

Materialist scientists believe everything can be reduced to matter, that there's nothing else of any importance in the universe, and because that's their reference frame they have to persuade themselves that there is no such thing as the supernatural. But I think they couldn't be more wrong. A point I often make is that materialist scientists, people like Richard Dawkins, author of *The Selfish Gene* and *The God Delusion*, will tell you straight-faced that there is no life after death. But they can't

possibly know that. That's not a scientific statement of fact, it's not based on empirical studies or surveys. That we don't know what happens after death is the truthful answer. We don't know whether we are nonphysical conscious entities temporarily incarnated in physical form, or whether the physical form is all there is to us. There are no facts in this area, only ideas, philosophies, and speculations. So I happen to be of the conclusion, and I prefer to put it this way, that reality is just much more complicated than we can imagine, and that we are presently tuned in to and interacting with a very tiny slice of reality. Our society strongly conditions us to interact with that tiny slice of reality, and seeks to persuade us that it is all there is. Perhaps because it would be destabilizing for our society if more and more people were to realize that this is not the case.

What's brought this home to me is my work with psychedelics, particularly with Ayahuasca, over the last dozen years or so. I would challenge any hard-

line materialist skeptic who claims there are no parallel realms, that this is all there is, to go down to the Amazon, have a dozen sessions with Ayahuasca, and then review their opinion. And to compare notes with other people who have drunk Ayahuasca, and they may find that they are meeting the same entities and exploring the same landscapes. Generally when a large group of people agree on the nature of certain experiences we conclude those experiences are real. And that's what's happening with altered states of consciousness and the realms they appear to open up to us. There's enough transpersonal work now to say that it appears we have a freestanding alternate reality out there, maybe many, and instead of dismissing it as mumbo jumbo, we should actually be devoting some of the resources of our society to exploring that. I think it would be a much more effective use of NASA's money. I'm not saying NASA are wrong to go searching for life on other planets, but I think they could have intriguing results if they were to go within as well and do targeted research projects with substances like Dimethyltryptamine, which alter consciousness radically, and see what comes out of those. Many people have supernatural experiences but they tend to be random, they tend to be unpredictable, and they're very elusive and hard to test. With Dimethyltryptamine, you have the opportunity to put people in a state of mind where they will have supernatural experiences. Then you can test those experiences, and you can compare notes between different volunteers.

So I think we are dealing with a complex, multilayered, nuanced reality, and I take the view of shamans, and ancient Gnosticism as well, that these nuanced and usually invisible levels of reality are interacting with us whether we like it or not. And it's better if we are proactive, rather than being the victims of those forces; that we seek to negotiate with them on equal terms. That's what

Graham Hancock studying the figure of a serpent with a peculiarly large head, carved out of the living rock, that emerges at the entrance of the Temple of the Moon, a cave shrine near Cuzco in the Peruvian Andes.

shamans do. Shamans are not in terror of spirits, they are the masters of spirits, their whole life training has been to become that, and I think there is a lot that we in the West could learn from them.

AJF: Your most recent fiction books, which are part of a larger series, are *War God: Nights of the Witch* and *War God vol. 2: Return of the Plumed Serpent*. They take place during the Spanish Conquest of The New World, with Cortés and his men conquering the Aztec Empire. In these books you vividly describe violent scenarios such as the Aztec human sacrifice ritual. Could you talk about what forces you believe lay behind the Aztec human sacrifice, is it an occult ritual, and what do you think were the supernatural ends of such a ritual?

GH: This comes down to the fundamental issue of good and evil. There is certainly good and evil in this physical realm. Some might say that these are just social constructs, but I don't happen to agree with that. I think there is fundamental good and fundamental evil. A friend of mine speaks of this physical world as a university of duality, that we're here to be taught by the choices we make between good and evil, between darkness and light. That's what defines us. And that's why it's an incredible privilege to be born in a human body, rather than a cockroach or a fruit fly. We've got the equipment to make very fine distinctions, and I would propose that we are all making those distinctions all the time. Sometimes it's at a very small level, in the case of your everyday average individual, the choices may be between small goods and small evils. Sometimes it's at a

massive level, where you have national leaders who are making choices and those choices may plunge millions into darkness, or offer the possibility of light for millions, as well. But it's a continuum: at the bottom of it is the process of choosing, because we always have that even in the most extremely difficult circumstances. Human beings always have choice. We don't have to do something wicked. We can choose not to do that. And if we do something wicked, I would say it is a choice, which in one way or another, in the long-term scheme of things, we will be required to account for.

The ancient Egyptians visualized this as the weighing of the soul and the scales of *Ma'at*, the goddess of cosmic justice and harmony, and in one scale is a symbol of the soul of the deceased and represents his heart, and in the other scale is the feather of truth and justice. In the ancient Egyptian system, they were tolerant, they understood human frailty. But the notion of life is that yes we make mistakes, we need not face eternal damnation, as the Catholics would say, for making a moral error. And yet we have long enough in life to put that right, to not repeat mistakes that we've made, to learn our lessons and to balance the scales in other ways, with acts of goodness. And I believe there is truth in that, that a human life is like a work of art, you should be able to knock off a few corners here and there and do some damage to your work of art, but also perfect aspects of it, and at the end of it stand and look back on it and say, "Overall, I did good."

Well there's good and evil in this realm, and there's good and evil in all other realms, in the so-called supernatural realms, in the parallel dimensions which

Graham Hancock (at right) talking with Professor Klaus Schmidt at the extraordinary 12,000-year old megalithic site of Gobekli Tepe in Turkey. Professor Schmidt, who passed away suddenly in 2014, was the discoverer and excavator of Gobekli Tepe, a site that has changed forever our understanding of human history.

Photo courtesy of Santha Faiia

interact with our own, as I said whether we like it or not. So when you go on a psychedelic journey, particularly with Ayahuasca, you are not only going to encounter beautiful glowing goddesses, you are also going to encounter demons. You are going to encounter psychic vampires whose entire purpose is to suck out your life force and leave you drained and empty. That's why it's no joke to undertake an Ayahuasca session. You have to gird yourself psychically for the challenges that you will face. Not everybody faces them, not all the time, but most people do if they do enough sessions. And again, you find yourself confronted by choice.

Now I think certain cultures in the past made deliberate choices for darkness, and perhaps they sought to be empowered by doing so. Yes, the Aztecs carried out the most ghastly human sacrifices. The evidence is that they took great pleasure in doing it, that they approached it with a kind of lust, that they humiliated their victims on their way up the steps of the pyramid and dressed them up in ridiculous clothes and daubed them with rubber and feathers to make them look foolish. They really were reveling in the suffering and pain that they caused even before the act of human sacrifice took place. And the act of human sacrifice was definitely about stealing the energy, stealing the life, stealing the soul of that person. So it's the ultimate act of intruding on another person's sovereignty. Let's call it what it is, it's murder. The act of murder is the intrusion on another human being's sovereign space, it's taking that away from them for your own benefit. I believe there are checks and balances in the universe that would not ultimately allow people to benefit from such actions,

but in the short term they might benefit. The Aztecs used human sacrifice as a way of terrorizing their neighbors. This was how they kept them under control. They would stage displays and bring chiefs of nearby tribes who might be becoming a bit disruptive, and they would sit them down and carry out grotesque human sacrifices—skinning people alive, for example, or cutting out their hearts—right in front of them. The message was if you cross us this is what's going to happen to you and your people—your men, women, and children—so don't cross us.

The interesting thing is that by doing that, yes the Aztecs did rise to power, but look what happened. When Cortés turned up on the coast of Mexico, huge numbers of people already hated the Aztecs. They hated them and feared them so much that when Cortés came with just 400 men and a promise that he would overthrow the Aztec hegemony, many local tribes joined him. So the security that the Aztecs thought they were buying with these ritual acts turned out to be illusory. In fact, it turned out to be the reason for their destruction because Cortés alone could never have defeated the Aztecs. He needed the local auxiliaries. So there was a direct karmic relationship there.

But this is not to say that Cortés is a good guy, because Cortés was a very bad guy. In writing the *War God* series I had a chance to get inside Cortés's head and to see how this man progressed through his life. He starts out as a rather cheerful, slightly immoral adventurer but ends up plunged in darkness and cruelty. He immerses himself up to the elbows in blood, and at the end of it he's a poisoned, tortured spirit. Now consider what the Spanish did when they burned people at the stake. We tend to say, "Oh the

Graham Hancock in the Urubamba Valley, Peru, hiking alongside the railroad track connecting Cuzco with Machu Picchu.

Aztecs were murderous savages, they cut out people's hearts and carried out human sacrifices"—well burning someone at the stake is an act of human sacrifice. That's what the Spanish were doing too, they were also feeding the dark side. And the irony is that they said they were doing it for a god that was good. That's what makes it even worse, you know. What they would actually do was take a human being, tie them to a stake, and then light flames under them. Imagine the state of mind it takes to put another human being in that place, to inflict that level of horrific suffering, and the Spanish did it lightheartedly. And in so doing, I maintain, they were carrying out acts of human sacrifice and seeking to energize the dark side of themselves.

So this is a realm where good and evil are found on both sides. One of the things in telling this story, for me, has been to find those characters who redeem the story, who even in the darkest situations with the most awful things going on around them find the capacity for love and principled courage, and act upon it. That's the beauty of humanity. We have all this complexity and an incredible capacity for wickedness, but also an amazing capacity for good, and for love and decency. I believe those capacities cross all realms and all realities.

AJF: Could you talk about the role of entheogens such as psilocybin mushrooms in the rituals of human sacrifice, particularly with reference to the last Aztec Emperor Moctezuma?

GH: Well again, this shows that with powerful psychedelics, the intention you bring to the experience is at least as important as the substance itself, because psilocybin can be used in very positive ceremonies. It can act as a liberating influence in people's lives. It so happens that that's not the way the Aztecs used psilocybin. They used psilocybin mushrooms to connect with demonic entities. The sacrificers frequently would have consumed psilocybin mushrooms before they embarked upon the grisly act of cutting out hundreds of living people's hearts in honor of their deities. So here we have a powerful vehicle for transforming consciousness, and the way that it transforms consciousness, and the direction in which it transforms consciousness, doesn't reside in the vehicle itself; it resides in the individual who is using it and the choices that individual makes. It's a bit like electricity. Electricity can be used for wonderful and positive purposes, but it can also kill people. And I would say the powerful entheogens are like that. The state of mind that you bring to the party is a crucial part of what will happen. You can invoke the dark side, and some people definitely do.

Ayahuasca was not known in Central America, but in South America where Ayahuasca is known it isn't only used for the light. The Ayahuasqueros I like to work with are the *curanderos*, the healers; they're using it for healing. But there are *brujos*, there are sorcerers, there are men and women who are using Ayahuasca and the vulnerability it brings to gain control over others, to infringe upon the sovereignty of others and take everything away from them. And this is something that the West should be aware of as we expand our relationship with Ayahuasca—and that's going very fast at the moment. You can drink Ayahuasca in most industrialized cities now, ceremonies are available—

under the radar of course—but they're there, and no one should imagine it's all sweetness and light in that garden, because it's not.

I happen to believe that there is a great entity of love behind the Ayahuasca brew, and in the West we call her Mother Ayahuasca. It's like an encounter with a goddess. Any down-to-earth materialist hearing me say this would conclude that Hancock is mad, and they're welcome to that view. But I say again, go to the Amazon, have 12 sessions with Ayahuasca, and see if you feel the same way. I have seen situations in ceremonies where people encounter this entity—I've encountered her myself—and have received fundamental healings as a result of that encounter. But I've also seen darkness come down in ceremonies and people seized and possessed by something very negative. I attended such a ceremony with a friend of mine and we

some human being has to teach. We don't need gurus in this area.

AJF: Very good advice. So, both Cortés and Moctezuma were in contact with divine intelligences, Saint Peter and Huitzilopochtli respectively, and furthermore the appearance of Cortés was seen by many as the return of the plumed serpent Quetzalcoatl, even that this reappearance had been long anticipated. It would seem that this whole ordeal was to some degree dictated and determined by outside agencies, by the supernatural world. Are these factual accounts, or something you've highlighted more intuitively in the *War God* books?

GH: First of all, in terms of those… let's call them spiritual encounters, the notion that I play with in the *War God* series

both experienced dramatic and terrifying effects, which affected the whole group, and Mother Ayahuasca appeared to my friend and said, "You needed to see this—now you understand what I have to deal with all the time." There's a strange vulnerability in a goddess there. Whatever they are, these entities are not all-powerful. They manifest in the material realm by affecting human consciousness, and some of them affect human consciousness very negatively, and some affect it very positively. So we must be strong when we go into that experience, and ideally we should be guided by a goodhearted person, a shaman who absolutely knows what he or she is doing, and who is not driven by ego. My advice to any person seeking out Ayahuasca is to gain knowledge of the shaman who will be offering you that brew, because if there's any hint of a personality cult around that person, run away as fast as you can. What you're supposed to be drinking Ayahuasca for is the lessons that medicine has to teach, not the lessons

is that the same demonic entity—these are shape-shifters, remember—that manifests to Moctezuma in the form of the god of war Hummingbird, they called him Huitzilopochtli, takes another appearance, another disguise, and appears to Cortés in the form of St. Peter. But actually it's all one demon. And he's doing what demons have always done throughout human history, which is to seek to maximize confusion and chaos and misery in the world. Cortés might imagine that he's talking to some saintly guy, but actually what he's talking to is a demon who is driving him to ever more wicked acts along his journey.

Secondly, this notion that Cortés's dream encounters with St. Peter were actually encounters with a demon, that's my suggestion. But he did have them—that's a fact. From his childhood Cortés believed himself to be inspired by St. Peter and had frequent encounters with the entity he construed to be St. Peter in the realm of dreams. He was reportedly saved from a fatal childhood illness by the intervention of St. Peter, and ever afterward St. Peter was his patron saint. Likewise, we know from the historical annals that Moctezuma felt himself to be in regular contact with Hummingbird, the god of war. And that contact was facilitated by eating what they called "the flesh of the gods," the psilocybin mushrooms, and he would enter a trance state and encounter this entity who gave him extremely bad advice and always wanted him to conduct more murders, to feed him the souls of more sacrificial victims. There's definitely a historical basis to both of these encounters, but the construal that I put on them is my own, of course.

AJF: What about Cortés being the return of Quetzalcoatl?

GH: Well now there's something very strange. There was a prophecy of the return of Quetzalcoatl. To summarize it briefly, there was in Mexico a classic battle between good and evil that was remembered as having unfolded in the year One Reed. So he fulfilled an undoubtedly real existing ancient prophecy, and he looked the part, too. He came in ships that moved by themselves without paddles—sails, the Aztecs had never seen sails before. He was equipped with all kinds of weaponry they didn't understand. There was a certain weapon spoken of in the ancient traditions of the Mexica called a fire-serpent, which bolts of fire would come out of and dismember human beings. It was a terribly powerful weapon. And the Spanish had fire-serpents, only they called them guns, and so many other aspects of the Spanish were mysterious and supernatural, including the very fact that they rode horses. Only 16 horses amongst the whole Cortés army, but 16 heavy horse coming down on them at 30 mph, both men and horses armored in steel, and the ground shaking underneath their feet—there were very few indigenous Central American armies that could bear that sight. They felt they were confronting gods. For a while, they really weren't clear that this was men mounted on the backs of animals, they thought they were dealing

distant past. There had been a deity in human form who was called Quetzalcoatl, which means the feathered or plumed serpent. He had been a god of peace. He forbade human sacrifice and enjoined people only to sacrifice fruits and flowers, never to take a human life, and he ushered in a golden age or reign of peace. But then there came a conspiracy of evil against him, demonic entities, with Hummingbird amongst them, who sought to overthrow Quetzalcoatl—and who succeeded and drove him out of Mexico. And he's said to have sailed from the coast of the Gulf of Mexico at a place called Coatzacoalcos, which means the serpent sanctuary, on a raft made of serpents. It's all very peculiar. But as he went, he promised that one day he would return and when he did he would come back with others, and that they would be in boats that moved by themselves without paddles, and when they returned they would overthrow the rule of evil and restore the rule of peace. Also that this would happen at a particular date in the Mexican calendar, which was the year One Reed. And it's a very bizarre thing that the exact moment Cortés landed in Mexico in 1519 was the beginning of the Aztec

with some kind of hybrid entity. Eventually this myth was punctured, but that was their first notion.

So they were at a huge psychological disadvantage. It really looked like the fulfillment of ancient prophecy, and Cortés cynically, calculatedly, took advantage of that. Cortés was a Machiavellian player. His principle was use anything that works and he saw that he could use this scenario, and he cleverly did use it. It's not that he even pretended to be a god, but he allowed that superstition amongst the Aztecs to grow to a massive level. So the first time Cortés and Moctezuma actually met face to face, Moctezuma was literally shaking in his sandals. Like all bullies put to the test, Moctezuma proved to be a complete coward, and Cortés had just played mind games with him for months before that, to the point where the man simply crumbled. It's a fascinating episode to explore, actually.

AJF: Indeed. There's such synchronicity there that it could hardly be called random.

GH: No, I don't think so. I think there's something deeper and darker at work in all of this. Because we shouldn't forget that in many ways the monstrous course that the world is set upon today had its beginnings in the Spanish conquest of Mexico. So many negative things came out of that. The Spanish set the example, it was suddenly okay to just go and take other people's countries. A few years afterward Pizarro went off to Peru with even less men than Cortés had, and followed the Cortés model and pulled off the same trick. Then you have the genocide of the Native American Indians in North America. Again, it all goes back to that time where Cortés got away with it, and it came to be seen as something the white nations could do to the other nations they encountered. How different it would have been had Moctezuma not been hated by all his neighbors, and if they had stopped the Spanish invasion on the beach. How much that would have required the Spanish to rethink their strategy and perhaps to operate in a different way. Who knows the direction the world might have gone in. We might have ended up where these two different cultures approached one another in the spirit of seeking to learn from one another. But it went down the way it went down, and our world today is a product of what happened between 1519 and 1521.

AJF: Switching gears here, in the 1990s your writing career was kick-started with the release of your book *Fingerprints of the Gods*, which received a variety of different reactions from the general public and the academic community. The book posits that the birth of human civilization is far older than conventional historians would have us believe; also that there is a connection to a now long-forgotten advanced culture. Nearly 20 years later, you're about to release the sequel to that book, *Magicians of the Gods*. Could you tell us how this new book came about, what it contains, and how it is designed to function as a sequel? I'm also interested in Göbekli Tepe, if you're going to be using that in the book.

GH: Certainly, the opening chapters are about Göbekli Tepe. Göbekli Tepe is a mysterious archeological site in south eastern Turkey, which has completely revolutionized our understanding of history. And that site was not discovered when I wrote *Fingerprints of the Gods*. It's one of the reasons I'm writing a sequel. To be clear, this new book *Magicians of the Gods* is not an update of *Fingerprints of the Gods*. It's a completely new book, filled with new evidence and new travels to places I didn't talk about before, as well as to some places I did talk about before but with a new perspective. And one of the key new sites is Göbekli Tepe.

What happened was this. In 1996 a German archeologist called Klaus Schmidt from the German Archeological Institute came across a site that had been surveyed twenty years earlier and dismissed by a couple of other archeologists. They had dismissed it because there were very fine bits of carved stone sticking out of the ground, and the work was so good that they concluded — they were looking for Stone Age stuff — that the site was Byzantine and from the Middle Ages, and therefore of no interest to them. They passed it by. But Klaus Schmidt

Graham Hancock at Borobudur Temple on the island of Java, Indonesia

had some experiences on sites in Turkey which led him to think again about that, and he went back and took another look at that site and began to excavate it. What he discovered was a gigantic megalithic complex. On the scale of Stonehenge, multiplied by fifty. It's just a gigantic place. So far 80% or 90% of it is still under the ground, but we know it's there thanks to ground-penetrating radar. What they've excavated so far are these circles of gigantic megalithic pillars, with some weighing 20 tons and standing 25 feet tall, with precise astronomical alignments and all beautifully put together.

Now here's the thing, the dating of that site is absolutely definite. It's very difficult to date stone monuments. Carbon dating won't do it. Carbon dating only dates organic materials. So when an archeologist tells you we've carbon dated this site, what they mean is that they've found a bit of bone or a bit of charcoal which is associated with the stone object and they've deduced that the stone object is of the same age as that piece of organic material. But that may not be the case. What's special about Göbekli Tepe is whoever made it around 11,600 years ago deliberately buried it around 10,000 years ago. They covered it in what appears to be a "pot-bellied hill." That's what Göbekli Tepe means in the Turkish language. And so for 10,000 years it remained untouched by the hand of man, sealed away like a time capsule. That's not true of any other megalithic site. You could go to megalithic temples in Malta, for example, which are thought to be 5 or 6,000 years old, and they've been tramped over by every human culture for thousands of years, and so the dating actually is, in my opinion, very insecure on those sites. We may be being misled to give falsely young dates by the introduction of later organic materials to those sites. That didn't happen at Göbekli Tepe. So it allows us to say for sure that this site is in the range of 12,000 years old. It may be significantly older than that—let's see what else comes out of the ground—but what they've got now allows us to be certain that it's at least 11,600 years old.

For those who haven't studied archeology and history, you might think, "Well, so what?" Well, here's what. Stonehenge is less than 5,000 years old according to the mainstream chronology. All the famous megalithic monuments of Europe are actually thought to date to that horizon—5,000 to 5,500 years old. Nobody is supposed to have been creating gigantic megalithic sites 6 or 7,000 years earlier than that. Why? Because our ancestors 12,000 years ago were what they call Upper Paleolithic hunter-gatherers. They are not supposed to have had the organization or the social structure that is needed to create a large-scale architectural project. It just doesn't fit into the pattern of history. Furthermore, evidence is now compelling that at the same time that Göbekli Tepe was being made—whoever made it—they also "invented agriculture." Suddenly agriculture appears in southeastern Turkey, at the same time that monumental architecture appears. So for me the interesting issue is, what's really going on here? Did a bunch of hunter-gatherers wake up one morning and think, "Ah, we're just going to create

There are 72 Buddha figures in the bell-shaped stupas mounted on the upper terraces.

this humongous megalithic site with really challenging engineering problems, which we've never encountered before, but we're going to do it brilliantly. And by the way, at the same moment, we're going to invent agriculture." Is that realistic, or are we looking at a transfer of technology? Are we looking at the survivors of a lost civilization who, after a global cataclysm, settled in Göbekli Tepe and used it as a center of innovation to introduce the notion of settled civilization to the tribes living in the area at that time?

You see, even today we have a global situation where we have advanced technological cultures co-existing with hunter-gatherer cultures. There are people in the Amazon who don't even know that the United States exists. They've had no contact with technological society at all. And I believe it was the case 10 or 20,000 years ago as well—that there was an advanced civilization on this planet, and that there were hunter-gatherers. And the advanced civilization was destroyed.

But another thing that's of great importance in the new book is that there are many other sites now being discovered—Göbekli Tepe is only one of them—which don't fit the paradigm. There's an incredible pyramid site in Indonesia called Gunung Padang, which also features prominently in my book. But more important than that, in a way, is that I have now what I didn't have in 1995, and that's a smoking gun. That is the work that's been done in the last 8 years by a large group of scientists (there are more than 28 of them), who coauthor the papers in journals like the *Proceedings of the National Academy of Sciences*, or the *Journal of Geology*, or the *Monthly Notices of the Royal Astronomical Society*, and what they've been demonstrating, not without opposition, is that our planet was hit by a comet 12,800 years ago. It's taken so long for the evidence of this to come out because there doesn't appear to be an obvious and immediate crater. The reason there isn't a crater is that the comet broke up into fragments—some of the fragments were very large, about a mile in diameter—and those large fragments impacted what was then the North American ice cap. North America, roughly from Minneapolis northward, was covered in ice two miles deep: this was the Ice Age. And so the impacts were on ice. Therefore the craters were transient; they were formed in two-mile deep ice. They instantly liquidized that ice. They caused cataclysmic flooding across what are called the Channeled Scablands of the Columbia Plateau. You can particularly see them in Washington State. And they caused unbelievable volumes of icy water to be released into the world ocean, disrupting the Gulf Stream across the Atlantic, discharging more icy water into the Arctic Ocean, and changing global climate.

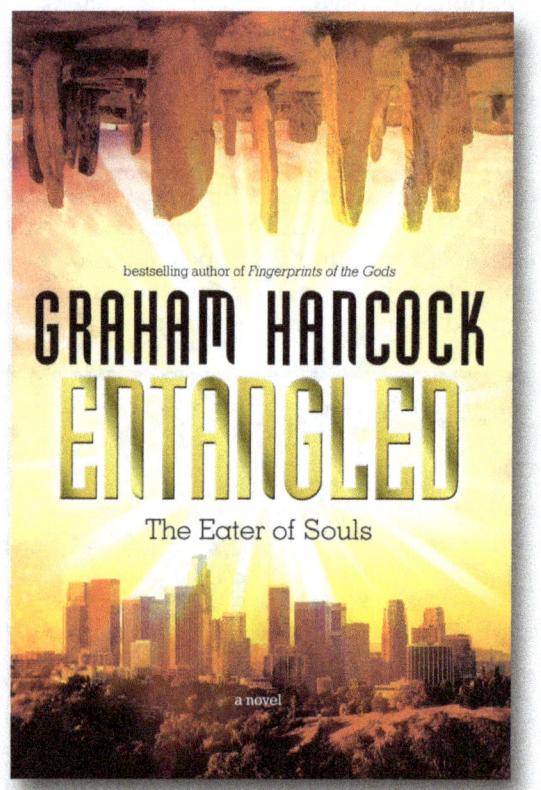

bestselling author of *Fingerprints of the Gods*

GRAHAM HANCOCK

ENTANGLED

The Eater of Souls

a novel

Now geologists have known that something weird happened then. 12,800 years ago is the beginning of a period geologists call the Younger Dryas. The world appeared to be coming out of the Ice Age, had been for a few thousand years, and then suddenly it goes back into conditions of extreme cold. It now appears that that was because of the comet impacts on the North American ice cap, and that that extreme cold resulted from the disruption of ocean circulation. 1,200 years later, 11,600 years ago, the exact date that Göbekli Tepe appears to have been founded, something else happens. The world suddenly reverses its climate again, the Younger Dryas ends, global climates shoot up by the order of ten or fifteen degrees in a single lifetime. But again, the comet explains this. The broad argument is that we are looking at what is called a giant comet, which originally had a diameter of 150 miles. This giant comet broke into fragments and 12,800 years ago about eight of those fragments hit the Earth, many big fragments as well as many smaller bits. It was an extinction-level event. This is when the woolly mammoths in North America went extinct. 1,200 years later, the Earth encountered the debris stream of the comet again. This time the impacts were in the ocean. They caused a huge cloud of water vapor to be thrown up into the upper atmosphere and created a dramatic global warming that resulted in the further climate change that took place at that time. So we have a period of 1,200 years, between 12,800 years ago and 11,600 years ago, when a previously undetected extinction-level event—on the scale of the event that made the dinosaurs extinct—happened.

Previously scientists used to think extinction-level events and encounters with asteroids and comets of a large size were very rare. Of course we encounter meteors all the time, but they're just harmless little firework displays. The big ones, they used to think they happened like every hundred million years, so archeologists have not been inclined to take them into account in the story of human history. The discovery of this comet impact totally changes all of that. What we're now having to come to grips with is that just yesterday, in historical terms, right at the beginning of the time when the story of civilization that's told to us by historians and archeologists seems to begin, there was this incredible punctuation mark, a global cataclysm on an unimaginable scale. So suddenly all the myths and traditions of a lost civilization, of a golden age, of global floods, they all make sense.

The point I'm making is that what we might call "the house of history" may have been well built by historians and archaeologists for the period of the last 11,600 years, but that it has foundations of sand because they are not taking into account what happened immediately before that, which is this extinction-level event. So I've written this new book to bring all this evidence—the archeological, the mythical, and the evidence regarding the comet—to bring it all together in one place and put it before the general public. That book is going to be published in November 2015 in the US, a bit earlier in Canada and the UK. But it's exciting for me to revisit this subject and to do so with completely new evidence. Because I took a lot of flak when I published *Fingerprints of the Gods* in 1995, and I can't begin to tell you the insults that were thrown my way by archeologists and historians—and their friends in the media—all around the world, who were absolutely convinced that their reference frame of history was right, and that there could be no lost civilization. What's happened in the last 20 years is a mass of new evidence that's come out, and that evidence needs to be put before the public in a coherent way, and that's why I've written *Magicians of the Gods*.

AJF: Well I'm very much looking forward to the book, it sounds fascinating. But returning now to your fiction work, obviously *War God 3* will be out soon?

GH: Absolutely, I'm so much looking forward to getting back to that. I had written 50,000 words of it before I had to break off to focus on *Magicians of the Gods*, but I'll soon be getting back and writing the further hundred thousand words that will bring that trilogy to a conclusion—which ends, of course, with the apocalyptic fall of Tenochtitlan, the Aztec capital, in August 1521.

AJF: Do you have plans for any other fiction projects besides that?

GH: I must finish the *War God* trilogy, so that's my first priority, and *Entangled*, my first novel, is part one of a two-part series, so I've also got about 100 pages of the second volume of *Entangled* written. But once those are finished, then we'll see. One day, distantly, this whole work that I've been involved with in the nonfiction field about a lost civilization, Atlantis by any other name, may take root as a novel. Possibly.

AJF: That would be great. That's been attempted a few times in some science fiction and fantasy books.

GH: It has.

AJF: But it's very fertile subject matter.

GH: It is, and people keep coming back to it again and again. Elements of it are in almost all post-apocalyptic fiction. And that's my guess, actually—that we are living in a post-apocalyptic world. Many writers go into this idea and do good stuff, and I hope that the fact that I spent 25 years working in this field as a researcher might enable me to bring some other good stuff to the party.

AJF: Most definitely. And so finally, could you tell our readers where they can find you on the Internet?

GH: The main thing is my website, grahamhancock.com, and on the front page of that there are links to the new book and there's also a link to my author Facebook page. I find Facebook a really interesting phenomenon, so I'm always very active there. I try as much as I'm able on my tight schedule to interact with the people who comment on the page. I can't tell you how many leads and useful bits of information have come my way because of this large Facebook community, so I highly value the interaction Facebook allows.

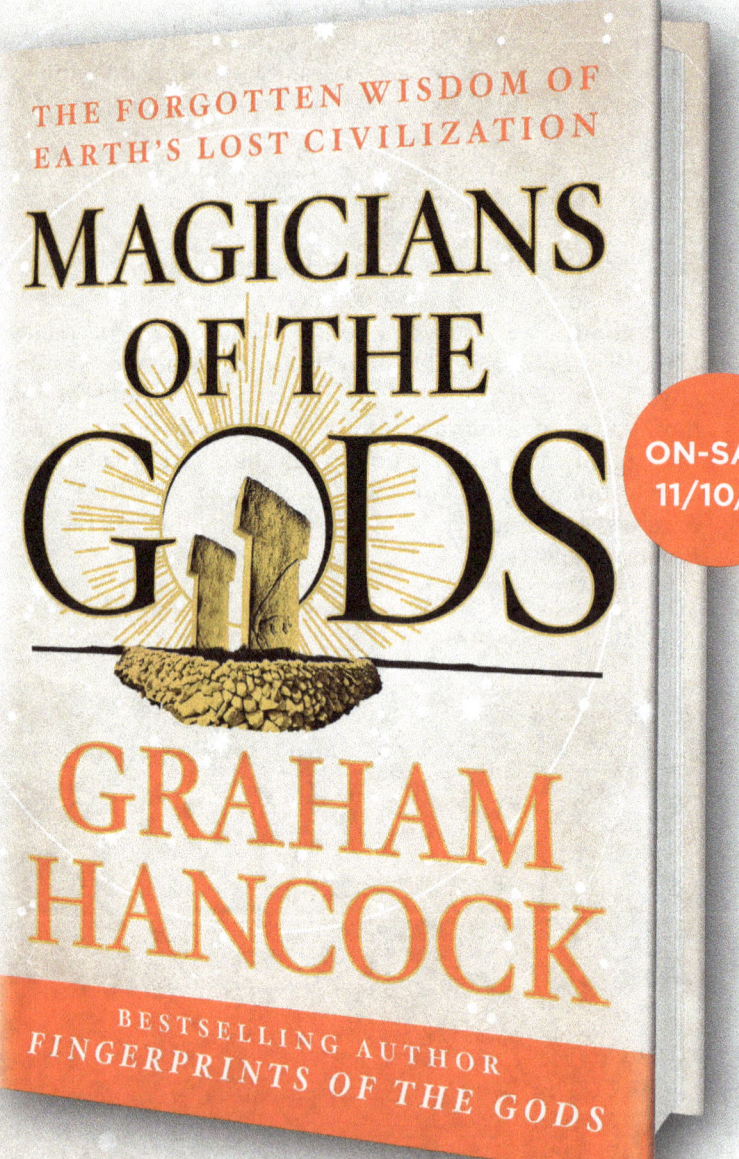

WAR GOD:
NIGHTS OF THE WITCH

(an extract)

BY GRAHAM HANCOCK

As Malinal's head began to clear from the beating she'd taken in the plaza she discovered she had somehow already reached the great pyramid and begun to climb the wide northern stairway. On both sides, stationed at every third step were guards holding guttering torches, and she saw she was part of a long line of prisoners ascending between them. She felt a helping hand pressed into the small of her back and turned to find Tozi right behind her. "Coyotl?" she asked, her voice cracking.

"Gone," Tozi said. Her chalk-white face was smeared with blood. "Ahuizotl put him in the other line. I've lost sight of him."

"It's my fault!" sobbed Malinal. Though she hardly knew Coyotl the intensity of the last hours was such that she was overwhelmed to be separated from the anxious, intelligent little boy and filled with guilt for her part in what had happened. "Ahuizotl did it to spite me. If I hadn't been holding Coyotl he wouldn't have taken him."

"It's not your fault that Ahuizotl is an evil, hateful old man," said Tozi. "You gave Coyotl love. That's what you should remember."

They were climbing very slowly, sometimes standing in place for a long count before shuffling up another step or two and halting again. The warm wind that had risen earlier was blowing more strongly now, overhead thick clouds raced across the face of the moon, and round Malinal's feet a foaming, clotting tide of human blood flowed from the summit platform and rolled ponderously down the steep narrow steps. It was slippery and treacherous. It accumulated in shallow pools spreading out across the plaza at the base of the pyramid. If filled the air with a sour terrifying stink.

Malinal's stomach cramped and heaved and bile rose in her throat. Though the cruelty and excess of the Mexica were nothing new to her, she was overwhelmed by the horror and depravity of this vast pageant of murder. Her stomach cramped again, this time she couldn't hold it back, and she threw up in a hot, spattering, choking gush.

"What a hero she is!" yelled one of the guards sarcastically.

"How brave!" sneered another. "A whiff of the knife and she spews her guts!"

There came the thumping, rumbling sound of flesh striking stone as priests threw a pile of a dozen bleeding torsos over the edge of the summit platform. They tumbled down the steps like clumps of viscid fruit fallen from some evil tree, trailing streamers of guts, rolling and bumping wildly until they came to rest in the plaza below. Something heavy and wet had brushed against Malinal's leg as they went past, and now her stomach heaved uncontrollably again, doubling her over, dry-retching, gasping for breath, to the general hilarity of the guards.

As the spasm passed, she straightened and spat, hatred scourging her like acid. What a vile vicious race these Mexica truly were—a race of arrogant, strutting, loud-mouthed bullies whose greatest pleasure was the desecration of others.

A race whose wickedness and cruelty knew no bounds.

Malinal was filled with impotent rage, wanting to punish them, to visit retribution upon them, to make them experience the same humiliations they inflicted, but she knew at the same time that none of this could ever happen, that she would continue to climb the pyramid, passive and unresisting as a dumb animal on its way to slaughter, and that when she reached the top she would be killed.

A soldier approached, carefully descending the steps, picking his way through the blood. Slung round his neck he carried a huge gourd containing some liquid and into it he dipped a silver cup that he offered to each prisoner in the line.

Most drank.

When it came to Malinal's turn she asked the soldier, who had a big, plain, honest, sunburned face, what he was offering her.

"Why it's *Iztli*, of course."

"*Iztli*?"

"Obsidian-knife-water." He glanced towards the summit of the pyramid, less than fifty paces above them, reverberating with the agonised screams of the next victim. "Drink!" He held out the silver cup. His tone was almost beseeching, his eyes level and kind, wrinkled with laughter lines. "Drink beautiful lady."

"What will it do?"

He looked meaningfully up again to the summit of the pyramid, then back down. "It will dull your pain lady."

As Malinal reached out, Tozi lunged up from the step below and knocked the cup aside. "It's not about dulling pain! Listen to those screams! They don't give a shit about our pain. They use *Iztli* to dull our wits. They use it to make us docile so we're easier to bring under the knife."

The kind eyes of the soldier had turned indifferent. "Your loss," he shrugged, refilling the cup and moving down past Tozi to the next victim, who drank greedily.

Malinal was thinking, *maybe I don't mind being docile so long as there's no pain when the knife opens my chest*. She was about to call the soldier back, but Tozi silenced her with a glance and whispered: "No! We have to stay alert. This isn't over yet."

Malinal looked closer and saw that something was back in the girl's eyes, a spark, a fire, that had fled after the fade and her subsequent catastrophic fit in the pen.

There was another outburst of horrific screams and the whole line, like some monstrous centipede, shuffled two steps closer to the summit.

"What are we going to do?" Malinal asked. The heart that was soon to be ripped from her chest was pounding against her ribs; the blood that was soon to be drained from her body was coursing through her veins and beating in her ears.

Tozi suddenly smiled and Malinal caught a fleeting glimpse of unsuspected depths in her strange new friend—of a sweet, otherworldly innocence beaming through the chalk and charcoal, and through the deeper disguise of the tough streetwise beggar girl in which she concealed her witchiness. "I thought all my powers were gone," she said, "maybe gone forever. But right after they took Coyotl something started to come back…"

The line trudged another dreadful step upward.

"I don't know what it is yet," Tozi continued. "But there's something there! I can feel it!"

"Will you try to fade us again?"

"No! It's not that."

"Why so sure?"

"I've tried already—before we started climbing the steps, just for a second or two—but it didn't work"

"Is it the thing you call the fog?"

Tozi shook her head: "No, not the fog."

"Then what?"

"I don't know! I wish I did! But there's something there I can use. I'm sure of that. I just have to find it."

More screams went up from the summit of the pyramid, close now, though still out of sight because of the steep slope of the stairway. There was the distinct wet *CRACK* the obsidian knife makes when it splits a human breastbone followed by a high-pitched gurgling screech and a sudden pulse of blood gushing over the top of the steps.

Ahead of them, her swaying pendulous buttocks pitifully uncovered by a flimsy paper loin-cloth, a young Totonac woman who had likewise refused the *Iztli* suddenly turned in her tracks, reached out her hand and gripped Malinal's shoulder. "I CAN'T BEAR THIS!" she screamed. Her eyes were rolling. "I CAN'T STAND IT ANYMORE." She gave Malinal a forceful shove, almost dislodging her from the slippery step and said: "Jump with me right now! You and me together! Let's throw ourselves down. The fall will kill us. It's better than the knife…"

A death chosen, rather than a death inflicted? Malinal could see the point of that. And it would have the added advantage of cheating the bloodthirsty gods of the Mexica.

But such a death was not for her while there was still hope, and Tozi had given her hope. She swayed, pulled her shoulder free of the Totonac's grip. "Jump if you must," she told her. "I won't try to stop you but I won't go with you."

"Why not? Don't you understand what will be done to us there?" The woman turned her face up to the summit of the pyramid, still hidden by the gradient.

"I understand," said Malinal, "and it's OK. You take care of your death and I'll take care of mine."

***

With groans of fear, whispered prayers, and the slack, dull faces of *Iztli* intoxication, the prisoners continued to shuffle upwards, pausing for long moments, then climbing again. Only those near the very top could see the altar and the sacrificial stone but the butchered torsos of women who'd climbed the steps moments before continued to be thrown down by the priests, a constant reminder of what was to come.

Up a step. Stop.

Up two steps. Stop.

Though the moon was again behind cloud, the whole summit was brightly lit by torches and braziers and Malinal began to see first the heads, then the shoulders, then the upper bodies of the team of sacrificers on the summit platform.

Ahuizotl was there!

How could he not be since he'd want to gloat over her death?

Her fingers curled into claws.

Beside the High Priest was Cuitlahuac who had also shared her bed.

And there, nude, bathed from head to toe in blood, working with furious efficiency, his face fixed in an ecstatic grin, was the coward Moctezuma, who she'd seen shit himself with fear.

WHACK! CRACK! In went the obsidian knife again, saturating the white paper garments of the next victim with bright red blood in an instant. Arteries were severed, more blood fountained into the air, and with a horrible, rending SQUELCH, the heart was out.

Malinal distinctly heard Moctezuma say, apparently to thin air: "Welcome Lord. All this is for you." Then at once another victim was stretched over the sacrificial stone and the Totonac woman climbed the final step to the summit platform and stood waiting, watching the killing team busy with their tasks. As the knife rose and fell she turned with a sad smile on her face, stretched her arms out beside her like wings and stood poised over the plunging stairway.

Cuitlahuac saw the danger first and barked an order for her to be held, but as the guards closed in she grappled with one of them, somehow unbalanced him, and tumbled with him over and over down the steep stairs, rolling and bouncing, their bodies pounded and broken into bloody shards long before they reached the bottom.

Malinal knew Moctezuma to be a superstitious man.

An ignominious suicide, carried out in his presence, snatching a beating human heart from Hummingbird's grasp, could never be anything other than a very bad omen indeed—one for which Ahuizotl as High Priest must surely be held responsible. The snakeskin drum, the conchs, the trumpets all instantly ceased their din and in the ghastly silence that followed the only sound to be heard came from Tozi. It was that same soft, insistent whisper she'd used when she'd faded them in the pen—and in the same way it now rose in intensity, seeming to deepen and roughen, becoming almost a snarl or a growl.

Ahuizotl took a step forward. His eyes found Malinal but drifted past her. He seemed shocked and disoriented.

Was he imagining the terrible ways Moctezuma would punish him?

Or was Tozi getting inside his head?

Malinal was beginning to hope her friend really had got her powers back when she felt Moctezuma's blood-rimmed glare drill into her skull as his four helpers grasped her by the arms and legs and threw her down on her back over the sacrificial stone.

***

It was truly a night of the gods, torn by winds and storm. Thunder rolled and huge black clouds harried the fleeing moon, sometimes reducing her to a flicker of balefire, sometimes allowing her furious and jaundiced face to peer through, sometimes shutting off her light entirely as though a door in heaven had closed.

Moctezuma had been killing since morning but now, in the depths of the night, his work illuminated by flickering torches and glowing braziers, he felt no fatigue. He had consumed two more massive doses of Teonanactl and the god power of the mushrooms coursed through his veins, making him ferocious, vigorous and invulnerable.

Far from tiring him, each new blow he struck with the obsidian knife seemed to animate him further. Should the priests find him five thousand more victims, he would kill them all. Ten thousand? Bring them on! There was nothing he would not do for his god.

Moctezuma felt preternaturally aware of everything. EVERYTHING.

Of this world of blood and bone, and of that other shadow world where he met and talked with Hummingbird.

The god had been absent for many hours while the new batch of sacrifices offered themselves to the knife but now he returned, with so little fanfare it seemed he'd always been there. He stood between Cuitlahuac and Ahuizotl unnoticed by them, his face sly and amused.

"Welcome Lord," Moctezuma said, holding up a palpitating heart, "all this is for you." He threw the streaming organ on the brazier, where it steamed and smoked, and immediately turned to the next victim, tore her body open and plucked her heart out too.

Everything was going wonderfully well, Moctezuma thought. He couldn't stop himself grinning and cackling. And why should he? The god was with him again, the downpayment on his price was being made in hearts and blood, and now he could expect divine help against the powerful strangers. No matter if they possessed fire serpents that could kill from afar! No matter if wild animals fought beside them in battle! With Hummingbird leading the way the Mexica were certain of victory and even if the strangers were the companions of Quetzalcoatl himself they would be vanquished! There was no other conceivable outcome.

The dream was sweet until Moctezuma heard Cuitlahuac shout "GRAB HER" and the scuff of bare feet behind him. He whirled round as the bloody corpse on the sacrificial stone was dragged aside to be butchered and witnessed something extraordinary and unbelievable. Instead of submissively waiting to take her place under his knife, the next victim was standing at the edge of the summit-platform, her paper garments flapping in the wind, her arms stretched out beside her like wings, poised to throw herself down the northern stairway. This must not under any circumstances be allowed to happen for it would bring the displeasure of the god. Moctezuma's heart pounded against his ribs and anger surged through him. He would have Ahuizotl's skin if the woman went through with it. Time seemed to race as guards moved towards her. One reached her. They wrestled on the edge of the abyss and then slowly, with the impossibility of a thing never seen before, both figures tumbled from view…

An awful sound broke the shocked silence that followed—an eerie, rough, whispering snarl that had the rhythms of magic. Moctezuma saw at once that its source was a dirty little female with wild hair. She was waiting second in the line of prisoners near the top of the stairway and staring straight at him.

Nobody looked the Great Speaker of the Mexica in the eye!

Yet this filthy child, whose heart he would soon cut out, showed no fear as she calmly met his gaze.

And she wasn't alone! One step above her stood another defiant figure. Tall, plastered chalk-white, hair roughly shorn, in the paper clothes of her humiliation, this woman looked nothing like a victim and stared him down with the same predatory anticipation as the child, throwing him further into turmoil.

Panic seized him as he sensed everything falling apart. The terrible omen of the suicide followed at once by the bizarre behaviour of these two females threatened to unman him completely. He sought out Hummingbird, fearing his anger, yet filled with a hopeless yearning for absolution, but the god who had been so present only moments before had vanished again, as silently and as mysteriously as he had appeared.

"Aaaah! Aaaah!" Moctezuma's bowels cramped and loosened, cramped and loosened, an ancient curse returning to haunt him, but he could not evacuate here at the top of the pyramid in full public view. It was simply unthinkable.

He clenched, tried to bring his emotions under control

and a renewed surge of the god power of the mushrooms pulsed through him, shoving a fist of vomit into his mouth, forcing him to swallow and gulp like a frog. The tall woman smiled.

Smiled!

How dare she?

Anger triumphed over fear and he began to think clearly again. The suicide was the worst form of sacrilege, yet amends could be made. The god had deserted him again, but he had done so before and there was still hope that the harvest of victims would lure him back. The only answer was to put all distractions aside and continue with the sacrifices as if nothing had happened.

Moctezuma signalled to the musicians to resume play as his four helpers seized the tall woman by the arms and legs, spun her round with practised economy of effort, and cast her down on her back on the sacrificial stone. He raised the obsidian knife, gripping its hilt in both hands, and muttered the ritual prayer — "Oh Lord, Hummingbird, at the left hand of the Sun, accept this my offering."

He was about to plunge the knife down when the voice of the god, loud and unexpected, boomed inside his head: "NO! I do NOT want this offering. You must NOT kill this woman."

Moctezuma froze in place, the knife poised: "But Lord, you told me to bring you hearts."

"You must still bring me hearts, Moctezuma, but not this heart. I have chosen this woman AND SHE MUST NOT BE HARMED. I have work for her to do."

"You have… chosen her, Lord?"

"Just as I chose you."

Suddenly the tenor of the divine voice changed and Moctezuma found himself once more in the presence of Hummingbird. It was as though they were both looking down on the victim from a great height. The war god's

skin glowed white hot. "Set her free," he commanded.

Moctezuma hesitated. Was he understanding correctly? Could there be some mistake. "Set her free?" he babbled.

The god sighed: "Yes. Free. Must you repeat every word I say?"

And at the same instant, in the world of blood and bone, Moctezuma felt Ahuizotl at his elbow, whispering alarm in his ear "You must NOT free her, Excellency! This woman must die! She must die! The god will not forgive us if she walks from the stone."

Moctezuma remembered that he alone conversed with Hummingbird, while for Ahuizotl and others it must seem he was talking to himself. "BE SILENT!" he roared.

"But Lord…"

"You know NOTHING Ahuizotl! I will have your SKIN for failing me this night."

The High Priest cowered and trembled, stammering apologies and then, unbelievably, the woman on the stone spoke! Her voice was rich and throaty, somehow familiar, and she seemed to look deep into Moctezuma's eyes: "Your priest is corrupt," she told him. "He broke his vow of chastity and took me to his bed…"

"LIES!" Ahuizotl screamed. "LIES! LIES!"

But Chuitlahauc had stepped close now and was examining the woman's face, rubbing at her chalk-white mask, revealing ever more of her skin. "Malinal!" he suddenly exclaimed. "This is Malinal, Lord Speaker! She was your interpreter when the messenger from the Chontal Maya brought tidings of the gods to you. You ordered her execution."

"Ahuizotl disobeyed the Lord Speaker," the woman said. "He keeps a secret house in the district of Tlateloco. He took me there from your palace four months ago. He used my body…"

"LIES!" Ahuizotl shrieked again. "All lies!"

"There's more here than meets the eye," Cuitlahauc said. He was known to be a stickler for rules and regulations, an enemy of Ahuizotl and a strong advocate of priestly celibacy. "The charge is grave. We must question the woman further and discover the truth."

"NO!" snarled Ahuizotl. "Kill her!"

Moctezuma's eyes darted back and forth between the two men and down to the prone, spread body of the woman.

Yes, he remembered her. His stomach cramped and his bowels rumbled. She had witnessed his shame and he had ordered her death; yet here she was four months later still alive.

How could that be if her story was not true?

As another devastating cramp gripped his stomach and a bubble of sour air burst from his mouth he made his decision. No questions could be asked. He would deal with Ahuizotl later, but the woman knew his secret and she must die with it now.

Her eyes, huge and dark, gazed up at him, catching and magnifying the flickering flames of the torches and the fiery glow of the braziers, seeming to burn into his soul. Resisting a powerful urge to recoil, even to run from her, Moctezuma jerked the dripping knife above his head, felt a thrill of pleasure as her pupils dilated with fear, and put all his force into a killing blow.

That never landed.

That never even began.

"You pathetic grubby little human," boomed the voice of Hummingbird. Unseen and unheard by all the others the god was still at his side, radiant as a volcano. "You will free this woman at once. You will send her from this city unharmed. I have spoken."

Moctezuma struggled, tried to move his knife hand and discovered that it was paralysed in place above his head. "Release her, or die," said the god. "In fact why don't you just die anyway? I think I prefer Cuitlahauc for your role."

"Bu… bu… bu…" Moctezuma tried to speak, but could not, tried to breathe but could not.

"Interesting, isn't it," said the god, "this business of dying? Fun when you're dishing it out, not so nice when you're at the receiving end."

Moctezuma gaped, his chest heaved, and yet no breath would come. It was as though a huge hand covered his nose and mouth.

"You are desperate to breathe," the god continued. "It gets worse. Very soon fear will overwhelm you, you will lose all control of your body and you will void your bowels. Tut tut! WHERE WILL YOUR SECRET BE THEN?"

"Gahhh, ahhh, gaargh…"

Moctezuma felt it coming now, felt death all over him like a swarm of bees, was shaken by another terrifying cramp and tried desperately to signal his surrender.

The god's smile was malevolent. "What?" he said. "What was that?"

"Gnahh, aargh…"

"Ah. You agree? Is that what you're saying? You will release the woman?"

His head spinning, his knees rubber, Moctezuma nodded his assent.

"Hmmm," said the god. "I rather thought you would. Well, I suppose I shall give you another chance. Grooming Cuitlahauc to play your part would be such a bore."

At once the sense of a hand clamped to Moctezuma's face was gone and he could breathe again. Gasping, heaving, his vision steadying, he turned on his four assistants. They held the woman stretched over the sacrificial stone, gripping her by her wrists and ankles, terror and confusion squirming on their faces. "RELEASE HER," he roared.

***

After she'd struggled to her feet Moctezuma ordered the woman to be taken from the pyramid, given clothes and sent on her way out of Tenochtitlan. The god had said she was to leave the city. The god had said she was not to be harmed. The god must not be denied.

Yet she refused to go!

Instead, looking him straight in the eye as though she were his equal, this woman, this Malinal as Cuitlahauc had named her, made a new demand.

"I was brought here with my friend," she said, indicating the wild-haired girl at the top of the steps. "I won't leave without her."

Moctezuma turned to Hummingbird, but the god had again deserted him.

He looked for Ahuizotl. The High Priest too had vanished.

He looked to Cuitlahauc, who knew Malinal, and to the other nobles. They stood in groups around the vacant sacrificial stone whispering to one another.

Whispering sedition.

"I remember our last meeting," Malinal said quietly. She looked pointedly at Moctezuma's belly: "It seemed the royal person was unwell. Allow me to express the hope that you have fully recovered your health." As she spoke Moctezuma felt the eyes of the woman's little ragged friend on him, heard the whisper of magic still pouring from her lips and helplessly doubled over as another agonising cramp struck him.

"Take her," he gasped. "Take her. I free you both."

Smeared with chalk and blood, Malinal seemed more demon or ghost than human flesh and blood.

"Wait!" she said. "There's one more thing."

~~~~~~~~~~~~~~~~~~

Read the rest of the novel *War God: Nights of the Witch* by Graham Hancock, out now from Peach Publishing, and available at all major online retailers. Also available now is *War God 2: Return of the Plumed Serpent*, and be sure to look out for War God 3, coming soon…

Occultists and Occult Fiction

BY DONALD TYSON

There's a definite link between the practice of the occult and the writing of occult fiction. Many great Western magicians over the past two centuries have also been writers of weird tales, and prominent writers of weird tales have dabbled in the study or practice of the occult. The best occultists are not the best fiction writers, nor are the top writers of strange fiction the most skilled occultists, but the crossover is common.

This should not come as a surprise when we reflect that reading science fiction has always been extremely popular among serious scientists, particularly those involved in the "hard" sciences. Many science fiction writers are themselves scientists, or at least have been trained in science fields. Why would stories of the supernatural not appeal just as strongly to those who study and interact with the supernatural every day? A study of the occult allows writers of occult fiction to avoid some of the more glaring mistakes made by their peers.

H. P. Lovecraft

The preeminent writer of the weird, H. P. Lovecraft (1890-1937), always professed to hold the practice of magic in contempt. When readers of his stories wrote to him and asked if he drew upon his personal experience in the black arts, Lovecraft would laugh at the very idea. Nonetheless, he did read works on Theosophy, including some writings by Madame Blavatsky herself. He found the grand concepts of Theosophy intriguing.

The Theosophists taught that there were successive ages of mankind before the present age, with different root races inhabiting the world, and numerous levels of existence through which the soul moved after death. Blavatsky also believed in the lost lands of Hyperborea, Atlantis, and Lemuria, and that the world was strewn with relics of ancient wisdom.

The sheer vastness of the Theosophical universe appealed to Lovecraft's conviction that reality extends far beyond the senses and the limited minds of humanity. There is an echo of Lovecraft's "spaces between the stars" in Theosophy's hierarchal astral planes, and something of his "old ones" in the seven root races.

Lovecraft was not, as many of his readers assume, a student of Western magic. In his stories he mentions historical texts on magic, mixing them in with the fanciful texts that he and other writers made up for their fiction, but he knew almost nothing about them other than their names, which he sometimes derived from the 11th edition of the *Encyclopaedia Britannica*, published in 1910.

The most famous book on magic, the fabled *Necronomicon*, was wholly Lovecraft's own invention. He dreamed the name, and in other dreams saw the book. The story fragment "The Book," which was written sometime around 1934, may perhaps describe Lovecraft's dream experience of encountering the *Necronomicon*, although the book

H. P. Lovecraft

Clark Ashton Smith

H. P. Blavatsky

Algernon Blackwood

described in this story fragment is not the *Necronomicon* but some other tome of black magic. At least it gives the sense of strangeness and wonder Lovecraft must have experienced in his dream upon finding the evil book:

> I remember when I found it—in a dimly lighted place near the black, oily river where the mists always swirl. That place was very old, and the ceiling-high shelves full of rotting volumes reached back endlessly through windowless inner rooms and alcoves. There were, besides, great formless heaps of books on the floor and in crude bins; and it was in one of these heaps that I found the thing. I never learned its title, for the early pages were missing; but it fell open toward the end and gave me a glimpse of something which sent my senses reeling.

Clark Ashton Smith

Lovecraft's good friend and fellow writer of weird tales, Clark Ashton Smith (1893-1961), who started his literary career as a poet, found the same inspiration in the wild ramblings of H. P. Blavatsky that Lovecraft found there. Smith did not belong to the Theosophical Society either, but he used its teachings as an esoteric well from which to draw story ideas. In a letter Smith wrote to Lovecraft in 1933, he admitted, "One can disregard the theosophy, and make good use of the stuff about elder continents, etc. I got my own ideas about Hyperborea, Poseidonis, etc., from such sources, and then turned my imagination loose."

H. P. Blavatsky

Madame Helena Petrovna Blavatsky (1831-1891) was what is known as a physical medium—a spirit medium who could not only talk to and channel spirits, but also cause physical effects to occur during séances, such as the sudden materialization of solid objects, an event known as an *apport*. As a girl growing up in tsarist Russia, she earned a reputation for finding lost objects, and for talking to unseen spirits. Stubborn, headstrong, reckless to a fault, she married at age 17, abandoned her husband three months later, traveled the world on her father's money, and founded the Theosophical Society in New York in 1875.

The basis of Theosophy was Blavatsky's claim to be in psychic communication with enlightened beings, called Mahatmas, who had agreed to teach her and her followers a secret doctrine. This pattern occurs repeatedly in Western occultism. Occult schools, or lodges as they are sometimes called, are formed when one or more individuals claims to have established communication with spiritual teachers. All of the occult schools mentioned in this essay were based on such communication.

Theosophy quickly gained a loyal following. Blavatsky cranked out two enormous works, *Isis Unveiled* (1877) and *The Secret Doctrine* (in two volumes, 1888-9). The material in these works was largely derived from other sources, but even so they are impressive if bewildering literary accomplishments.

In 1885, Blavatsky was "debunked" by Richard Hodgson of the Society for Psychical Research. He published a report in the December issue of the SPR magazine in which he claimed to show that her apports had been faked, along with her materializations during séances of enlightened masters.

Blavatsky probably did use physical trickery to impress those attending her séances. However, this does not mean she should be dismissed out of hand. She was a gifted spirit medium and possessed other unusual esoteric talents. I have no doubt that she was, indeed, in psychic communication with beings who claimed to be enlightened masters. That she could not make them appear at will to others during séances does not disallow such communication.

Blavatsky dabbled in occult fiction, but in a minor way. Her short story "The Ensouled Violin" is fairly well known and often appears in anthologies of ghost stories. A short form of the story was published in the January 1880 issue of the periodical, *The Theosophist*, and a longer version was included in a collection of Blavatsky's fiction titled *Nightmare Tales*, published in 1892. This book contains five of her spooky stories, with the "Ensouled Violin" occupying the place of honor at the end. It involves a violin in which a soul has been trapped in order to produce music of unearthly beauty. More recently the Theosophical Society published nine of Blavatsky's stories under the same title.

Algernon Blackwood

A number of Theosophists, although they did not attain great fame as magicians or mediums, became better-known as writers of occult fiction. Algernon Blackwood (1869-1951) joined the Toronto Theosophical Society in 1891, when he was just 21 years old, and was made the First Secretary of that Theosophical lodge. In 1899, when he returned to his native England, Blackwood became a member of the London Theosophical Society. He was also a member, for a short time at least, of the Hermetic Order of the Golden Dawn.

The Blackwood story that best expresses the vastnesses of worlds within worlds and dimensions beyond the stars that so attracted H. P. Lovecraft and Clark Ashton Smith to Theosophical teachings is "The Willows," a strange tale of two men making their way down the Danube in a canoe through some of the bleakest wilderness of Europe, who get stranded on a small island that is being eroded away from under them by the river. For reasons not given in the story these men are noticed by alien intelligences that are unseen but ever present. The power of the story stems not from what Blackwood describes but from what he intimates about these unseen others. Lovecraft, in his essay, *Supernatural Horror in Literature*, wrote of this story, "Here art and restraint in narrative reach their very highest development, and an impression of lasting poignancy is produced without a single strained passage or a single false note."

Blackwood is perhaps best remembered for his recurring story character, John Silence, a master of magic who went around solving supernatural mysteries for the betterment of humanity. He is described in a

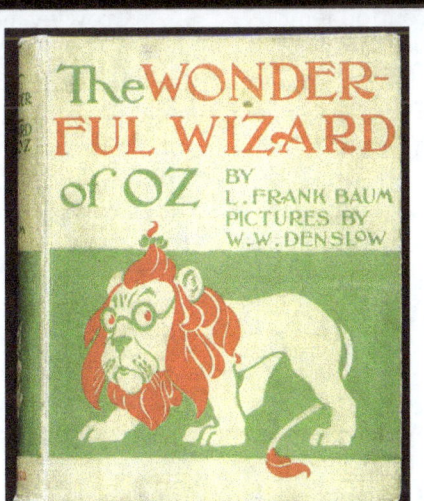

L. Frank Baum

series of six stories, the best known being "The Nemesis of Fire," which concerns the awakening of a protective fire elemental by the removal of a scarab brooch from an ancient Egyptian mummy.

The 1908 story collection *John Silence—Physician Extraordinary* is mentioned by Lovecraft in his essay. It contains five of the John Silence stories—the sixth, "A Victim of Higher Space," was published some years later.

Silence, as a character, is a bit stuffy and heavy-handed. It may be that Blackwood's practical knowledge of occultism inhibited the freedom of his creativity when he came to write about his magician detective. Blackwood's treatment of occult topics in his stories, on the other hand, is first rate. No one else has described a fire elemental with such chilling accuracy.

In the story, Silence instructs his assistant to construct a protective psychic barrier around himself. This shows a knowledge of practical occultism on Blackwood's part:

> "And, for your safety," he said earnestly, "imagine *now*—and for that matter, imagine always until we leave this place—imagine with the utmost keenness, that you are surrounded by a shell that protects you. Picture yourself inside a protective envelope, and build it up with the most intense imagination you can evoke. Pour the whole force of your thought and will into it. Believe vividly all through this adventure that such a shell, constructed of your thought, will and imagination, surrounds you completely, and that nothing can pierce it to attack."

This is a perfectly workable occult technique, although it requires years of rigorous mental training before it can be done effectively.

L. Frank Baum

Another Theosophist who used the society's teachings to expand his imagination was L. Frank Baum (1856-1919), author of *The Wonderful Wizard of Oz* and other Oz books. For a time he was editor of the *Aberdeen Saturday Pioneer*, and in 1890 he wrote in that newspaper, "Amongst the various sects so

Aleister Crowley · A. E. Waite · Dion Fortune

numerous in America today who find their fundamental basis in occultism, the Theosophists stand pre-eminent both in intelligence and point of numbers." This shows that he was under no illusions as to the occult nature of the society's teachings. Baum and his wife joined the Theosophical Society in 1892. *The Wonderful Wizard of Oz* was published in 1900.

Hermetic Order of the Golden Dawn

In 1888, thirteen years after the Theosophical Society was founded in New York, three Freemasons established the London temple of the Hermetic Order of the Golden Dawn, a Rosicrucian society devoted to the study and teaching of practical magic in the Western tradition.

The Golden Dawn attracted many intellectuals and artists, among them writers such as the poet W. B. Yeats (1865-1939), who joined in 1890 and was a key member for many years. Before joining the Golden Dawn in London he had been heavily involved in Dublin with hermetism and theosophy. Yeats actually practiced ritual magic, and the influence of the Golden Dawn teachings upon his work was profound. For a time he headed the London temple.

About his occult studies, Yeats wrote, "If I had not made magic my constant study I could not have written a single word of my Blake book, nor would *The Countess Kathleen* ever have come to exist. The mystical life is the centre of all that I do and all that I think and all that I write."

The Golden Dawn was notable in spawning a trio of dedicated occult writers who were also practicing occultists and who went on to found their own occult societies. Each dabbled in occult fiction.

Aleister Crowley

The most notorious of the three was Aleister Crowley (1875-1947), wayward son of a wealthy English brewer. He joined the Golden Dawn in 1898 and quickly rose to the higher ranks of the order. He was utterly devoted to the practice of magic, to the exclusion of all other considerations, yet he still somehow found time to climb

mountains, write poetry and play chess at the master's level. He was instrumental in the schism that broke the original Golden Dawn into two rival factions, and began the long and tortuous dissolution of the order.

In 1907 Crowley founded his own occult order, the Order of the Silver Star, and began to teach pupils on an official basis. He believed himself to be the Great Beast foretold by the biblical Book of Revelation, who would usher into the world the Antichrist and initiate a period of destruction and suffering.

The central principle of his cult of Thelema was the power of the human will. *"Do what thou wilt shall be the whole of the Law"* became his primary motto, a line taken from his prophetic and spirit-dictated *Book of the Law*, which he received psychically through his guardian angel in Cairo in 1904.

Thelema, in a nutshell, is the performance of one's True Will, the thing one was intended to do from birth, as opposed to ordinary willfulness. It does not mean doing whatever you want, it means discovering what you were created to do above all else, and doing it. This brings happiness, contentment, and fulfillment.

Crowley wrote a huge number of nonfiction books about Thelema and about magic in general, but he also found time to write some fiction. Like Blackwood, he created an occult detective. Crowley's detective is named Simon Iff. Six of these stories were collected together under the title *The Scrutinies of Simon Iff*, published in 1917-8 in New York. Crowley later wrote three other collections of Iff stories, *Simon Iff In America* (12 stories), *Simon Iff Abroad* (4 stories), and *Simon Iff Psychoanalyst* (2 stories). The character Simon Iff also appears in the novel *Moonchild*, which details the ritual creation of a magical child. This involved impregnating a woman under suitable occult conditions, and then specific rituals and meditations, along with a controlled diet and a symbolic environment throughout the term of pregnancy, so that a desired spirit could be drawn into the fetus.

A collection of three other stories by Crowley was published in 1929 under the title *The Stratagem and other Stories*. In 1902 he wrote a play title *Tannhäuser: A Story of*

All Time. His production of poetry continued throughout his lifetime and may be roughly divided into mystical and sensual poetry. Needless to say, there is a crossover between the two types of poems—Crowley believed ecstasy to be a pathway to spiritual enlightenment.

A. E. Waite

Another man who led a version of the Golden Dawn for a time was the writer Arthur Edward Waite (1857-1942), who was initiated into the Golden Dawn in 1891 along with his wife. He was never comfortable as one of the rank and file members of the order and had frictions with some of its leading lights. Crowley despised Waite as a plodding, pedantic fool, and Waite equally despised Crowley as a degenerate and pervert. When the Golden Dawn split into factions in 1903, Waite took over the running of the London temple and renamed his faction the Order of the Independent and Rectified Rite.

In 1915, Waite broke away completely from the Golden Dawn and formed his own independent occult order, the Fellowship of the Rosy Cross. He was a mystic rather than a practicing magician, and never liked the emphasis the Golden Dawn placed on the mastery of practical magic. In drafting the constitution of his new order, he wrote, "The Fellowship of the Rosy Cross has no concern whatsoever in occult or psychical research, it is a Quest of Grace and not a Quest of Power."

Waite's output of nonfiction text on various aspects of occultism was immense, but he also wrote two fantasy novels, *Prince Starbeam: A Tale of Fairyland* (1889) and the *Quest of the Golden Stairs* (1893).

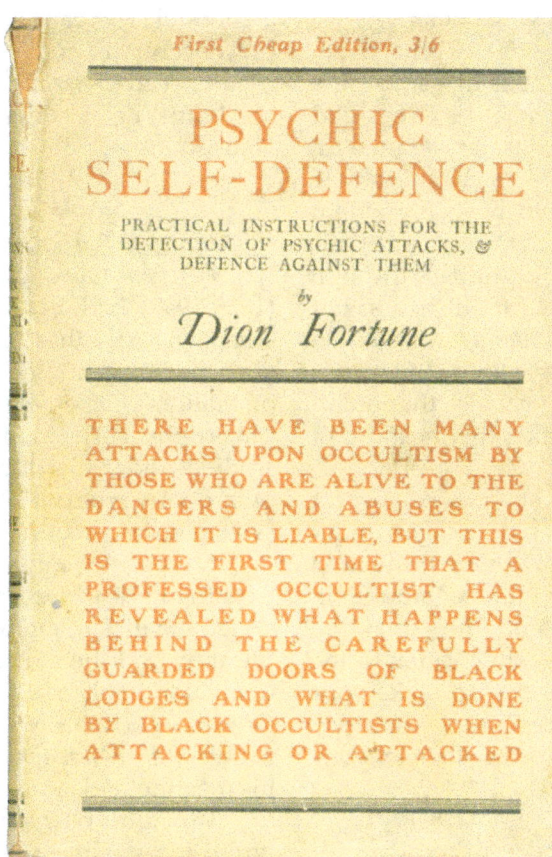

First Cheap Edition, 3/6

PSYCHIC SELF-DEFENCE

PRACTICAL INSTRUCTIONS FOR THE DETECTION OF PSYCHIC ATTACKS, & DEFENCE AGAINST THEM

by

Dion Fortune

THERE HAVE BEEN MANY ATTACKS UPON OCCULTISM BY THOSE WHO ARE ALIVE TO THE DANGERS AND ABUSES TO WHICH IT IS LIABLE, BUT THIS IS THE FIRST TIME THAT A PROFESSED OCCULTIST HAS REVEALED WHAT HAPPENS BEHIND THE CAREFULLY GUARDED DOORS OF BLACK LODGES AND WHAT IS DONE BY BLACK OCCULTISTS WHEN ATTACKING OR ATTACKED

Concerning the first novel, the reviewer for the *Saturday Review* of October 11, 1890, wrote, "Full of dark things and occult, too sad and too secret, we fear, for dimmed earthly intelligences, is *Prince Starbeam*, a tale of Fairyland." The book reviewer of the *Spectator* wrote in October, 1890, "As a fairy-story it is too long and diffuse, and though we do not fail to recognise a certain beauty of imagination and smoothness of diction, it is not of that simple and true fairy-tale type which should clothe even the highest efforts."

The *Quest of the Golden Stairs* was republished in 1927 by the Theosophical Publishing House. The book reviewer in the July 22 issue of the *Spectator* for that year described it as a "fairy story" and wrote of Waite's novel, "It is an escape from the world into an enchanted kingdom, and we advise the reader to set out on a pilgrimage with Prince Starbeam and see with him the Phoenix, the Daughter of the Stars and all those who wear white or green samite."

Dion Fortune

The third in the triumvirate of notable occultists of the Golden Dawn to write fiction is Dion Fortune (1890-1946). Her real name was Violet Mary Firth. As a child growing up in Wales, she had visions and flashes of psychic ability. She joined Theosophy, and then in 1919 was initiated into the Golden Dawn in London, while it was being run by Moina Mathers, the widow of one of the original founders, or chiefs, of the order, Samuel Mathers. Both women were strong-willed with decided opinions. Fortune bristled under Mrs. Mathers' control, and in 1922 she left the Golden Dawn to form her own occult order, the Fraternity of the Inner Light (later known as the Society of the Inner Light). She did not entirely forsake her interest in Theosophy—in 1925 she became, for a brief period, president of the Christian Mystic Lodge of the Theosophical Society.

Fortune was paranoid about being under magical attack. Her popular nonfiction book *Psychic Self-Defence* (1930) is based on this paranoia. It is quite chilling in places, and reads like a suspense thriller. She believed that Mrs. Mathers was working malicious magic against her, and that she had to defend herself with magical means. It's worth noting that Aleister Crowley thought exactly the same thing about Samuel Mathers, when Crowley split away from the Golden Dawn.

Her order taught a mix of Golden Dawn magic and Theosophical cosmology, with an emphasis on the then very highly-regarded fields of psychotherapy and psychology, which Fortune had studied at the University of London. She wrote numerous nonfiction works on various aspects of occultism. For the most part they are somewhat vague and lacking in practical application. Her *Psychic Self-Defence* is the exception to this rule, which is why it is so popular.

Fortune also wrote a large amount of occult fiction. Her prose fiction is the best that has been written by a leading occultist. Crowley's fiction has flashes of brilliance, but overall Fortune's fiction is superior. In her novels she described some of the practical techniques of magic she picked up in the Golden Dawn. Indeed, I find that there is more to be learned in a practical way from Dion Fortune's fiction than from her nonfiction.

Her fiction is concerned with classical mythology and

with the legend of the Holy Grail, which also preoccupied Arthur Edward Waite. She even made her home in Glastonbury to be closer to the roots of the Arthurian legends. Her most intriguing character is Vivien LeFay Morgan, the direct descendant and reincarnation of the Arthurian figure, Morgan LeFey, Arthur's half-sister. A nonfiction work by Fortune, *Avalon of the Heart* (1934), was said by the fantasy writer Marion Zimmer Bradley to have been the inspiration for her own popular novel *The Mists of Avalon*.

Fortune wrote five novels. In *The Demon Lover* (1927), an evil magician plots to use an innocent girl against rival magicians, but ends up falling in love with her and sacrificing himself for her. *The Winged Bull* (1935) is about a neurotic woman psychologically damaged by her involvement with an evil adept, who is restored to health, and awakened to the power of her own sexuality, with the help of a male companion and a wise old magician. *The Goat Foot God* (1936) is about a man driven by the karma of a previous incarnation to invoke the Greek god Pan. In *The Sea Priestess* (1938) a man has an affair with Vivien LeFey Morgan, a mysterious enchantress. He later marries, but is disappointed with his wife, whom he compares unfavorably to the enchantress, until his wife learns to channel the power of the Goddess through herself and wins his love. *Moon Magic* (unfinished at her death; published 1956) finds Vivien LeFey Morgan in London, where she is setting up a temple to the Mysteries. She undertakes to restore to its proper balance the soul of a brilliant neurologist who has forgotten the meaning of happiness.

Dion Fortune published a collection of a dozen short stories about an occultist who is also a psychologist under the title *The Secrets of Dr. Taverner* (1926). In her introduction to the collection, Fortune called her stories "studies in super-normal pathology" and wrote, "They may be regarded as fiction, designed, like the conversation of the Fat Boy recorded in The Pickwick Papers, 'to make your flesh creep,' or they may be considered to be what they actually are, studies in little-known aspects of psychology put in the form of fiction..."

G. I. Gurdjieff

Before I close, let me mention a man who is seldom regarded as a magician, but whose esoteric influence over the minds of others has been considerable. George Ivanovich Gurdjieff (c. 1866-1949) was, like Madame Blavatsky, a product of pre-communist Russia. The two share much in common. They both claimed mysterious adventurous lives. They never ceased lying about themselves, so that it is impossible to be sure what is true and what is false in their histories. They both possessed magnetic personalities that charmed, captivated and overawed other human beings.

Gurdjieff's central teaching was that human beings are asleep without knowing it, but can only achieve their full potential when they wake up. His system involved exercises designed to wake up the mind from its deep

slumber. This involved destroying every belief, every conceit, every truism, held by an individual, leaving the mind naked and vulnerable to the implantation of new beliefs. In effect, it was a form of brain-washing.

His writings consist of a trilogy of works called *All and Everything*. The first part is titled *Beelzebub's Tales to his Grandson* (Russian, 1924; English, 1950). The second is *Meetings with Remarkable Men*. The third part is *Life Is Real Only Then, When 'I Am'*.

Beelzebub's Tales to his Grandson may be regarded as a work of fiction. It consists of the entertaining chatter of a space alien named Beelzebub to his grandson, Hassein, as they journey through space on the spacecraft Karnak. Beelzebub relates the strange experiences he had on the planet Earth while dealing with the race known as man.

Gurdjieff deliberately made his first book as difficult as possible to read, with the purpose of challenging the preconceptions and complacency of his readers. I have tried to read *Beelzebub's Tales to his Grandson*, and can only say I must be very deeply asleep, because I could find no value in it.

P. D. Ouspensky

Perhaps Gurdjieff's star pupil, Peter D. Ouspensky (1878-1947) had better luck with Gurdjieff's first book. Ouspensky, another Russian, wrote many nonfiction books about his master's teachings, and his own understanding of reality. Ouspensky was attracted to the teachings of Theosophy early in life. He met Gurdjieff in 1915 and studied under him for ten years. In 1922 he founded his own occult group in London to teach the *fourth way*, the system he had acquired under Gurdjieff.

Ouspensky's nonfiction books are more scientific in tone than the works of other Western magicians. He was a mathematician and a rationalist. He tried to express the uncanny and the miraculous in scientific terms. His main nonfiction books are *The Fourth Dimension* (1909), *Tertium Organum* (1912), *A New Model of the Universe* (1914), and *In Search of the Miraculous* (1949). The last was an account of his meeting and association with Gurdjieff.

I include Ouspensky in this essay because he also wrote the strangest novel I have ever read, *Strange Life of Ivan Osokin* (Russian, 1915; English, 1947). It is about a man who relives in exact and excruciating detail all the events of his former life after he is reincarnated. The first half of the book is a telling of Osokin's life. The second half of the book is a *retelling* of Osokin's life, with only the very smallest differences is wording.

Ouspensky intended it to indicate how robotic our lives are, and that we cannot change even when we know we must. Knowing that he must relive his entire life, Osokin finds himself forgetting the past and becomes lost in the trivialities of everyday living, so that he ends up repeating all the same mistakes a second time.

THESE THINGS, THEY LINGER STILL

BY DAMIEN ANGELICA WALTERS

People don't come to her lightly. They come when they've exhausted every other option, when they're broken and desperate. They come with shaking hands, trembling voices, shattered souls. She takes, and she gives.

   If secrets have ghosts, she fears one day they'll wake and demand the justice they were denied. What *she* denied them.

  Shouldn't there be a price to pay for what she's capable of? Shouldn't there always be a price to pay?

***

Robyn is sitting at the table closest to the window of the coffee shop, and even from outside, through glass partially covered with gilt signage, even without being able to see her face, Leah knows it's her. Her hair is shorter but the color, a distinct shade of coppery brown, is unmistakable.

Leah slows her pace. Curls quivering fingers toward palms and catches the inside of her cheek between her teeth. It isn't too late to turn around. She isn't even sure why she agreed to meet. It's been a long time, and the last time she and Robyn were in the same room… Leah blinks away the memory of shouting, the steady thump of clothes thrown in an overnight bag, the slamming door, more goodbye than a word could ever hold.

Maybe she's wrong, maybe Robyn just wants to talk, to apologize. Leah grimaces. And maybe they're in the middle of a movie—one of the silly romantic comedies they watched together so many times—and they'll put all their puzzle pieces back together and walk out hand in hand, all laughter and forgiveness, while music plays triumphant in the background. A pretty fantasy and nothing more. She erases the grimace on her face and puts on something not quite as grim.

Strange how heartache can linger; strange how old wounds can still bleed, though she of all people understands such truths better than most.

Robyn turns in her chair when Leah walks through the door, and their gazes lock. Robyn smiles, but it can't banish the secret in her eyes, the dark ribbons almost obscuring the green of her irises. Tiny eel-motes in an ocular ocean no one without magic would see. Her slumped shoulders show it all too well, though. Secrets have a weight, a way of making themselves known.

It's much worse than it once was. So much worse.

In spite of the darkness in her eyes, Robyn's full lower lip and strong cheekbones send Leah's heart racing and fill her smile with real warmth. They embrace, quick and almost-impersonal, and her stomach tightens with a remembered frisson.

"You look good," Leah says.

Robyn cocks an eyebrow. Grins. "You never could lie worth a damn. I ordered you a coffee."

Leah takes a sip, and of course it's exactly the way she likes it. They were together for less than two years, but sometimes it doesn't take long to get to know someone, to let them in so they know you back.

"How are your parents?" she asks.

Robyn barks a laugh. "My dad's the same. A year after my mom got sober, she got cancer and a year later, she was gone."

"I'm so sorry."

Robyn shrugs and Leah stares at her coffee mug. She shouldn't have asked; Robyn was never close to her parents, and her relationship with her mother was contentious at best, even after Terri quit drinking.

"But it doesn't really matter now. I didn't ask you here to talk about her or anyone else. I want to hire you."

The words hover between them, guillotine sharp.

Leah clears her throat. "Robyn, I can't. I—"

"I wore you down, I forced you to do it, and I'm sorry. I'm sorrier than I can say. And then I treated you like shit, and you probably hate me for it. You *should* hate me for it.

I would."

"That has nothing to do with what you're asking. Don't you remember the way things went that night?" Leah drops her voice to little more than a whisper. "We could have died."

"But we didn't, and it's been four years. Four *years*. A lot can happen in four years and people change. We're strangers now, or close enough, and it only works with strangers, right? Isn't that why you said it didn't work?"

Leah swallows hard. Nods.

"Look at me. I know you can see it. Do you think I'd ask if I didn't need to?" Robyn reaches across the table, grips her hand hard enough to hurt. "Please. I can't take it anymore. I've tried and I can't, I just fucking can't. Please help me. Please at least try, and if it doesn't work, you'll never hear from me again."

Her eyes are glittering with tears, and Leah blinks her own away.

"You could just tell me and—"

Robyn squeezes her hand even tighter. "Don't. Don't you dare. Talking won't fix this. It wouldn't then and it won't now. Will you help me or not?"

Leah pulls her hand away, drops it in her lap. "I'll think about it. That's the only answer I can give you right now."

Robyn looks away; when she glances back, her eyes are dry and hard, her mouth set into a thin line—the same expression she wore the night she stormed out of their apartment and out of Leah's life. "Fine," she says, pushing away from the table hard enough to send coffee splashing over the rim of Leah's mug, and she's out the door before Leah can take another breath.

***

Leah arranges her legs beneath her on the sofa and turns the television on, set to mute. With a wine glass cupped between her palms, she stares at the flickering images onscreen until her vision blurs.

A knot twists in her gut. She should tell Robyn no. It's what her mother would do, what she would tell Leah to do, too. Ten years in her grave, but Leah can still hear her saying, strong and sure, "There will always be another client, another secret. The world is full of them. Don't bleed for them, do what you're paid to do and move on. If you have any doubts, be smart and leave the secret where it is."

Then she'd tell Leah to remember her lessons and trust the magic. Respect and follow the rules: Never care too much, never believe the secrets belong to you, and never take a secret from someone you love.

Until Robyn, Leah followed them all.

The first time they met, Leah saw the secret in Robyn's eyes—how could she not? She ignored the scattering of dark specks, but after she saw the scars on Robyn's shoulder and belly, she couldn't keep quiet. Robyn refused to talk about it, said it was a long time ago, said it had nothing to do with them.

Most of the time, it didn't, but sometimes Robyn grew cold and silent and sometimes her words turned cruel, with little provocation. In those moments, the specks in her eyes swirled like bits of storm. Leah tried to let it go. She did. But you can drown in someone else's secret as easily as you can one of your own.

So she pushed. She insisted if Robyn talked about it, it would get better; Robyn laughed, called her an armchair shrink, and told her to sell her bullshit to someone who wanted to buy it.

The dark specks grew larger; the silence even more so. They were *both* drowning, and then on a rainy morning, right before leaving for work, Robyn leaned close and whispered, "Fine, then take it away. If you love me, take it away."

Leah knew better. But Robyn kept asking, demanding, *taunting*, and one night while they were in bed, pretending to sleep beneath cold sheets and the frantic heat of yet another quarrel, she gave in. Out of love or anger or a desperate wish for it all to stop, she still doesn't know, but she remembers what she said: "I think you're a coward, but I'll take it away if it's what you really want."

Robyn smirked and said, "Do it."

A challenge Leah accepted.

But the rules were in place for a reason. Because the bond of love was strong, magic and secret locked together and refused to budge. Growing up, Leah heard stories about her great-great-grandmother who tried to take a secret away for her husband. A neighbor found their bodies the next day, their faces contorted in agony, their eyes gone black as pitch.

Leah isn't sure what gave up first that night, her magic or Robyn's secret, but the tearing sensation when it did is seared in her memory, the way she and Robyn remained immobile for hours, each trapped in their own sphere of hurt, the way the pain lingered for days, the way things fell apart so quickly afterward.

Sometimes she thinks if she'd left it alone in the first place, Robyn's secret would've stayed quiet, buried, and none of the rest would've happened, yet that's bullshit. Secrets don't stay secret forever. It would've come up, come between them, one way or another.

But maybe it would've done so when Robyn was strong enough to deal with it, when they were strong enough to deal with it together. The regret is bitter on her tongue. If her magic *had* worked, would she taste regret of a different kind? Would Robyn?

Do *any* of her clients regret it? It's a question she once asked her mother; her mother said, and Leah can't recall if there was a slight pause beforehand or not, "Don't be foolish, why would they?" Still, sometimes Leah wonders, as futile as it might be. What's done is done and can't be undone.

She presses her fingertips to her temples. Squeezes her eyes shut. Obviously she still cares or she would've said no outright, but does she still love Robyn?

No. She doesn't, not in the way that matters.

But does she *not* love her enough? That remains to be seen.

Finally, the memory of Robyn's tears, more than the dark strands in her eyes, speaks to Leah, makes the magic ripple inside her, makes the decision for her. She never saw Robyn cry before, not even at the end.

Maybe Leah owes her this much.

She dials Robyn's number, doesn't wait for her to say hello. "Okay, I'll try."

"Thank you," Robyn says.

"I'll come tomorrow." She takes down Robyn's address and disconnects the call before Robyn can say anything more, before she can change her own mind.

***

Robyn's house is small, the lawn well-manicured. A pot of marigolds sits on a small table off to the side, which surprises Leah. Robyn was never one for flowers.

The door opens as she's preparing to knock a second time. Without a word, Robyn ushers her into a living room with a wall of bookcases and gestures toward the sofa. Her face is all wide eyes and rapid blinks; twin spots of color sit high on her cheeks. The darkness in her eyes coalesces, breaks apart, gathers together again.

"Is this okay?" Robyn asks. "We can go in the kitchen instead, if that'll be better."

"No, this will be fine."

"Okay, good." She steps closer, then back, rubbing her jaw. "Can I get you something? Coffee, water?"

"Water would be great, thank you."

Leah folds her hands in her lap, linking her fingers tight to keep them still. The sofa isn't the same battered, ugly thing they sat together on so many times, watching movies or making love, but it feels achingly familiar. On the bookcases, Ursula Le Guin, Octavia Butler, and Stephen King sit alongside Shakespeare, Shelley, Jackson, and Poe. Almost a mirror twin to her own collection. Funny, until they met Robyn wasn't much for reading, either. Her lips quirk into a wry, one-sided grin.

Robyn comes back with the water and then turns around again. "Sorry, I forgot your fee."

"No, you don't have to—"

Robyn holds up both hands and drops her chin. "This is a business transaction, right? If you didn't know me from Adam, you'd charge me, right?"

"I would."

"Okay, then."

"We don't have to do this," Leah says, her words fast and whispery.

Robyn's face turns harsh, but her voice is soft. "Don't. Please."

Leah swallows the rest of her words, and when Robyn returns, she tucks the money in her pocket where it burns like a brand, like shame. Robyn takes the seat beside her, but she doesn't sit so much as she sinks, and Leah thinks if the cushions opened up to reveal a chasm, Robyn would let herself fall. Although she's still blinking too much and her hands flutter here and there, the pink on her cheeks has faded.

Their gazes meet. The darkness in Robyn's eyes blooms, an evening primrose beneath a twilight sky.

"I trust you," Robyn says, but there's a tremor her words can't hide.

"Fool," Leah returns, softening it with a smile as close to real as she can manage. "Close your eyes." She flexes her fingers; a slight tremble remains but she's slipping into a mode she knows well, the calm before the storm. She lets everything go. Inside, the magic awakens with a familiar flutter. This is the easy part. Seven generations of women in Leah's family have had the same ability; possibly more, but the family records only go back so far. Magic wasn't exactly wielded in the open. They burned women for far less.

"Take a deep breath," Leah says. "Good. Now I'm going to press my fingers against your temples. Just breathe normally."

Leah hesitates, but only a moment—*please let this work*—then Robyn's skin warms beneath her touch. She closes her own eyes, and the magic inside her emerges, flows. A sensation of cold floods her veins. A sea, crashing against her shores. It finds the secret and wraps around it, gripping it tight, and Robyn draws in a hiss. Inside, Leah is iceberg and snowmelt; she clenches her jaw to keep her teeth from chattering. She yanks the magic back, and there's a hint of resistance. Fear coils in her belly, then the secret rips free and a million icicles impale her from the inside out as the magic returns with its captive. Robyn cries out, shudders; Leah remains silent and still.

"It worked," Robyn says. "It really worked." She takes an audible breath, her shoulders noticeably straighter, and lets out a quick laugh. Her eyes, unencumbered by the strands of black, are bright, but there's a kiss of sorrow, too, and Leah suspects it's in *her* eyes as well. This, more than anything, is proof that what they once were is no more.

Silence stretches between them, and Leah drains her water glass more for something to do than from thirst.

"Listen, you could stay here," Robyn says. "I remember it gets rough after, and I could help. I could take care of you."

Her eyes hold sincerity, but Leah shakes her head. "No, we both know that's not a good idea." She hands back the glass. "I need to go."

"Okay. You'll call me if you need anything, if it gets too bad, won't you?"

"Sure," Leah lies.

The silence stretches even more, until they say their goodbyes with their eyes, not their lips, and Leah races to her car, blinking back tears. Robyn's secret swims through her abdomen, her back, the hollow of her throat.

By the time she pulls into her apartment complex, her mouth is filled with the taste of seaweed and rot. Her body is ice and fire, a war of goosebumps rising on her arms and sweat beading her forehead and slicking the serpentine length of her spine. Hands over her belly, she staggers to her front door. The secret is a strong one, and as she collapses on her bed, she prays it won't take long.

***

In sweat-soaked sheets, Leah tosses and turns, raging with the ebb and flow of sharp pains and dull throbs. She stifles her moans into her pillow and shoves tangles of hair from her eyes. The first two days are always the worst; even though she should be used to it by now, she isn't.

Years ago, she saw a documentary about oysters and pearls and she believes the magic behaves much the same. Deeming the secret an irritant, it surrounds it with its own version of nacre until it can't hurt anyone anymore. In truth, isn't her pain a small thing balanced against the

suffering of those she's released? Who can say an oyster doesn't suffer the same?

She presses a palm to her chest. If she cracked open, would the secrets spill out onto the floor, tiny poison barbs made safe, or would they break free and return to their rightful homes?

Secrets never die easily; they do not go quietly or gently into day or night, but on the third day, when relief usually begins to spread, it's as though tiny, serrated teeth are nibbling away at her from the inside out.

Robyn calls and leaves a message asking if Leah is okay. Leah sends a text back telling her everything is fine, taking care to spell every word correctly, to give nothing away.

The fourth day is a blur of hurt. On the fifth, Leah wakes, if the gray state can properly be called sleep, and the foulness in her mouth is thicker, coating her teeth and tongue. The pain is brighter and bigger than it should be, and beneath it, over it, is a heaviness, a sense of being pressed in from all sides at once. She can't straighten her shoulders or her spine, can't breathe without her ribcage aching.

The secret is waging its own war, and it's winning.

She curls into a ball and wads the sheets in her fists. Maybe it has nothing to do with the secret all, maybe there was enough love left deep inside to bend, to break, the rule, and now it's going to break her. Maybe she's wrong and only needs to give it another day or so. She squeezes her eyes tight, tries to swallow her fear.

***

Sunrise creeps through the slats of the window blinds, and Leah pulls the sheet over her head. The secret isn't merely fighting, but devouring. Her magic is seeping from her as surely as if she took a straight razor and opened a vein.

She scrubs her face with her hands, fumbles for her phone. She has no choice. She has to give the secret back. She's never tried it, doesn't even know if it will work, and she doesn't want to do it, but she can't keep it inside. Robyn has to understand.

The call kicks to voicemail. Leah closes her eyes, recalls the quick trill of laughter once Robyn realized the secret was gone, and tosses the phone aside.

As dusk begins to fill her room with shadows, she dials Robyn's number again but disconnects before it can even ring.

***

Hunched and trembling, Leah grabs her car keys and staggers out to her car. Her fingers can't make the seatbelt click into place, and when she tries to slide the key in the ignition, her key ring slips from her fingers to the floor mat. She rests her head on the steering wheel with one hand on her chest. Her magic is still there, but it's thin and small, little more than an echo.

The secret is no longer targeting her magic alone. Its teeth press against her heart, its claws against her soul. It's going to kill her, or at least get close enough to make the distinction between death and life a moot point. There are many ways to die; not all of them require dying. But whatever wrongs she committed, whatever mistakes she made, this price is far too high. Even for someone she once loved, this price is too high.

She drags her fingers back and forth across the floor mat until her index finger hooks through the key ring, her breath a shudder in her lungs, her pulse a trapped rabbit. Hair slicked to her forehead and neck, she climbs from the car. There has to be another way. There's *always* another way.

***

Obey the rules. Trust the magic.

Leah closes her eyes, follows the trail, and there, a trace of her magic curled like a nautilus deep in its shell. It still

man stands over her, a hunter with his prize, shoots again. And again. Then he aims the weapon at Robyn. And she's screaming, screaming, screaming, until she can't scream anymore…

When there's nothing left to see, nothing left to know, the secret nestles its weight in the pit of her stomach. Leah sobs into her hands, but all the tears in the world won't wash away what she's seen.

***

The street could be anywhere; the houses all long and low, the trees old, their branches pruned carefully away from the overhead wires. Leah wipes her palms on her thighs, takes a deep breath, and gets out of her car. Her family's been wrong all along. Secrets shouldn't be dissolved or

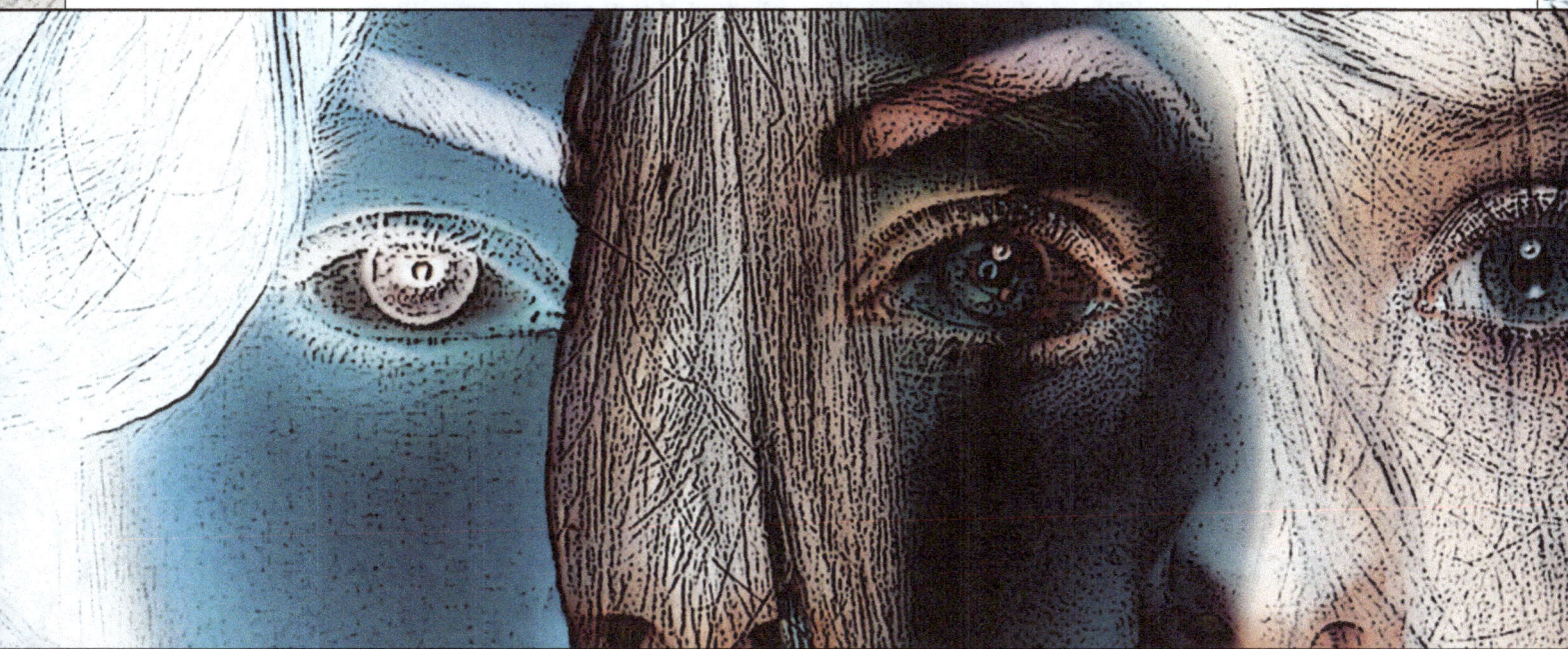

holds a pulse, albeit a thready one. She coaxes it open, feels its fragility, its smallness, and bites back tears. She needs it to be strong enough, not to fight, but to give in. The secret doesn't truly want to kill her, doesn't want to destroy her either; it wants its due.

Time to give it what it wants. She hurts too much to fight it anymore.

But she whispers "I'm sorry" first.

It takes far less of a push than she expected for her magic to penetrate the secret's heart. There's a stillness inside her, a pause, and then the secret breaks, crashing into her mind:

A kitchen, a woman with hair and eyes the color of Robyn's standing at the stove. The ghost of bruises clings to the side of her face, but she's smiling. A young Robyn, young enough to have all her baby teeth and a round, chubby face, sits at the table, empty plate before her. The smell of bacon frying in a pan. A clock ticking on the wall. A door swings open, and a man walks in, his face blank, his eyes, rage. The woman says, "You can't be here, Michael. You can't be here anymore." And he says nothing, nothing at all, pulls a gun from his pocket instead. The woman doesn't have time to scream; Robyn does it for her. The woman's body hits the floor with a heavy thud, and the

forgotten, and although magic chooses you, you get to choose what to do with it.

The man wasn't nearly as hard to find or as far away as Leah expected. His face is a study of wrinkles; his chin and cheekbones of similar shape to his daughter's. He has to know she survived, in spite of her wounds, and was adopted. But does he know he broke something precious and innocent that would never heal? Would he even care?

Did his time in jail—not even close to long enough—show him the truth of his own heart? He has a wife and a stepson and a step-grandchild on the way; do they know what he did? These are the questions Leah's asked herself as she's watched him, learning his routines.

Dressed in sweatpants, a t-shirt, and tennis shoes, he emerges from his house just as Leah reaches the sidewalk at the end of the street. She's dressed much the same, sweat making the fabric of her shirt cling to her back, and she fights to keep her hands from clenching into fists. He's walking fast, but it doesn't take long for her to catch up. She keeps her gaze focused on the distance, not his face.

What if it doesn't work? What if it makes things worse?

Her lips pressed tight, she forces her feet to keep moving. Pretending to stumble as she passes, she rests one hand briefly against his bare forearm, the warmth of his skin a shock against her own. The secret, now a tamed beast in a cage, leaps out of her and into him with a rush that feels like triumph. Like justice.

"Sorry," she mumbles.

He speaks with a voice of sandpaper and stone—"Clumsy bitch"—and she darts a glance at his face. The secret is already threading its black into his eyes, and she bites the inside of her cheek to hold in a smile.

But once she's back in her car, driving safely away, the expression breaks free. Small threads of guilt tighten in her chest, falling away when she thinks of the terror in Robyn's face and the sound of her screams.

***

Robyn's late and Leah worries she changed her mind. This time of day, the park is busy with parents and children, and there's a hint in the air of the autumn chill to come. A few minutes later, Robyn, two cups of coffee in hand, crosses the green. She takes a seat next to Leah on the bench, their thighs a whisper away from touching.

The coffee is perfect, of course.

"You look good," Leah says.

Robyn beams. "Thanks to you. You look good, too, but you always do. Don't even bother rolling your eyes."

Leah does anyway.

"I owe you big time," Robyn says, her words soft.

Leah shrugs. Touches the piece of paper in her pocket.

"And I'm sorry. For the way things happened, for, for everything."

"I'm sorry, too," Leah says.

They finish their coffee in silence, and Leah pretends it's the kind of perfect silence that holds no awkwardness.

Robyn rakes her fingers through her hair and lets her smile slip for the briefest of moments in such a way only someone who once breathed in her exhalations, who knew the hollows of her body as well as their own, would notice.

"Sometimes I feel its absence and it's heavy, almost as heavy as the thing itself. Funny, don't you think? I tell myself it's better this way and I'll get used to it, but would it feel the same way if I'd just told you? Would *I* feel the same? And if I had, where would we be now?"

Leah fights against the lump in her throat, fights for the right words, but the only thing she can say is the truth: "I don't know."

"Anyway, like you always used to say, what's done is done, right?" Robyn stands, brushing imaginary debris from her pants. "It was good to see you again, really good," she says, but she looks away as she speaks. "We should get together and grab lunch sometime."

"We definitely should," Leah says, but they both know they won't.

Leah wants to tell her she finally understands the power secrets hold. Wants to ask her forgiveness and tell her she's sorry in a way words could never convey. Wants to tell her he suffered for six months and it wasn't nearly enough, but it's too late for that. It's too late for any of it.

If this were a movie, neither magic nor secret would matter. Everything good between them would come rushing back, and they'd live happily ever after. But what's done is done. Leah watches Robyn walk away, takes a deep breath, and crumples the obituary in her pocket.

Everyone has a secret. This, then, will be hers.

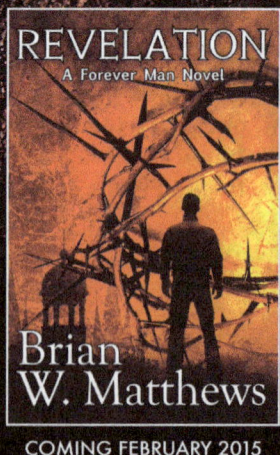
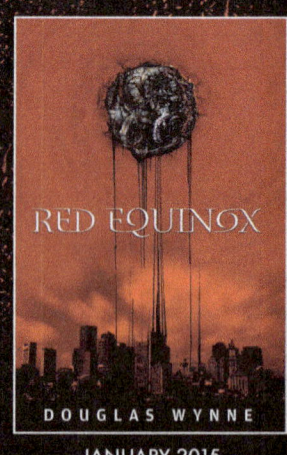

Double X Chromosome

BY
YVONNE NAVARRO

THE OCCULT AROUND US

© June 2015

Photo courtesy of Yvonne Navarro

So I've been thinking about this issue's theme, "The occult in dark fiction." The occult is there, of course, but it's in much more than just "dark" fiction. Google's noun definition for occult is this: "supernatural, mystical, or magical beliefs, practices, or phenomena." Miriam Webster's noun definition is "matters regarded as involving the action or influence of supernatural or supernormal powers or some secret knowledge of them," and states the first known use of the word was in 1923.

I'm not try to go religious here, but isn't the belief in some Greater Being, be it God or Allah or Gaia or whom/whatever, at its core a belief in the occult? That belief is all around us—we pray to deities we can neither see nor prove exist, we cross our fingers, we knock on wood three times, we don't open umbrellas indoors, and somehow believe that a life can be ruined for the next seven years if we break a mirror. Just this morning as I ranted about still not being able to assemble our Murphy bed after a year and a half, a friend told me it was Murphy's Law, and I should never buy anything with that name in it.

Speaking of friends, I have those who cleanse houses of spirits using sage and spells, who read the Tarot but each in different ways. Crystals catch not only the light but good luck, and a charm on the doorknob can bring both good luck and money. Always carrying a penny in your purse to ensure you're never broke, and never write in your checkbook in red (whether you're overdrawn or not).

Sounds like superstition to me.

But isn't superstition the belief in the occult?

Fire and brimstone, good and bad, heaven and hell.

Prove it's there.

Prove it's *not*.

Prove God is real.

Prove He's *not*.

The inexplicable.

But since part of the key phrase is "in dark fiction," let's talk about books.

Witch Ball – Hung in the window, it captures evil spirits before they can enter the house.

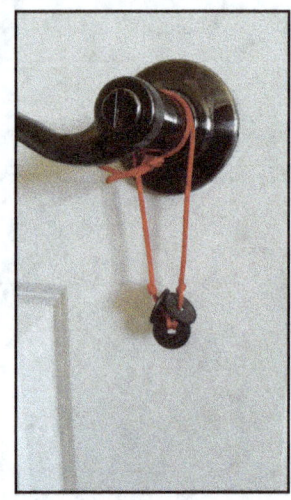

Wiccan Prosperity Charm – Hung on the doorknob to an office to ensure luck and money.

The term "dark fiction" is an enigma in itself. Is it dark fiction because it has an occult-based story? That can't be true, because there are entire genres that have, at least in my not-so-humble and extremely biased opinion, dark themes—mysteries, true-crime, war stories, psychological thrillers, tales of abuse and the myriad number of terrible things that mankind does to mankind. Yet none of those genres are considered "dark fiction." So for fiction to be "dark," it almost requires some sort of supernatural. Some instance of *occult*—an occurrence of something we cannot explain. Leave that out and it no longer seems to fit into the genre.

I've written a lot of books—twenty-four, to be exact—but only one (That's Not My Name) could be considered a straight thriller. It's the only novel that has no supernatural basis for any part of the plot. It involves deceit, kidnapping, murder, solving a crime, lies, and bigotry, but no one would ever call it "dark" fiction. I've sold many copies of that book at conventions where folks would stop by the table and, when I ask what they like to read, answer something that effectively means "nothing I can't explain." That means, to me, no monsters, no supernatural, no vampires, no ghosts, etc. They want to read about the kinds of things that could happen in the real world because the fictional world frightens them too much.

I'm just the opposite. My reading preferences run very strongly to dark fiction—the supernatural, the occult. I'll take They Thirst (Robert McCammon) or Daughter of Smoke & Bone (Laini Taylor) over Crazy for You (Michael Fleeman) or Bogeyman by Steve Jackson, and give me Seal Team 666 (Weston Ochse) over the newspaper any day of the week. I'm astounded that people can be scared more by things

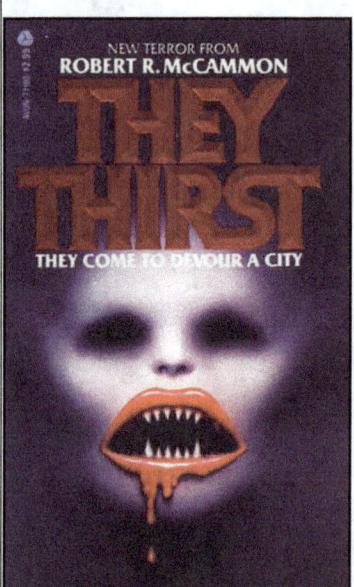

A Native American Dreamcatcher – Captures nightmares.

that *don't* exist than things that do. As far as I can tell, the only tie between the two is the dark and what you *don't* know that might be in it, but I can tell you with certainly that I think the shadowed corridor between two houses in a big city has the possibility to hide something dark in the form of a human monster. When people have asked me during panel appearances "What scares you?" my answer has always been the same: "Human beings."

Think about it in terms of down-to-earth reality. For all the occult's adrenaline-inducing ability, do you really think you're going to look out your second story window and see a vampire floating past? Or that the dead will suddenly dig themselves out of their graves when you go place flowers on Grandpa's headstone this Sunday? The delicious lure of the occult in fiction, on screen, or in the everyday, is that it's all about what we don't know, what we can't see, or at its most basic, what we can't *control*. We could go on to talk about the perception of "control" and how what folks think they can control can differ mightily from what they really can, but that's a bunch of words for some other time or column.

To give a true example, I'm going to talk about my faux-daughter, Clara, and the night I invited (which might be a synonym in my world for *insisted*) her over

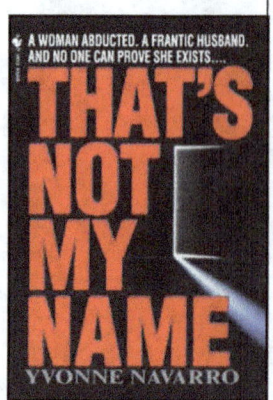

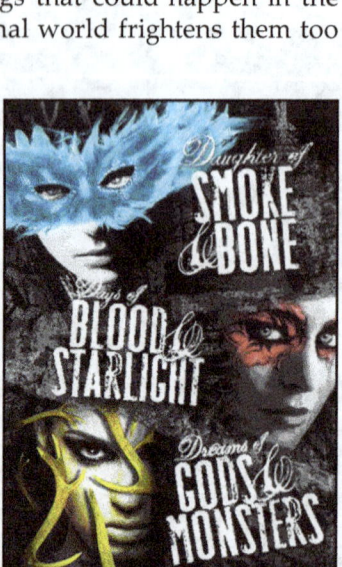

Mexican Crib Angel – Hung above an infant's crib to protect the child.

to watch the movie, 30 Days of Night. My husband was deployed to Afghanistan, so we turned off all the lights and ate pizza while we watched what one writer acquaintance terms "sharks with legs" run rampant in Barrow, Alaska. Clara was cool as ever, logical and firmly fixed in reality. "I don't believe in that stuff," she said, and although she did jump a few times, she insisted, "That really wasn't that scary." End of movie, Clara goes home.

But not end of story.

Clara lives in a duplex, and a day or two later Clara mentions that the next time she sees her neighbor, the woman asks her why she parked so close to the front door of her apartment (under the carport). It would seem that for the first time since she's lived there, Clara became a wee bit suspicious of the surrounding dark and wanted to make sure the trip between her car door and her front door was minimized... so much so she barely left room between the car and the door.

Methinks disbelieving in the occult might be believing you have control over things, more than a few of which you actually can't even see...

By the way, it was Clara who told me I shouldn't have bought anything with the name "Murphy" in it.

~~~~~~~~~~~~~~~~~~~~~

Here's a megadose of occult—vampires, witches, voodoo, and all manner in between. To order, visit the Crossroad Press Store at:

http://store.crossroadpress.com/ and search for "Yvonne Navarro."

Comments? Questions? Yvonne Navarro can be reached via her Facebook page (www.facebook.com/yvonne.navarro.001), or at her Dark Discoveries email: yvonne@journalstone.com.

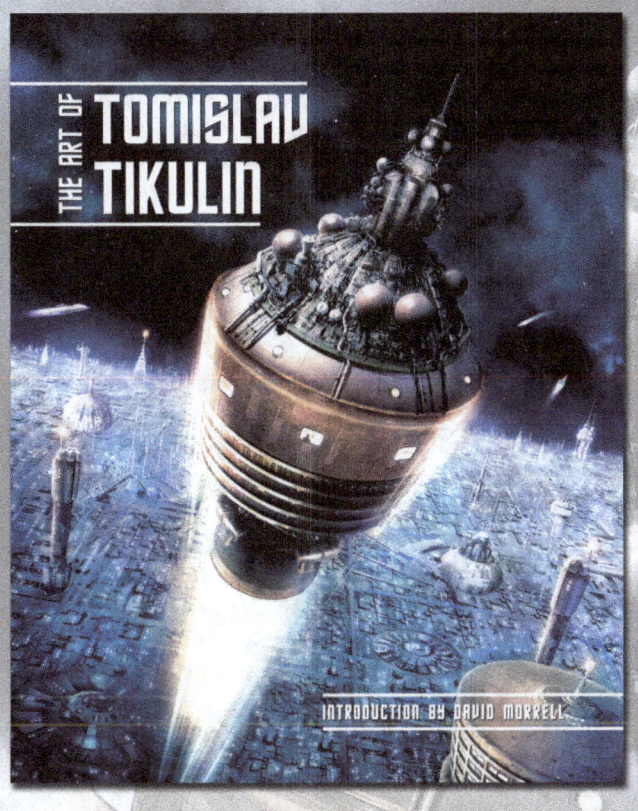

Weird Fictionist & Esotericist Arthur Machen

BY MARK VALENTINE

Arthur Machen (1863-1947) was probably the first Welsh author since Geoffrey of Monmouth to create a British national myth. They came from the same part of Wales, the border county that Machen always called Gwent, preferring the Welsh name. The medieval chronicler's *History of the Kings of Britain* was highly influential on later literature, and was instrumental in forging the foundation myths of the country. Machen created the enduring modern legend of the Angels of Mons, celestial beings who aided British troops in retreat during the Great War.

Incidentally, there is not much doubt that he *did* create it, despite those (rather obtuse or wishful, as I think them) who believe that he merely reported the myth. There is not the slightest shred of any evidence of any alleged sightings of the Angels before Machen's story appeared in his paper, the London *Evening News* on September 29, 1914. After that, of course, there was a slew of anecdotal (nearly always second- or third-hand) reports of the incident, but all plainly derivative from his original tale. And Machen himself gave a clear account of how it came to him: while in church, meditating on what he had heard of the retreat, his imagination roamed in the "medievalism that was always there" in his mind: and the idea of a heavenly intervention by St George, a radiant host and the ghostly shapes of the (Welsh) bowmen of Agincourt came to him.

The legend of the Angels remains the likeliest point of recognition for many people when Arthur Machen is mentioned. But he has also always been a favourite of those who savour outré and unfashionable literature, a genuine "cult" author, in and out of print often, but always collected. The roll-call of those who admired, respected, even revered him is itself strange and various, as will be seen in this very small sample: John Betjeman and John Masefield; Mick Jagger and Mark E. Smith of the Manchester band The Fall; the recent Archbishop of Canterbury, Rowan Williams, and Aleister Crowley, who recommended his work to his occult students.

The irony for Machen was that 'The Bowmen', the tale that gave rise to the Mons myth, was one of his slightest pieces, yet it brought him more fame (in a slightly backhanded way) than any of his other work. He was for many years a prophet without honour not only in his homeland of Wales, but also in Britain more generally, though a French critic had acclaimed a book of his "le renouveau de la Renaissance" and American enthusiasts in the Nineteen Twenties thought his neglect was a crime of the sort that should be "shouted from the rooftops."

His masterpiece was the spiritual romance *The Hill of Dreams* (1907), but he was best known in his time for the Victorian horror tale *The Great God Pan* (1894), and there will be those who will argue that his first volume of autobiography, *Far Off Things* (1922), is his lasting testament. It is a wonderfully evoked memoir of the life of a lonely, bookish young man in rural Gwent in the Eighteen Seventies and Eighties. Quite apart from the fine writing, it tells us much of the country, the families, the conventions and the eccentricities of this lost domain.

After he left his rectory home in Llandewi, near Caerleon, as a young man, Machen subsisted on very meagre fare in a London garret, while trying to write and earn a living. He was a very *antiquarian* young man: his education, at Hereford Grammar School, had been sound but perhaps somewhat old-fashioned; he had learnt, probably from his father, the Rector, a habit of introspection and studiousness. He barely got by on cataloguing second-hand books, editing, tutoring and similar odd jobs. But at last he achieved fame—or notoriety—and an income of sorts, usefully supplemented by an inheritance, with his novella *The Great God Pan*.

The story was a "shocker." That was the term the later Victorians applied to such tales. Stevenson called his *The Strange Case of Dr Jekyll and Mr Hyde* (1886) this. Machen was very fond of Stevenson's work and the influence is evident in his own tale, as the critics were not slow to point out. The tale is propelled, like Stevenson's, by an experiment in science that has more devastating consequences than was intended: and it is also a study in the dissolution of personality. It is laced, too, with the same hints of unspeakable vices and crimes that Mr Hyde is suspected of: and, while Stevenson's book is set in a very Edinburgh London, Machen's begins in Gwent before moving to the streets of the capital he had come to know so thoroughly, as he walked them wearily to escape his attic room.

Machen benefited, though also, in the eyes of some contemporaries, was tainted by, an association with the decadent, fin-de-siècle mode seen in the books issued by his publisher John Lane, with their weird themes, Beardsley illustrations, ornate styling, and "daring" subject matter. The author took a perverse delight in the pungency of some of the reviews he attracted: but Machen was also apt to underplay those that were more positive, which compared him favourably to those masters of the macabre, Poe and Le Fanu.

The Great God Pan can still be read today with relish, and as more than just a period piece. Even the most devoted Machen admirer would admit it has faults: as H.G. Wells

macabre tale, is a detective story: the influence of Conan Doyle's Sherlock Holmes is evident in the amateur investigating and deducing that Machen's flaneur Mr Dyson gets up to. The creator of the Great Detective admired Machen's work: after a book of his had been lent to him by Jerome K. Jerome, he remarked, so Jerome reported, "Your pal Machen may be a genius alright; but I don't take him to bed with me again." The story has all the satisfactions of the Sherlockian detective yarn, including (what is often overlooked in discussions of Conan Doyle) the sheer strangeness of incident. But the achievement of the story is in the way Machen makes the landscape of Wentwood, the great forest he could see from where he lived as a boy, convey the evil that is afoot: twisted trees, haggard rocks, dark hollows all hint at the torture of a human soul.

That use of natural forms to convey supernatural forces

pointed out, in an unenthusiastic notice, the characters (so many men-about-town) are insufficiently differentiated; and the structure is rather awkward. But the strangeness of the idea, the well-achieved descriptive writing of the opening chapter set in Gwent, and the sheer gusto of the plot, are all still attractive.

In his introduction to a 1916 edition of *The Great God Pan*, Machen described, with an aching tenderness, the genesis of the work in the "wonderful and enchanting country" where he grew up, around Llandewi: and then descending into reflections on the gap between what he dreamt and what he could write. The Irish novelist George Moore was unimpressed by Machen's books, but thought that the Welshman's introductions were nearly as good as his own writing: this was intended, as Machen wryly observed, as a rare compliment, and he added, with characteristic good humour, "and so it was."

The Great God Pan was not long enough to make up a volume on its own in Victorian times, and Machen wrote another for the John Lane volume. This was "The Inmost Light," certainly the superior of the title piece in its integrity of plot and rather more oblique, transcendental horror.

"The Shining Pyramid," another classic Machen

is even more evident in the "The White People." This is often regarded as one of the finest tales of supernatural horror ever written, usually alongside Algernon Blackwood's "The Willows," which similarly evokes wild nature to convey wonder, awe and terror. The force of Machen's story, however, derives equally from the conviction he achieves by casting the narrative in the form of a young girl's diary. Her tone and manner of description, as rendered by Machen, are mesmerising in their blend of innocence and complicity, her raw trust tainted with the knowledge of secret things.

As Ramsey Campbell has observed, Machen is also adroit at letting the reader piece together what is happening in his stories, rather than by telling them outright, often narrating through multiple voices and only in fragments, with differing registers of tone, an approach Campbell sees as particularly modern.

It is a technique he deploys still more in his second book with John Lane, the episodic shocker *The Three Impostors* (1895, and a favourite of the critic Cyril Connolly's). The tale-following-tale, episodic structure was derived from Stevenson's *New Arabian Nights* (1882). But, although this was also moderately successful (and equally reviled by the stiff-collared among the critics), Machen perceived that he needed to shake off the Stevenson influence. He set himself, in a highly conscious, careful way, to create a style of his own and a book nearer to the dreams and visions he saw. The process was laboured and painful: pages and chapters were discarded; he spent hours staring at the blank paper. But he got his theme: the story of a young man who is marooned, like Robinson Crusoe, thought not on a desert island. He would be utterly alone, spiritually alone, in the teeming streets of the capital.

Stevenson had not been the only influence upon him; in his earliest work he had drawn on the ornate, studied, consciously worked prose style of the three literary Thomases who remained dear to him; Sir Thomas Browne, Thomas de Quincey, and Sir Thomas Urquhart, the Scottish eccentric who translated Rabelais in a highly inimitable (and often wholly original) way. Their taste for the arcane word, the archaic expression, the serpentine sentence, the paragraph as labyrinthine plainchant, never quite left him. But what he was able to do with *The Hill of Dreams*, the "romance of the soul" he at last completed, was to fuse their richness of language with the finer suppleness he had learnt from Stevenson, into a style that no-one else could achieve. It was this style, and not only the rare, strange and tragic theme, that was to attract to the book such praise as "the most beautiful book in the world" and "the most decadent book in English literature."

The style alone was not what drew such ardent readers, though. The theme was intensely compelling for a certain sort of reader: how a sensitive, dreaming, artistic youth, Lucian Taylor, suffers from the materialistic and philistine world around him, and retreats instead into a gorgeously-evoked fantasy world of Roman gardens, temples and taverns. The huddled, dreary, shrunken little town of Caerleon-upon-Usk, Machen's birthplace, is transformed in his protagonist's mind into what it might have been, idealised, fifteen hundred years ago, a great classical citadel. Haunting flute music, rare wine in stone flagons,

statuettes of lost gods, white marble and carved amber are beautifully evoked. And the author suggests that this is more than mere daydreaming: that the true quest of the alchemists, the transmutation of lead into gold, was really an allegory; that the dull world around us can be transmuted too, by the spiritualised imagination, into something infinitely wonderful and strange.

Ending a story or book was never Machen's strength: often he over-ended, with too much explication; sometimes he just petered out. But in *The Hill of Dreams*, rather against the odds, he gets it about right, with an image that flickers back to the opening of the book, a lingering, oblique mystery, and a final, devastating irony.

The book was rejected by John Lane when Machen submitted it in the late Eighteen Nineties: and rejected by the even more daring publisher Grant Richards early in the next century. It made its first appearance, bizarrely enough, serially, in *Horlick's Magazine* during 1904. This was the trade journal of the famous malted-milk-drink company. The magazine was edited, very much as he liked, by Machen's close friend, the esotericist and occult scholar, A.E. Waite, and the company were probably unaware of the decidedly unsoothing content, in contrast to their product, of Machen's romance.

The Gwent author had to wait until 1907 before Grant Richards changed his mind and published *The Hill of Dreams*, which was Machen's own favourite and finest work, in book form. Then, at least, Richards did him well, with a design and quality of production that was admired even by the arch-Aesthete Ronald Firbank, who demanded his own books should have the same design. Machen continued to write supernatural fiction and essays on the byways of history and folklore for another thirty years, but never quite regained the fervent artistry of this book.

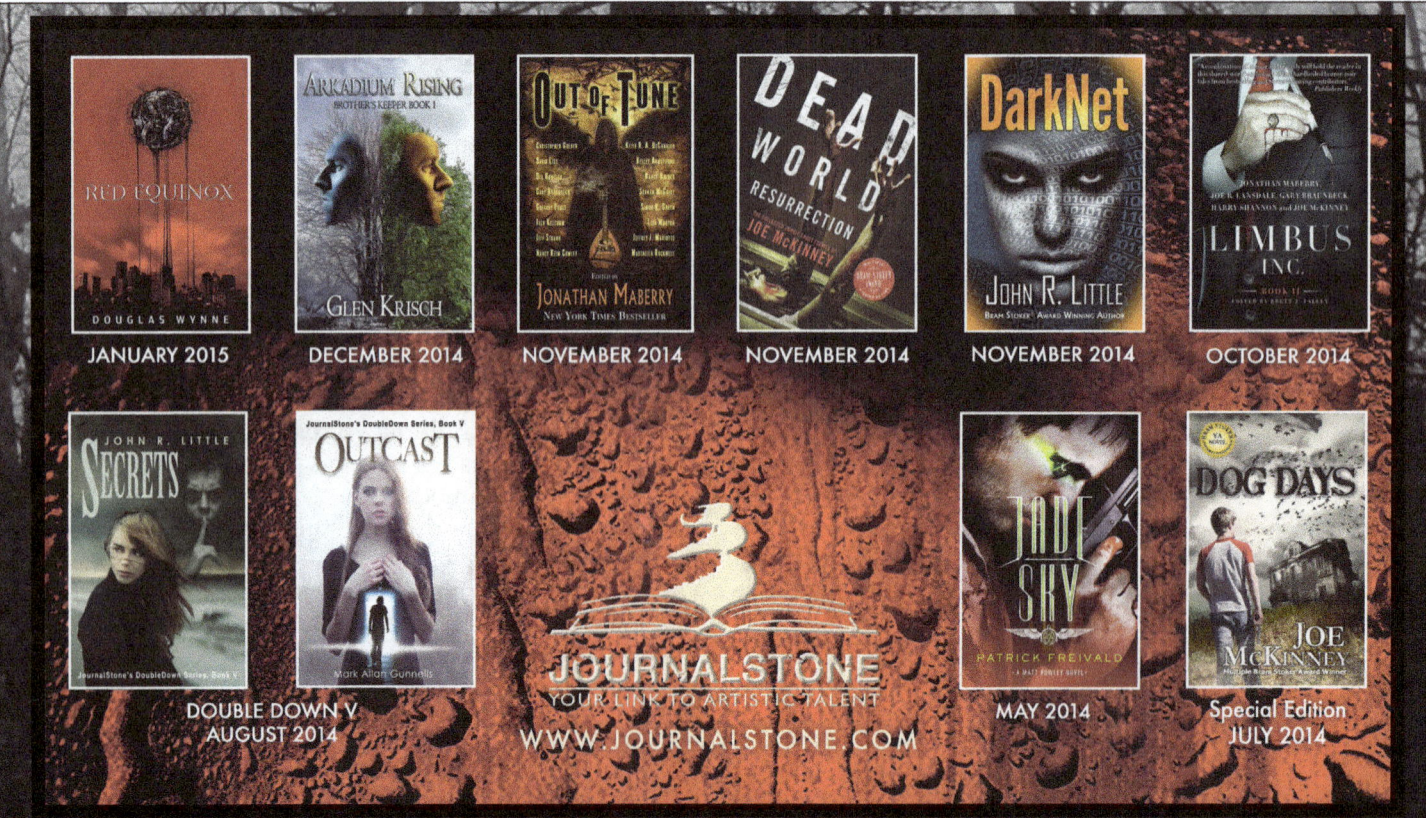

The Wine of the Serpent

By Mark Valentine

When he awoke in his dock at SleepCube Central, there were images fleeing from him. He tried to grab them back but they were gone too quickly. But he knew for sure he had been in the rooms again, unfolding one after another, and each with their shaded niches where there were things he could only half-see. He flicked on his *life*™ and sent a message at once to his community: drmt rms agn; wa?

In a few minutes he had 217 replies. He put them through the mincer. This left 23. Some said it was just retinal or mental residues from whatever game he'd been playing before he fell asleep. He thought about this. His game just now was *Master Connoisseur* where he roamed the world finding precious objects each guarded by an evil spirit, and each harder to avoid than the last. He was up to plane 13 and it was hard. But he couldn't see the link with his repeated dreams of the rooms. The edgier members of his community had a different take. The 'They' were trying out a new wave of beta sleep apps on him: without his knowledge, he was part of a select experiment on advanced users. Could be.

But most of the replies just wanted to tell him about their own weird dreams. These were not very interesting: random, colourful, highly-charged, yes, but not like his. The rooms dream came about every seven nights and was always pretty much the same. He is walking in a floating kind of way through high empty chambers with a silvery light. There is something ancient about them, like they were old Greek or Roman ruins that were unruined. Between each room is a tall doorway with stone pillars and above the doorway is a cut circle of stone. The doorway has no door: at least, he thought, not a material door, but there is something there that is like a door would be if it wasn't physical. This is an idea he can feel but cannot explain to himself very well.

He skimmed his replies again. There was maybe a handful who asked him a question, like they were really interested in him. One said: "what's in the rooms?" Another: "do the rooms change?" His fingers left the pad for a very long time—it might even have been more than five minutes—while he thought about this. The things in the niches he could never quite see properly were sort of human faces in stone, with blind eye-sockets. But there were carvings on the faces that were of other things, like lions, roses, stars, hounds, so it was like looking at carved monuments of a hybrid, part mortal, part emblem. Easy effect to get, sure: but whenever he stared at them they seemed to waver, as if in transition from one thing to another.

He replied, saying a bit about what he saw. Came one reply: U bn brwsng Brit Muse? Flippant, maybe, but kind of right. He had been flickering the exhibits in the museum's e-galleries, picking up clues for the game. They'd streamed through his brain at high speed and some might have left themselves there to be retrieved later. One reply was more troubling though: it proposed a pick-up. "Me too. Meet Y01 1AZ noon?" Stalked? Couldn't be: all his community were high-end screened.

A few minutes later his entire *life*™ was deleted. All right, yes, *he* was still here. But everything else was gone. Total delete. All his friends, groups, communities: nil, zero,

blank. He tried every reboot, recover, rezip mode, nothing. On his wrist now was just a piece of dumb chrome and plastic. Somewhere in the building there was a morgue, he knew, a place for people without their own *life*™ who could pay to get on some truly ancient device for a few minutes. Like he really wanted to go there alongside all the old fumblers. But he forced himself to find it, next to the vending machine alley, which stank of stale coffee and seaweed vita-soup, and went in, loudly saying to nobody in particular, and everybody, how his own *life*™ was totally wiped.

After long minutes he got on to *life support*™. Useless as always: couldn't even trace him, though he'd registered, got deals, offers, from them every day. They said they would get back to him. How? He'd have to be back in the morgue later. How much later? Couldn't say. Great. He was not planning to spend his day in the morgue. Hey, do one thing for me before you go. Sure. Send me a route from here to, uh, YO1 1AZ. Ok, done. Hoo, it's a church. Say a prayer we get your *life*™ back eh? Ma ha ha. Yeh, great.

***

He had to copy the route out by hand. It felt strange to wrap his fingers round the pen he'd borrowed from the old guy next to him, and for a few moments he couldn't get the right pressure on it to make any marks on the paper. It made his hand ache to write out the many turns, and he knew he would look weird walking about carrying this sheet instead of listening to the precise voice of the *life*™ street guide in his ears. So he tried to stroll casually, just sneaking a look at the scrap of notes when he had to.

Even with the route, the church was well-hidden. It was in pale stone that the city had grimed black. It was as if clusters of shadows had been caught, and smeared onto its outside. The street led nowhere else and the church backed onto the old city walls. From within the gloom of its porch with its pointed arch, he saw a figure move. That figure saw a young man with a bare austere flint-knapped head, hair cut short but not stubbled, and with a quirky tuft like a coconut sticking up from the crown. The youth wore a black plastic tunic like an artist's smock, but with a hood not up, dark drainpipe jeans, ankle boots. A candy-striped soft shirt in blue and red could be seen below the tunic and at the neck. The eyes, as he'd expected, were like polished obsidian: the sort of dark that seems to keep a deep light captive.

He advanced.

"DanDK?"

The youth nodded, not removing his hands from the long pockets of his black tunic. It didn't seem strange to be called by his online name: he spent more time in it than with his given name.

"Revel14. Let's go inside."

When DanDK had been in churches before, not very often, they had been cold, seemed empty even with people in, and smelt musty. But this one had a warm honeylike atmosphere as soon as he stepped through the door. And there was a smell he couldn't track at first: something like woodsmoke or joss-sticks, but very subtle. Otherwise it was like any other church he'd encountered in games:

wooden pews, brass fittings, stained glass, stone font, pulpit, altar. Except, except…let into the white walls on either side were little scooped-out hollows like the niches in his dreams. But they were empty. He stared at them. They stayed empty. But the noon sun, streaming through the stained glass, seemed to refract into coloured shapes, rose, green, purple: and some of these swirled over the niches as if they were trying to form something there.

He could see Revel14 watching him. An older guy, twenties? Wore his black hair long, like a cavalier in *English Revolution*. Big dark cloak.

DanDK shook his sharp head. The tuft played like a brown fountain.

"So: same dreams uh?" he asked the stranger.

"Almost the same. Anything happen this morning?"

"Yes: *life*™ packed up. Extinct."

"Uh. Yeah. That was Us."

He could hear the capital letter in 'Us' and he didn't like it. He didn't want anything to do with any Us.

"You…? Us?"

"It was for your safety."

"Waa? *You* did DEL on me, totally?"

"Sure. Not DEL though. ESC—or ALT, if you prefer."

"Get it back."

"Not advisable."

"Suppose I decide that."

"You don't need it. You got it already. "

The boy withdrew the device from his pocket, flipped his fingers over it. Nothing.

"I don't. Look…"

The 'cavalier' sighed, and smiled.

"In here."

He lent forward and tapped the youth's left temple. DanDK recoiled from the contact. Maybe this was a stalk, after all? He shrunk back inside his dark outfit. There was silence. Should he feel unsafe? He couldn't even press alarm mode with the device dead. Yet inside the church he didn't feel threatened. He looked at the light playing through the stained glass and felt a surge within him, as if with the right command he could make his own body as bright and fluid, as full of strange colours as this.

"Who is this *us* then? I thought you were just a friend."

Revel14 just stared at him.

"We are. Hey, Dan, you like history. Give me a bit of time. Listen to this."

The youth shrugged. Guy might be a creep. But with no *life*™: what else to do?

"This window here. What do you see?"

He looked at it. The tall glass held a single figure in sumptuous colours of scarlet and green. He had a white face with golden hair, almondine eyes, long elegant pale limbs, and rich vivid drapings. His jewelled hands held something: a vessel. At his feet creatures crouched: they had scales, wings, talons, teeth, but did not seem to quite cohere into an exact form.

"Some saint, I suppose."

"Some saint. Ever play *Beast of Beasts*?"

"Yeh."

"The original writer. St John the Divine. The author of *Revelation*."

This interested DanDK. He put aside the suspicion that the 'cavalier' might turn out to be a religious freak.

"Look at the hair quite carefully. See anything?"

The artist had given the saint curling yellow locks and, with his sensitive features, there was just a suggestion of the girlish about him. That was no bother to the boy. Regendering, neugendering, went on all the time. It was good. No worries there. Interesting that this most ancient designer had thought of it too. But now, what was he meant to be looking for? He shifted his gaze so that it was no longer directly focused on the figure's hair but was more aslant. For a moment it was as if the hair writhed, like a helmet of golden serpents, but that quickly passed. He felt a thrill of the noon sun streaming through the hued window pass into him, warming his blood as if with its colours. And then he saw that at the brows of the saint the artist had very artfully limned-in a curl on each side that just suggested, just hinted, at a pair of horns.

Revel14 had been watching him.

"So, you've seen. Now here's a tip. Next time you dream of the rooms, don't look straight at the niches. Look at them like you looked just then. "

DanDK turned quickly towards him. He knew at once, with a deep instinct, that this was right. But he also sensed he was getting into stuff that he was wary about, that might just be a plane too far.

Despite himself, though, he was curious. He gestured to the figure.

"What's he holding?"

His guide smiled again: the right question.

"It's a cup."

"There's something coming out of it."

"Yeah. See what it is?"

Dan stared hard at it, then remembered what the man had just said. He relaxed his gaze and looked at it sidelong. There was a silver flicker with a dark forked tongue.

"Snake. Why? What's that got to do with some saint?"

A shrug of the dark cloaked shoulders.

"A biblical legend. A witch tried to poison his wine. He knew what she had done and cast out the poison: so the snake leaps out of the cup, see? Symbolism."

There was a brittle silence in the church. Oh god, thought Revel14, oh gods, now, now. Let him be a knower.

The boy looked thoughtful. His dark eyes gazed up at the figure. A quiver, like the quick, sensuous movement of the snake's tongue, tasting the air, scenting, rippled through him, as if his whole body was an alert instrument. Then he shook his pale, carved head.

"That's not it at all."

The cavalier kept his stare calm but could not stop himself swallowing hard.

"No? What *is* it then?"

There was another lunge in the youth's body, firing his imagination like the swift flame from a salamander's tongue.

"The cup is a vessel—like him, you—me. The snake stands for secrets. For knowledge, and for, for something else. I can't quite get the something else. It keeps wriggling away from me."

Revel14 gave a very deep sigh and could not stop a broad grin.

"Let's sit."

They took places a little distance from each other on the hard polished wood.

"All right. This is going to sound like a game scene, right? It isn't. It's real."

The boy nodded.

"Don't just trust me. You will know it's real because something in here will tell you it's real."

He reached forward and touched the boy's face again. DanDK felt the impress of his fingers on his forehead. He wanted to reach up and wipe away the slightly clammy spot where they had rested, but some sense of courtesy stopped him.

"It will be like you remembered it," the dark man said.

***

"In the days before technology, before printing," he said, "knowledge was only held in two places: in manuscript, and in memory. The art of memory was much more refined and developed than it is now. Those who had perfected it were much in demand. They were like, if you can imagine, living memory sticks, yes? These were used for diplomacy, commerce, espionage, and in the arcane. Everyone knows of the Knights Templar, sure: they safeguarded treasure; the bankers of Christendom. And not just Christendom: they worked with the Saracens too. And also the Knights Hospitallers, their great rivals: the knights of St John of Jerusalem, a different St John that is, not ours, not the Revelation guy. They looked after pilgrims, travellers, had hospices, then hospitals. So, you see? That's money and health covered, and what could be more than these?"

He paused. DanDK did not fill in the gap. Already he knew this was just A, B, C.

"Only one thing," went on the stranger. "Secrets. Our secrets. And those who looked after the secrets were good at it: so good they were themselves completely secret. No page, no word ever survived about them; they existed only in the minds and the memories of their members, and their very selected clients. A different order to those other two. They were called the Knights of St John the Divine. Him."

He pointed to the window.

DanDK followed the gesture. But he did not look upon the face of the saint: he watched the silver twist of the snake.

"Messengers, emissaries, ambassadors, interpreters, translators," Revel14 went on, "they moved between nations and faiths, carrying locked away in them the most secret of secrets of the great men of the ages. Whatever could not be written down. So—you guessed the rest. That's us. You, me—him. And you know what? We are still needed today. Things so severe, so critical, they cannot be put on any device, any network, anywhere. That's what we know. That's what we transmit."

The boy shook his head.

"That's not it."

Revel14 looked startled, and tried quickly to cover this up.

"We're not just some glorified courier service," said the boy. "All this you just said is just another disguise. It's a masque."

This was interesting, Revel14 thought. He'd accepted it was "we" not "you" anymore. And he already spoke as though with authority. A shrug seemed best.

"You know more than I do, then."

"I'm not saying it isn't so. Just that it isn't all."

His guide looked at him curiously. Perhaps he hadn't, after all, got it.

"Look, let me impress on you. What we deal in are the very uttermost secrets of the world; only a handful of people know them. They might be military, political, religious, royal, financial, but these are very precious keys."

The boy's pale, sharp face remained unimpressed.

"Oh, yes, I see that. But they are still just keys to the world. What he saw—" (he gestured to the horned saint) "—was much more than that. He held the key to the beyond, to the beginning, and the end. The something else I could not quite see in the rooms in my dreams, that thing that kept writhing away from me."

The cloaked figure inwardly uttered a huge oath. It figured: but this was getting way over his powers. He had better get him to the House and let them listen to him.

DanDK was already staring intently again at the stained glass window of the saint with the serpent in the cup, but in the oblique way he had learned earlier, as if from the edge of his eyes. Revel14 felt the silence in the church becoming more intense, more fragile, diamond-sharp. The scent of ancient essences seemed deeper, felt as if it was pervading his whole body, his veins, his bones, his senses. He knew that he could not move, that he must stay within these moments. He looked up at the window of St John the Divine, at the horns so artfully concealed in the golden hair, at the creatures of wings and scales, and at the cup held by the pale fingers. Some shadow must have passed across the gilded pane, because it seemed to him that the silver of the snake twisted quickly, as if it was rising from the vessel.

The boy looked at the pale stone niches and the colours from the sun-illumined glass playing upon them. It was as though figures were trying to form there, as if the scarlet, green and purple reflections might with a sudden lunge become embodied creatures. He raised his hand to his left temple and felt a surge course through his mind. And then, though he was awake, he was again racing through the halls and corridors, and the light streaming in the niches in the church was now within him. On either side of his vision the stone masks and their emblems, the lions, roses, stars, hounds, and the many others, flickered, wavered, became form, then un-form, resolved themselves into a hundred different hybrids, all possible semblances of creatures and symbols, in an endless parade of impossible unities, each one suggestive of a vast creative power, eternal yet ever-changing. And as these forces cavorted in his mind, DanDK clung onto a single strong thought, a truth that was like a blue fire. This was how the world was meant to be, this was how we were meant to be: all potentialities, human, animal, celestial, co-existent in constant flux and mutability, fluid, unseparate. And then it was as if there was no difference between the vision within him and the play of light upon the niches in the church. The ever-changing images were coming into existence in the world. ◆

THE LEGACY OF C. M. EDDY, JR.

BY K. H. VAUGHAN

Clifford M. Eddy, Jr. (January 18, 1896 – November 21, 1967) is a name that aficionados of pulp-era fiction should know from his connections with H. P. Lovecraft and Harry Houdini and his infamous tale *The Loved Dead*, which appeared in Weird Tales May/June/July 1924 issue. However, there is more to the C. M. Eddy, Jr. story, and his grandson Jim Dyer has been working to secure Eddy's legacy with the establishment of Fenham Publishing. Eddy's involvement in fiction, theatrical booking, music, and magic made for a rich and fascinating life. With interest in weird fiction continuing to rise, fans of the genre may wish to pull back the curtain on the Rhode Island native.

C. M. Eddy, Jr. and his wife Muriel were amateur writers (there is an extensive collection of fiction, essays, poetry, and music between them), who lived not far from H. P. Lovecraft's Angel Street residence in Providence. Like many other amateur writers, Muriel Eddy reached out to him. Her mother knew Susie Lovecraft socially—it is reported through the women's suffrage movement, although there isn't evidence that Susie was particularly active in this—and an arrangement was made for the exchange of letters. Despite his reclusive ways in this period, Lovecraft was an active correspondent. His mother, however, shielded him from social contact and discouraged him from significant socializing. It was not until after she died in 1921 that Lovecraft was able to accept an invitation to visit in person. Once he did, he became a regular guest of the Eddys until his death in 1937, and was famous for showing up in the late hours of the evening to read his latest stories and to take long walks exploring areas of Rhode Island with C. M. Eddy, Jr. Despite Lovecraft's exaggerated reputation as

an eccentric recluse, the Eddys, as did most of the people who knew him personally, enjoyed his company and did not think him odd. He would play with the Eddys' young children and bring them snacks when he came to visit, and the Eddys' fondness for him comes through in their reminiscences.

Eddy accompanied Lovecraft on many late-night walks though Providence and on longer excursions as well. Among the more famous of these was their August, 1923 day trip to Chepachet in northwestern, RI in search of a mysterious Dark Swamp off Putnam Pike. This apocryphal location was rumored to be so dense that the light could not penetrate it, and there were sinister whispers of strange events and disappearances. A long day of walking and questioning locals produce some vague stories and a possible location, but by the time they had established their firmest lead they were exhausted and did not pursue it to the end. Some seventeen miles on foot in a humid August day in RI had bested their curiosity. They never returned to try again, but the trip and people they talked to may have influenced Lovecraft's The *Color Out of Space* and Eddy's *Black Noon*, which was incomplete at the time of his death, but has been published posthumously. For the adventurous, the probable route for this excursion can be found at https://stonewings.wordpress.com/2012/05/23/417/, but proceed at your own risk.

On another occasion, Lovecraft persuaded Eddy to join him on a late-night excursion to visit Poe Street, then and now in a marginal neighborhood one might normally think twice about visiting after midnight. This adventure may have been a higher risk proposition than their trip to the wilds of the Dark Swamp, for more mundane, practical reasons. Eddy also took Lovecraft on a trip to the Newport Tower, in Newport, RI, a mysterious stone structure some twenty-eight feet tall built in the 1600s. The original purpose of the edifice remains open to speculation, but Lovecraft's notes include reference to a similar tower south of Arkham that is thought to have been inspired by this trip. August Derleth used this fragment as the basis for *The Lurker at the Threshold* (1945).

Eddy wrote a number of stories for *Weird Tales* under the editorship of Edwin Baird and Farnsworth Wright, and for other pulp magazines of the period. His most famous piece is *The Loved Dead*, a story of sexually-motivated murder, necrophilia, and suicide that was controversial at the time. When it appeared in *Weird Tales*, there was some uproar over the lurid content and it was pulled from some newsstands as a result. However, improved sales from the scandal proved a windfall for the struggling magazine and it is sometimes credited with saving it from bankruptcy. The cover for the May/June/July, 1924 issue featured *Imprisoned with the Pharaohs*, ghostwritten by Lovecraft for Harry Houdini and appearing in Houdini's name. *The Loved Dead* has since been reprinted at least a dozen times in various anthologies and collections. Eddy's fiction in this and subsequent issues of *Weird Tales* appeared alongside fiction and article by Houdini on debunking fake spirit mediums, stories by Frank Belknap Long, and H. P. Lovecraft, and poetry by Clark Ashton Smith.

There is some debate in the literature about Lovecraft's contribution to four of Eddy's tales. HPL's "revisions" included *Ashes*, *The Ghost-Eater*, *The Loved Dead*, and *Deaf, Dumb, and Blind*, all of which were published in *Weird Tales*. These have been reprinted in various anthologies with permission of Eddy's estate, including *The Horror in the Museum—Revisions*, edited by August Derleth. Some writers have suggested that Lovecraft was largely responsible for *The Loved Dead*, but Muriel Eddy and August Derleth have said he did no more than offer some suggestions or touch it up. With its strong sexual themes, it is certainly not a typical Lovecraft story.

Eddy wrote on various themes, including supernatural horror tales, crime and detective fiction, and fantasy adventures involving prehistoric cave men. Although he continued to write after the 20s, Eddy did not publish a great deal of fiction after his early success with *Weird Tales*. He was by no means idle, however. Eddy was a theatrical booker for many years and an investigator for Harry Houdini. Houdini was famous for, among other things, his efforts to expose fraud spirit mediums. Such con artists would rig their studios with primitive special effects to levitate furniture, create disembodied spirit voices, turn on Victrola record players, and create light and sound effects. As a stage magician, Houdini determined that he could replicate these tricks and demonstrate that these spiritualists were frauds. As part of his crusade against psychic trickery, he employed investigators to do legwork on specific mediums before he would go to confront them directly. Eddy's role was to secretly investigate potential mediums in the New England area and brief Houdini in advance. He would also sell Houdini's pamphlets in the lobby of Houdini's shows, some of which he had ghostwritten himself. After Houdini's last show in Providence, Lovecraft, the Eddys, Houdini, and his wife Beatrice all dined at the Waldorf. Eddy and Lovecraft were both involved in the planning of a book Houdini was writing entitled *The Cancer of Superstition*, and Eddy completed three chapters of it before Houdini's death. The book was subsequently cancelled by Houdini's estate and was never completed. As a theatrical booker, Eddy knew many vaudeville performers, magicians, comedians, and burlesque dancers and left behind significant memorabilia from this golden age of stage entertainment. He also ran a successful music publishing business, composing lyrics and melodies individually and in collaboration with other artists. Songs such as *Dearest of All*, *Sunset Hour*, and *Hello Mr. Sunshine (Goodbye Mr. Rain)* did not reflect the dark imagination behind his fiction, but the image of poppies surrounding a sleeping child on the sheet music for *Every Little Lullaby* could be suggestive.

C. M. and Muriel Eddy enjoyed ongoing correspondence with many writers and fans of Lovecraft long after his death, and wrote a number of essays about their relationship with him for his adoring fans. They continued to be involved in the local Rhode Island writing scene and each served on the Board and as President of the Rhode Island Writers' Guild, which was founded by their daughter Ruth and remained active from 1950 through 1980. Save for a few reprints of his stories connected with Lovecraft, he might have faded into obscurity outside Rhode Island circles. After Muriel's death, two of their daughters attempted to publish a number of his stories through Dyer-Eddy Publications in the 1970s. These rare editions appeared in soft-covered saddle-stapled format and can occasionally be on the collectables market. Since that time, horror and weird fiction have increased in popularity and his friend and collaborator H. P. Lovecraft's star has become increasingly ascendant. The stars may be right for a C. M. Eddy, Jr. revival as well. Collections of Eddy's published work and previously unpublished stories from his archives are currently being released in new editions by Fenham Publishing at www.fenhampublishing.com.

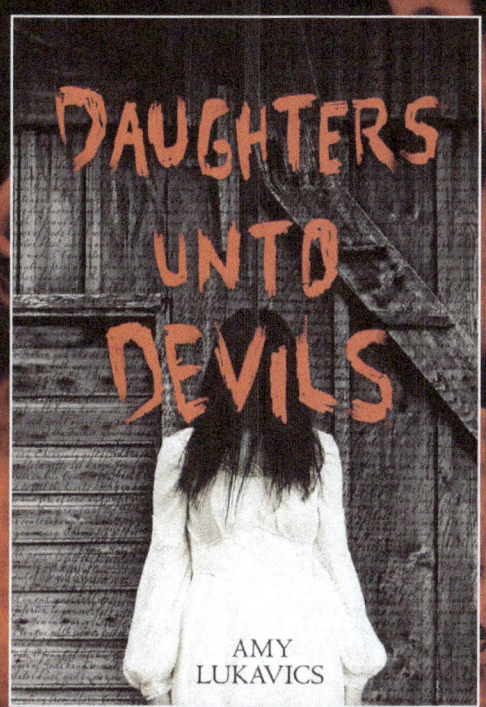

Daughters Unto Devils
by Amy Lukavics
amylukavics.com

Slasher Girls & Monster Boys
Stories selected by April Genevieve Tucholke
slashergirlsandmonsterboys.com

Sanctum
by Sarah Fine
sarahfinebooks.com

CHECK OUT THE HOTTEST TITLES IN YA HORROR!

Photo courtesy of Jim Dyer

Magic and the Outré: A Discussion on C. M. Eddy, Jr.

By K. H. Vaughan

"It is midnight. Before dawn they will find me and take me to a black cell where I shall languish interminably, while insatiable desires gnaw at my vitals and wither up my heart, till at last I become with the dead that I love." —C. M. Eddy, Jr., *The Loved Dead.*

Jim Dyer is the grandson of C. M. Eddy, Jr., a weird fiction writer and a friend of both H. P. Lovecraft and Harry Houdini. We met at his house in Narragansett, Rhode Island's historic district to discuss the life and work of Eddy, one of the original pulp writers. He showed me a selection of ephemera from Eddy's career, including letters, photos, and sheet music from Eddy's music company while we talked.

K. H. Vaughan: So, tell me a little about your grandfather.

Jim Dyer: Well, my grandfather was C. M. Eddy, Jr., a writer in Providence, Rhode Island. He wrote a lot of short stories during the 1920s, a lot of horror, science fiction, fantasy, and supernatural stories. I look at them as *Twilight Zone* kind of stories, *Alfred Hitchcock* kind of stories. He was friends with H. P. Lovecraft and Harry Houdini during that time. Lovecraft and my grandfather would meet, usually after midnight.

Lovecraft would come over to the house and knock on the door and they would go for walks around Providence, and they would trade story ideas. They would go back home and write them, and would meet up afterwards and read the stories aloud to each other. And then they would critique them and get them ready to be published and send them in to *Weird Tales*. Keep their fingers crossed that they would accept them. A lot of times my grandmother [Muriel Eddy] would type up the stories for Lovecraft, because he hated to use the typewriter. I mean, he did if he had to, but he did everything in long hand, same as my grandfather.

My grandfather and Lovecraft were both ghostwriters for Houdini, but my grandfather was an investigator for Houdini as well. Toward the end of Houdini's life, he liked to expose the fake séances. Houdini was actually looking to talk to his mother. He really wanted to talk to his mother, so he employed a lot of people around the country, and one of them was my grandfather for the New England region. He would go to séances and talk to the people to figure out how they did all the fake things. Then he would report back to Houdini and Houdini would come a week or two later with the newspapers and make a scene as if he had just figured it out on the spot.

KHV: But, it sounds like Houdini was originally sincere in hoping that he could find someone that was legitimate but was never able to?

JD: Oh, yeah. He really wanted to talk to his Ma, and he was looking for someone who could do that, but he realized that they were cheating everybody. And, I think he may have felt a little guilty because that's how he first started out too, I believe. But then he decided that he was just going to expose it because, back then, people were making a lot of money in it. A ton of people were interested in it so there was a ton of money being made off of people.

KHV: Yeah, spiritualism was very big then, and there were a lot of frauds. There was definitely money to be made from conning believers. How did an investigation work?

JD: Well, from what I understand, from what I found in my grandfather's things, he would go to the séance undercover. They asked him questions but he wouldn't give them the right answers. In one of them they had him start to talk with his mother, but his mother was still alive. And then, the table would start to lift and all those hokey things… he would try to figure out how it happened. Before an investigation he would read about the tricks and even try to do some of them so he would know how they did it. And I'm sure Houdini would say "well, they might try this or that" and they'd get specific for what to look for.

KHV: And then Houdini would swoop in and put on the show and take credit.

JD: And take all the glory. I mean, it's showmanship. That's what he did.

KHV: Right. Now the writing…

JD: My grandfather wrote, I think about seven or eight stories for *Weird Tales* from 1923 to 1925.

KHV: Under his own name.

JD: Right, under his own name. And the Houdini stories, Houdini paid for them. I do have some stories that my grandfather wrote for Houdini, but they never got published because Houdini passed away, so I'm working on a book on that. There are maybe three or five of those.

KHV: So, these have never seen the light of day? No one has read them?

JD: No one has. And some of them have the notes from Houdini saying "well, why don't we do this?" and so on. So, hopefully that's going to come to fruition at some point.

KHV: So, when you were growing up, did you have a sense of Eddy's place in weird fiction or is this something that you discovered later?

JD: No, I always knew. My grandfather passed away when I was nine, but I still have good memories of him. I always knew about Lovecraft and Houdini from talking with him. Back then, everybody used to go to Sunday dinner and he would talk about them. And I read some of his stories. Not a lot of them when I was nine, but after he passed away. My grandmother was still alive for a while after and I always asked questions about them, so I knew. But, he didn't make a big thing out of what he did.

When I was going through his things I found his papers from the 1920s. Letters from Lovecraft, Houdini. Stories for Houdini. And I found a lot of letters from *Weird Tales*. In a few of the letters, they talked about *The Loved Dead*, and how they weren't sure if they wanted to publish it because of the nature of the story at the time—the necrophilia. And one of them said—actually, this wasn't from *Weird Tales*, but from another magazine—you're never gonna get this published in America. Bring it to France and maybe then, because they have the *Grand Guignol*. That's the only place you can do it. When he sent it into *Weird Tales*, they were very hesitant about publishing it. They did, and then the editor sent a letter to my grandfather saying what an uproar it caused. The Indiana PTA took an injunction out and made all sorts of noise about it. But then, what happens when you do something like that? Everybody buys the magazine.

I don't know if that saved *Weird Tales*. People have said it did because they were going bankrupt at the time. They couldn't pay anybody, and after that they started publishing more regularly. The issue that it was in was a three-month issue because they couldn't afford to publish on schedule. I don't know if it saved it. I'd like to think that it did, and that it helped the careers of a lot of people. Because everybody that came after that, all the stories they ran… they probably would have got published but it would have taken more time.

KHV: Some of them might not have been. A lot of the pulps were on shaky ground.

JD: Yeah, a lot of them didn't even last a year or two and then went out of business. So, I'd like to think that he helped.

KHV: Lovecraft suggested that editors were scared to publish some of his pieces after *The Loved Dead* came out because of the reaction.

JD: I know! And *The Loved Dead*, some people say Lovecraft wrote it, but I have the original handwritten manuscript, and there are some Lovecraft annotation on it—he touched it up a bit. My grandfather wrote it in 1919 before he knew Lovecraft.

KHV: You have the original.

JD: And I have letters from other publishers from before he sent it to *Weird Tales* as well. As I said, they would read stories to each other and touch them up. Lovecraft did ghostwrite for a lot of people, and when he revised for some people he basically threw it all away and kept the title of the thing, but with my grandfather's stories he just touched them up. They were friends. They talked and made suggestions, and my grandfather did the same for him. Lovecraft asked for advice and he would give it, just like if you and me were writing stories and you said "hey, read this."

KHV: Like a critique circle.

JD: Right. And with the manuscripts they would have what they called the "travelling copies," which, what they did was, they would write a story, in the Lovecraft circle, and hand it around, and everybody had a hand in it. It's like, when someone writes a song and the band plays it, the drummer and the guitarist, they add things to it, but the original person wrote the song.

KHV: Lovecraft described different levels of "revision" and getting paid to substantially revise or completely rewrite other people's work, but that's not how he describes the stuff he does with Eddy. He's not getting a check for it.

JD: Through the years different people have interpreted it differently, and well, it's up to them. That's what happens.

KHV: But you have the manuscript.

JD: Yeah. I think part of it, when *The Horror in the Museum* came out in 1970… we have a letter that August Derleth wrote my grandmother—when he was working on the anthology, my grandfather was still alive and he said "I'd like to include these three stories and I knew Lovecraft didn't write them, but was it o.k. to put them in there?" and I think that's where it started. Because Lovecraft's name was on the cover, through the years it kind of morphed. That's my feeling. In the beginning of *The Dark Brotherhood*, August Derleth writes that the stories that are in *The Horror in the Museum*—*The Ghost Eater*, *The Loved Dead*, and *Deaf, Dumb, and Blind*—he writes that with these stories H. P. Lovecraft revised very little—I don't have the exact words there, but that's what he said.

KHV: S. T. Joshi has written that *The Loved Dead* was more Lovecraft than Eddy, but he based that on his subjective impression. I saw an interesting statistical analysis that disputed that conclusion. [Note: *Stylometry and Collaborative Authorship: Eddy, Lovecraft, and "The Loved Dead"* by Alexander A. G. Gladwin, Matthew J. Lavin, and Daniel M. Look. In Digital Scholarship in the Humanities (forthcoming).]

JD: Oh yeah, that was Gladwin. We corresponded while he was working on that—it's an interesting way to look at it.

KHV: From a methods perspective, I thought it was a good piece of work. That kind of analysis has its limitations, but he acknowledges them and his conclusions were reasonable.

JD: People can think whatever they want. I don't worry about that.

KHV: You mentioned *The Twilight Zone* and *Hitchcock* earlier. Are there underlying themes or philosophies that you see in Eddy's writing? In the way Lovecraft is centered around cosmicism, for example?

JD: No, I feel he wrote more classic stories. He actually wrote for whatever magazine he was writing for, so I don't think he had that larger thought or philosophy. He was just writing stories, I think. Somebody else might have another idea. He wrote stand-alone stories, whereas Lovecraft wrote stories that were more connected. He did more like the classic werewolf story or vampire story but he'd put a twist on it. His first story was in *Mystery Magazine*. He wrote a detective story that came out in 1919, and it was a little unusual in that it featured a female detective, and that was unique. Edgar Allan Poe had started detective stories and they were becoming popular, but a female detective wasn't something you'd see. His name was on the cover of that issue.

KHV: How many did he publish?

JD: About twelve to fourteen, most of them in *Weird Tales*, but also in *Muncey's Magazine, Action Stories, Snappy Stories*. You probably don't remember some of these because they only lasted a year or two, but the majority of his stories appeared in *Weird Tales*.

KHV: In recent years some of these older weird fiction writers—Lovecraft, Chambers and so forth—have grown in popularity. Are you seeing more interest in Eddy's work?

JD: Oh, yeah. I've been doing a lot of conventions and people are definitely interested. I think people discover Lovecraft and they get interested in the other authors from the same time. So, yes, I do see a lot more interest in his writing. Weird fiction in general. I was at an event recently and I had a big stack of ads for NecronomiCon [NecronomiCon - Providence, August, 2015]. People who weren't necessarily even horror fans were very interested—people took them all.

KHV: When did you found Fenham Publishing?

JD: In the year 2000. So we've been doing it about fifteen years.

KHV: Why "Fenham?"

JD: I named it "Fenham Publishing" because many of my grandfather's stories were set in a fictional town that he created named "Fenham." *The Loved Dead, The Vengeful Vision, Black Noon*, and *Deaf, Dumb, and Blind* are examples of some of the stories where he used Fenham as a setting. And we did it because, over the years, everything was put away in trunks and bureaus and we had a ton of papers and nobody in the family looked at it for probably forty years. I just wanted to get my grandfather's stories back out there. They had been published through the years, the majority of the ones from *Weird Tales* anyway, in different anthologies, but not all of them and I wanted to put them all together in book form. When I first started doing this, some of the small presses contacted me and said they wanted to do it but I looked at it and said "How hard can it be? I can do this." And then I started and found out how hard it can be.

KHV: Really hard.

JD: Yeah [laughs]. You know, it's just something I wanted to do. I designed the books myself, print the material. I wanted to do it a certain way and pay homage to him. Right now, we have two collections of his work, *The Loved Dead and Other Tales* and *Exit Into Eternity: Tales of the Bizarre and Supernatural.*

KHV: Plus, you also have *The Gentleman from Angel Street.*

JD: Yes, *Memories of Lovecraft* is the subtitle. Through the years, everybody asked my grandparents what kind of person Lovecraft was. Not a lot of people knew him. They knew him from his letters, but not as much personally. So, they wrote essays for different fan zines and magazines about Lovecraft, how they knew him, what they used to do. This is a collection of a few of these. It's a more personal view of Lovecraft, because a lot of the biographies out, people take information from the letters. When someone writes a letter, even now if you write an email, it can be hard to interpret. If you tell a joke in text, you don't get the inflection, so often in the letters I think Lovecraft is joking but you can't really tell if you didn't know him personally.

KHV: It seems pretty clear to me that in his correspondence he often wrote in an exaggerated tone or wrote things that he did not expect the recipient to take seriously if they knew him.

JD: Right, but someone can take that as being serious. I mean, my mother met Lovecraft when she was young, and he would come over and play with the kids. A lot of people when I tell them that think, "what?" Because they have that whole impression of him as a dark, serious person, and he was just a regular person. He joked around. One time he came over with James Morton, and they and my grandfather went walking around the East Side [of Providence]. They went in the First Baptist Church and he tried to play the organ and sang "Yes, We Have No Bananas" but he couldn't get the thing going. It tells the kind of person that he was.

KHV: If you look at the large number of friends that he had... you know, you've really got to like a guy if you're going to tolerate him showing up at all hours of the night and dragging you off on these long walks. People spent a lot of time with him, so he must have been a warm and enjoyable person to be around.

JD: Charismatic, yeah. He was a regular guy. He just had a really over-active imagination. A fantastic imagination to create what he did. He considered himself a little upper class, but otherwise a regular guy. He had a lot of friends.

KHV: I read that your grandparents received some of his household goods when he moved, does any of that survive?

JD: Yeah, we still have a lot of my grandparents' things, I think a bureau...

KHV: I remember a foldaway bed?

JD: Yeah, the foldaway bed, that's not here anymore. That mattress... [laughs] that mattress is long gone. Through the moves we lost some of that, but the bureau we have. We didn't have Lovecraft's typewriter. My grandmother afterwards said she wished she'd had that—that would have been the piece to keep. But we do have the typewriter that she used to type his manuscripts. Back then, he always wanted carbon copies and she always used to say she wished she'd kept an extra carbon of some of those stories. But, back then, he was just a friend.

KHV: None of them knew that he was going to have the kind of success that he did. Why archive it? Were your grandparents friends with other writers?

JD: They were. They started the Rhode Island Writer's Guild in 1950 and they met with a lot of the local writers during that time. I remember being young, they'd be at the house. It was a support group. People used to come see my grandparents because they knew Lovecraft. One time, when I was young—this was after my grandfather passed away, I forget how old I was—but it was a Sunday and my mother and aunt were having tea with this guy. She said "This is Mr. Bloch" and I said "hi" to him and talked to him. He was a really nice guy, joking around. I didn't find out until later that it was Robert Bloch. I had no idea who he was then. He used to come visit. I have letters from him to my grandfather. They kept in contact with a lot of people.

KHV: There's a book right there: the correspondence with other writers.

JD: Yeah. L. Sprague de Camp, Morton. August Derleth, obviously, from when he first started Arkham House until he passed in 1971. Derleth acted as my grandfather's agent for reprints, followed by his daughter April after he passed away. He was very happy with Derleth's representation, always got paid. He kept in touch and came to see them when he was in Providence. And Lovecraft's wife Sonia Greene—my grandmother kept up with her after the divorce. She sent a lot of letters and pictures from when she was living in California. They had a lengthy

THE GENTLEMAN FROM ANGELL STREET

MEMORIES OF H.P. LOVECRAFT

MURIEL E. EDDY • C.M. EDDY, JR.

correspondence and talked about everything. Sonia sent pictures of herself from when she was living in a nursing home or elderly home. I have a ton of those pictures. She talked a lot about Lovecraft in those, and her husband at the time too, of course.

KHV: She went on to have a long successful life after Lovecraft.

JD: She did. I forget how old she was when she passed away but we have a letter from the nursing home to my grandmother saying she had passed. Incidentally, when Lovecraft went into Jane Brown Memorial Hospital before he passed, the nurse at the hospital wrote to my grandmother, back and forth, about how he was doing. This is all stuff that we put away and it sat for decades.

KHV: Your grandfather was also a booking agent.

JD: Yes, he was a booking agent, and he would book performers into theaters in New England. Providence then had a lot of theaters and vaudeville shows—he would book the comedians, the burlesque dancers, and different performers. We have all these old headshots and contracts from vaudeville performers. That's how he got to know Houdini too, he booked him. He knew a lot of magicians from Rhode Island and outside the area. He was always really keen on magicians. The RI Society of Magicians, that's a chapter of the national Society of American Magicians that Houdini was president of back in the twenties. The RI chapter is named for C. Foster Fenner, who he booked. They have

meetings every month, and they invited me to talk about my grandfather and Houdini. I brought some papers and photos of some of the magicians he booked, and people were like "oh, yeah," they knew the names from the old days.

KHV: So, he was right there when burlesque and vaudeville were going into decline and got to see the tail end of that era.

JD: He ended up working as a clerk for the State of RI for a few years. He continued writing, but the pulp magazines, the music, the vaudeville dried up and he had to get a real job. I hate to say that, but he had a family to support, too. And that's why he did so many things, because when he knew Lovecraft and Houdini he had three little children. I always thought it was funny, because Lovecraft would come over after midnight and they'd go out and my grandmother was o.k. with it. One o'clock in the morning and you're walking around the streets of Providence.

KHV: You can't do that with a regular nine to five.

JD: It cracks me up how they stayed married because who knows what time he would come home, but he was out being creative.

KHV: He was also in music publishing and writing.

JD: He wrote a lot of music. People would send him words or music, or he would write his own lyrics and put them to music on the piano. He collaborated with a lot of people. He had his own company called Success Music Publishers, that started in the 1920s and probably lasted into the 1930s or 40s. Back then, they didn't have much recorded music on the radio, but they would have a live band, and some of his music was introduced live on WPRO in Providence. People would buy the sheet music. Another side note, when Houdini did his live shows, he would have musical interludes and used my grandfather's music. He didn't want people to know that my grandfather worked as an investigator for him, so he'd pay him to include the music in the shows too.

KHV: He had an interesting life.

JD: Yeah, he was a low key guy. Throughout his life people wanted to know about Houdini, but he had sort of a gentleman's agreement that he wouldn't talk about the investigations. He'd probably get mad at me for talking about it now. He was o.k. telling people that he worked for him, but he didn't want to reveal any of the actual specifics.

KHV: And he was at Houdini's funeral.

JD: Yeah, if you see the biography with Adrian Brody, at the end they show actual footage of Houdini's funeral, and coming out of the Elks Club, the pallbearers bringing the casket to the hearse, one of them looks exactly like my grandfather. I know he went to funeral and I have the picture of the pallbearer but I can't prove it's him.

KHV: What would he think of the weird fiction and horror environment today?

JD: I think he would be excited, because weird fiction and horror are in kind of a revival. It's always been around but, especially with shows like The Walking Dead becoming more mainstream, I think he'd be happy. Some of the horror is very graphic and goes for more shock value than for horror, and I think he'd be taken aback by that. He was like Lovecraft in that he wanted it to be more psychological and not come right out and say things. It's the things you don't say that make you scared more. It's how you allude to things. I think that's what he would say. I don't want to speak for him, but both he and my grandmother liked things more subtle. I think he'd be happy that more people enjoy it.

caulbearer

BY rebecca cantrell

gnes drifted along with the peyote, not worrying about her contractions. There was time for the baby to come. Time for everything.

She crawled across the cold plank floor and lay her head on the quilt. Under her cheek interlocking buttercup yellow and ruby red rings glowed. The wedding ring pattern. She imagined many pairs of withered hands stitching it. A simple design now infinitely complex. When the next contraction hit she gazed into the weave of the fabric, seeing how it all connected, loomed by the universe. The colors blazed so brightly they pealed like cathedral bells.

"I don't want to get all heavy on you." A woman's voice drifted in from far away. "But what did you take, honey?"

Agnes laughed at her. She had secrets. Things she wouldn't tell these strangers who had taken her in out of the driving Alaskan snow. When her son slipped between her bloody legs into the world, she still held onto her secrets. She told no one her name, what she had taken, or what she intended to do in the morning.

The woman helped her into bed and placed a wet warm creature on her naked stomach. Agnes stared at the baby's head, its ebony curls plastered against its skull with fluid from her body. She shuddered. She touched a strand, repelled at the sliminess. Such night-black hair. How had something so dark been birthed from her own light body? Once part of her, their connection now sundered.

The woman severed their umbilical cord with giant shears.

"His face?" Agnes pointed to a white membrane that covered his eyes and forehead.

The woman lifted the membrane off with a piece of dark flannel. Agnes smelled the tang of soap. It rang warm against the metallic scent of blood.

"It's a caul," the woman said. "Happens only once a thousand births."

Agnes stared at the heartbeat pulsing in the soft spot on top of his head, quick like a lizard's. "Did it hurt him?"

The woman shook her head. Each strand of her long hair floated and swung from side to side like a spider web in the lightest of breezes. "Doesn't he have beautiful eyes?"

Agnes avoided the warm wetness that were eyes, still mesmerized by the leathery spot on his head, pulsing at her in time with the rhythm of the universe.

The woman ran a trembling index finger along a strawberry birthmark on the left side of his chest. Light glittered on its crimson surface. Agnes touched it with a fingertip, expecting it to be hard and cold like a ruby, but it felt warm and soft, like the skin of her eyelids.

The woman cleared her throat. "A caul means many things. A caul with a birthmark like this means it is his fate to know true connection." She dropped her voice. "If he can give away that which matters most to him."

Not listening, Agnes answered, "I will call him Rainbow. After the colors of the sky."

The next morning she wrote his name on a piece of crumpled paper she left on the cleanswept pine floor before she slipped out the back door into the frigid December air. She had not looked at his eyes. And she never would.

***

Thirty years later, Rainbow, who had long since changed his name to Ron, sat in his divorce attorney's office, tapping his fingers on the arm of an ergonomic chair that looked like something a space alien would use for a long voyage. A space alien with a different configuration of limbs than humans.

"Sign here and I'll file them Monday." His lawyer, Aloysius Slade, slid papers across a polished black desk. Ron's reflection in its shiny surface took them. With his newly balding head, Ron looked like Darth Vader. Darth signed, pen bleeding black ink into the paper. Now his wife's fishing company, the one that he had saved from bankruptcy and rebuilt from the boats to the smokers, would become solely hers once she countersigned.

Behind Slade's chair, snow swirled in the darkness beyond the plate glass window.

"It's not my place," Slade drawled in a honeyed Southern accent. "But do you have to marry them all?"

Ron held out the papers, light glinting gold off his wedding band. "It's not your business, Aloysius."

Slade took the papers, tapped them square, and slipped them into a manila folder. Ron shivered, and goosebumps raised on his arms.

"I have to turn down the heat in here." Slade wiped his brow with a handkerchief.

How could Slade be hot? The room felt like a meat locker.

"It warmed up outside when it started to snow," Slade said. "Must be twenty out there."

Ron stood to go. He wasn't paying good money to listen to small talk about the weather. When Slade rose too, Ron noticed how much weight he'd packed on. Getting fat off Ron's money, like everyone else.

"Why do you do it?" Slade asked, as if he just couldn't help himself. He pushed round glasses up his sweaty nose. "Third time you've been in here in three years. Each divorce costs more than the last."

"I believe in giving away my heart in marriage." But the marriage was over, or soon would be. Ron rubbed his cold palms together. Justine, his soon-to-be-ex-wife was always cold.

"You don't believe in it for more than six months at a time." Slade opened his office door, and they strode out into the hall. "You should try something less binding."

Ron ignored his comments. This time, the divorce had been her idea. "I'm looking for the right one. And when I find her, I'll know."

"So why do you keep marrying the wrong one?"

"I think it's the only way. To really connect. Activate

your heart." Ron sounded certain, but he wasn't. Not anymore.

"Activate? You make it sound like a bomb." Slade sighed when Ron walked past the elevators toward the stairs.

"Maybe it is a bomb."

"So far it's been exploding dollar bills all over my office pretty regularly." Slade panted from trying to keep up on the long walk down the hall. Ron quickened his pace.

"It's only money." Ron paused, hand on the door to the stairwell.

"You sound like some kind of hippie. Not the ruthless businessman I know."

"Maybe I'm a lot of things you don't know."

"I know some things about you, Ron."

Ron took the stairs two at a time down to the ground floor. In spite of his words to Slade, he felt discouraged. Tonight was his company Christmas party, and he resolved, for the first time, to go home from it alone. He zipped his coat, stepped past two smokers sneaking a cigarette in the stairwell, and went out into the chill of the storm.

***

White-shirted waiters circulated in the ballroom of the Anchorage Hilton with trays of salmon puffs, stuffed crab, and platters of finger foods. Ron knew he'd need to eat a bucket of each to get full. Yet another way his soon-to-be ex-wife, Justine, wasted money. She had ordered the food, as if anyone came for that. Everyone was most interested in the free bar till midnight. Between that and the cabs he had on hand to drive the drunks home, the event would set him back more than he had budgeted. Still, it had been a good year for the business, his legacy. He raised a Champagne flute to his lips.

"Hello, Ron," a familiar voice spoke from directly behind him.

Ron turned to face her. She wore a long gold dress with complicated black straps. She reminded him of a yellowjacket. "Justine."

She snagged two Champagne flutes off a tray with the easy grace he'd once so admired. "Beautiful event."

"Last one they'll probably see. The new owner is too damn spoiled to run it."

Justine smiled, showing sparkling white veneers. "Why, Ron! What a rude thing to say about the woman who was almost the mother of your children."

Ron downed his Champagne in one gulp. Justine handed him her extra. He took it without a word of thanks. "So you're not going to cannibalize the business now that it's officially yours? Lay off everyone and dump the money into your account?"

"I forgot to wish you happy birthday." She clinked her glass against his. "And let's say merry Christmas and happy new year too, because I don't think we'll be seeing each other then."

Ron knocked his glass against hers. "I'll miss you, Justine."

"Too bad I'm not your soulmate," she said icily. Her eyes flicked past him.

Ron could tell by her suddenly jealous expression that a beautiful woman must be standing right behind him, so he turned. His elbow jostled an attractive woman in her twenties he'd once marked as a prospect, before he'd started dating the boss's daughter. A few drops of Champagne glistened on her front.

"I'm sorry." He wished he had a napkin and the balls to blot the bubbly drops off her breasts. Out of the corner of his eye he saw Justine stalk away.

"My bad," she gushed, in the way that secretaries do to the man who ran the company. Or used to run it.

"Think nothing of it." Ron ran his eyes down her body. Firm and curved, she wore a tight red dress with white shoes and a white belt.

"I'm Candy." She held out her hand for him to shake. "I work in shipping."

He took her hand. Electricity jolted up his arm when he touched her warm and very soft fingers. Perhaps he should reconsider his resolution about going home alone. "I'm Ron."

"Oh, I know," she said. "I've walked by your office like a hundred times."

On the other side of the room, Justine flirted with Bill. A fisherman on one of Ron's boats in the summer, he ran a trapline in the winter and didn't come into town much, but he'd come into town for the Christmas party. He didn't have an ounce of fat on him, plus he had a full head of curly blond hair. Why did it have to be Bill?

"What do you do over in shipping?" he asked, smiling down at Candy. When she stepped closer to him she smelled, improbably, of mint and vanilla.

Before Candy could answer, pain cut across Ron's right hand. He dropped his Champagne flute on the floor, where it shattered. A cramp?

"Did you cut yourself?" Candy asked. "Hold it above your heart and apply direct pressure."

He grabbed his uninjured palm with his left hand, following Candy's instructions. But he could see that he hadn't been cut.

Candy took his hands and raised them up over his shoulders, proper first aid if he'd actually been cut. Oh Lord, Justine would be frosted if she saw him holding hands with Candy.

Behind him, Bill's voice yelled, "Justine!"

Ron turned, Candy still holding his hands. Justine sprinted out of the ballroom.

"Your hand's fine." Candy massaged it. "Probably a cramp."

Ron pulled his throbbing hand free from Candy's and hurried after Justine. By the time he got through the front door, Justine's dress flashed gold from halfway across the parking lot. "Stop!" he called. "I need to talk to you."

Bill appeared beside Ron, holding a mink coat in his work-roughened hands. "You forgot your coat!" he yelled after Justine.

Justine ignored them both, yanked open the door of a Lincoln Navigator with her left hand, climbed in, and slammed the door shut.

Though still sheltered in the entryway of the building, Ron shivered. Had he made a mistake? He stared into the darkness of the parking lot.

Candy opened the door. "What are you two doing out

there? Come inside before you catch your death of cold."

Bill followed Candy inside. "What're you drinking?" he asked.

Ron too stepped back into the warmth, eyes drawn to Bill's muscles, bulging like the Incredible Hulk's.

***

Two hours later Ron sat up next to Candy with a scream. He rolled out of bed and landed on her shag carpet groaning.

"What's wrong?" Candy ran her fingers through mussed light blonde hair, sleepy eyes alert.

"Call 911," he choked out.

Candy was on the phone in an instant, barking out orders like a doctor. In spite of his pain, he listened, impressed. She was wasted over in shipping.

She knelt next to him, bare knees warm against his side. "Where does it hurt?"

"My right hip." He groaned again as fresh pain lanced through him. "I think it's broken."

"Broken?" She ran her hands deftly along his naked hips. "Maybe it's referred pain."

"What the hell are you talking about?" He tried to breathe through the agony.

She held his wrist lightly. "Your pulse is racing. Do you have anxiety attacks?"

"Hell no!" He shifted on the carpet and pain seared up his back. He gasped.

She raised a plucked eyebrow skeptically. She picked her red dress off the floor and pulled it over her head. "I'll let in the EMTs."

He wanted to beg her not to leave him alone, but he bit his tongue and focused on his breaths. You could rise out of your body, he'd been told by a shaman once. He concentrated. The pain abated and he lay still on Candy's floor, staring at a velvet chair covered with teddy bears. His head cleared enough to think.

He sat up, his back to the bears. If it wasn't his pain, it must be Justine's.

Justine was the one.

He felt a strong urge to sleep, but beat it back. Far away, he felt Justine slip into unconsciousness, and his pain vanished.

With shaking hands, he pulled on his pants and buttoned his dark shirt. He had to find her, had to save her. He had to undo the worst mistake of his life.

He surprised Candy by the front door. "Call them back," he said. "I'm fine."

She dimpled up at him. "You're quite the roller coaster, Ron."

"Now, please."

She shook her head and called off the EMTs.

"I think Justine's been hurt." Ron slipped on loafers, wishing he'd worn boots to the party.

She blinked a few times. "Your ex-wife, Justine?"

He nodded, knowing how crazy it was.

"So you have some kind of psychic ESP powers?" She put her hands on her slim hips.

He shrugged.

"This is why you should never sleep with your boss," she said. "You find out things you don't want to know."

"I'm serious, Candy." He pulled on the coat he'd worn to the party, too light for the weather. "Give me your keys."

"I'm sure you're serious," she said. "And I'll drive."

He didn't argue. If Justine woke, he'd likely drive off the road and then they'd all three be done for.

Once on the road heading toward his old house, where Justine now lived alone, he slumped against the seat, exhausted and cold, staring at the plastic heart hanging from Candy's rearview mirror. A crack ran down the middle.

"I think she had a car accident," he said. "Call the police. And turn up the heat in here."

"Car accident?" Candy turned the fan on full blast. "What makes you think that?"

"Just a feeling... Call the police." Even though the air from the heater blew so hot that it was drying out his eyeballs, he felt bone cold.

She turned her gaze on him. "I called the EMTs the last time you had a spirit vision, Ron. It's your turn. And don't use my phone."

He sighed. She wasn't one to cut him slack, and as soon as he heard her words, he knew how stupid he sounded. No one would believe him. He pushed buttons anyway, fingers clumsy with cold.

"911. State the nature of your emergency." The woman on the other end seemed professional, but rushed.

He took a deep breath. "There's been a car accident."

"How many vehicles involved?"

"I don't know." He stared into darkness. Snowflakes melted on Candy's windshield.

"Where are you located, sir?"

"On the Glenn Highway, between Anchorage and Eagle River." Dark pines flowed by outside the window, only the tops visible over the ten foot high berms of snow plowed up onto the sides of the road.

"Is anyone hurt?"

"I think a woman's broken her hip. And maybe also her shoulder. She's unconscious."

Candy rolled her eyes.

"Anyone else hurt?" the dispatcher asked.

"I don't know."

"Where exactly is the accident?"

"I don't know." He wished he did. A jeep covered in multi-colored Christmas lights passed them.

"What's your name?"

"Rainbow," Ron said. Candy snorted. "I mean Ron. Ron Matheson."

"Have you been drinking, Mr. Matheson?"

"No. Not much." He fought to keep desperation from his voice. "You have to get there soon or she'll die."

"Where are you?"

"I'm in a car driving toward Eagle River, but I don't know where she is."

Cold silence answered him. Candy hummed *Somewhere Over the Rainbow.*

"How do you know she's been injured. Did she call you?"

"Sort of." He shot Candy a look, and she stopped humming.

"Did she call you on a phone?" The dispatcher sounded wary now.

"No." He felt a flush spread up his neck. But he had to help Justine. "More like a psychic call."

"Do you know that there are penalties for making false 911 calls, Mr. Matheson?"

He hung up the phone.

"Glad I didn't make that call," Candy said.

He stared out the window at the white snow walls closing them in. A giant yellow GIVE MOOSE A BRAKE sign flashed by. It told him that there had been 147 road kills that winter. "Stop!"

She pulled over, coasting to a standstill. "I don't see anything."

"She's close. I can feel it."

Candy glanced back at the wide sweep of highway behind them, snow glittering in the moonlight. "It must be ten degrees out there."

He pulled open the car door, wincing at the pain in his hand. It was no cramp. He walked along the side of the road, searching for tire tracks. Snow blew into his face, caught in his eyelashes. He missed Candy's warm bed.

Behind him the car door chimed. He turned to see Candy climbing out. Her coat reached to the bottom of her dress, her legs bare and pink. Neither of them was dressed for this expedition.

She pulled on heavy white bunny boots. They looked so incongruous against her nude legs that he laughed.

"Girl's got to keep her feet warm. Especially if we're going to be tromping around here until the police arrest you." She flicked on a flashlight and swept it over the ground. "For making a false 911 call."

He jogged along the highway, loafers squeaking in the snow. The apex of the curve lay dead ahead. If Justine was speeding, that was the most likely spot for her to lose control.

He spotted a break in the snow wall. He knelt in front of it and stared at tire tracks, visible under a thin blanket of new-fallen snow. Justine.

His teeth chattered, and he wrapped his arms around himself.

Candy shone her flashlight at him. "Best to keep your feet warm. You know…" Her voice trailed off as she looked at the hole in the snowbank.

She stepped next to him and poked her flashlight through the hole. A Navigator lay upside down a few yards away, dome light casting a gold coin of light in the darkness.

"Holy crap." Candy ran through the snow toward it, sinking above her knees with each step. He slogged behind, shivering.

She yanked open the car door. Metal crunched as it plowed through snow. "Justine, can you hear me? It's Candy. I'm here with Ron."

He felt a weight pull his eyelids down to his kneecaps. His eyelids creaked open and blinding pain returned. He grabbed the side of the upside down car. His head rang with pain. He vomited in the snow. It steamed.

"I couldn't stop," Justine said. She closed her eyes and moaned. She held her freshly bandaged hand out.

Ron collapsed on the snow, twitching. Candy took Justine's hand.

"For Christ's sake, Ron." Candy flipped open her cell phone. Her red thumbnail dialed 911.

Ron closed his eyes.

***

When he opened them again, he was laid out flat in the snow. Candy must have zipped his coat and put up his hood. He glanced toward the car. Candy tromped back and forth in front of it, rubbing her bare arms and swearing. Her coat draped over an ominously still Justine.

He licked his cold lips. "Candy?"

She ignored him, staring past him at lights on the highway.

"We're down here!" Candy swept the flashlight from side to side. "Hurry!"

Two burly EMTs waded through the snow toward them, one carrying a stretcher, uniforms dark against the white.

"She's in bad shape," Candy said quietly to the EMTs.

The EMTs talked in low tones to Justine, but she never opened her eyes. Together they undid the seat belt and eased her onto the stretcher. Ron and Justine cried out in unison.

"Was he in the accident too?" a deep voice asked Candy, starting toward Ron.

She shook her head, eyes on Justine. "He came with me."

"Is he hurt?"

"Not a mark on him," Candy said.

The EMT checked out Ron, being thorough until Candy picked her jacket off the snow and wriggled into it, distracting him from his work.

He drifted in and out of consciousness listening to the EMTs. They agreed with Candy. He wasn't hurt.

"But he'll freeze to death," the deep voice said. "We can't leave him here."

He wondered if they would.

***

He woke in the hospital waiting room, stretched across a row of seats. Candy sat near him, sipping a coffee. He groaned.

"Don't think the theatrics are helping." She dumped another sugar into her cup and stirred.

"How's Justine?" he whispered. He felt weaker than he ever had in his life.

"Don't know," Candy said. "I'm not family. They won't tell me anything. Who's her family? Someone should call them."

"Is it that bad?" Panic shot through him, overlaying pain. Would Justine die? For a selfish moment, he looked forward to being free of pain.

Candy shrugged. "Maybe. Can you call them?"

He shook his head and rattled off Justine's mother's number.

Candy flipped open her cell phone. "No reception in here. I'll make it outside. Will you be OK here?"

"No."

She gave him a scathing look and clomped toward the front door in her bunny boots.

He rolled himself off the chairs onto the black-flecked linoleum. Pain seared into his bones, but he levered himself up onto all fours and crawled across the floor. He didn't try to look where he was going. He knew he would find her if he kept crawling. Linoleum flowed ahead of him like an endless river.

Eventually he pushed through a set of swinging doors. Feet and legs rushed to and fro, tending to someone. He looked up. Justine.

Bright lights burned into his brain, and he retched.

"What the hell are you doing here?" asked a man in a white coat.

"She's my wife." And, legally, it was still true.

Two nurses grabbed him under his armpits and flung him in a chair next to her bed. He shivered, arms and legs icy.

Golden hair pillowed Justine's beautiful pale face. He remembered how she'd looked on their wedding night, hair long then, too.

He winced when someone stuck an IV into her arm.

He watched liquid flow down it, felt it enter his own arm like ice, soothing cooling ice. He and Justine moaned with relief at the same instant.

She turned to him. Her glassy brown eyes widened, and he knew that she felt the connection. He smiled and tried to shake off the stoned feeling from the painkiller.

"I love you," he said and, for the first time, he meant it.

"The brakes failed," she whispered. "But you know that. And why."

"I'm sorry." And he was.

He squeezed her icy hand. He felt her wedding band clink against his. Comfort flowed through their hands. Comfort they could have shared for a lifetime. "I didn't know this would happen."

A force pulled him down a night-black well.

"We're losing her."

It was the last thing he heard.

On *Occultism* in F. Paul Wilson's *The Keep*

BY MICHAEL R. COLLINGS

We live in a world in which words and their meanings are increasingly vulnerable. Whether through the carelessness, ignorance, or willful intent of speakers and writers, words are shifting meanings, perhaps more rapidly than ever before. Within a few years, for example, *literal* has completed a complex transformation and now means both *literal* (i.e., 'true to fact, not figurative or metaphorical') and its diametrical opposite, *figurative* ('metaphorical and not literal'). *Privilege* has been reversed, so that what once identified 'opportunities or benefits available exclusively to a few' now denotes 'opportunities or benefits available exclusively to the majority.' *Equality* has become a touchstone term that often is forced to link essentially and inherently *unequal* persons, institutions, or ideas. Recently, the venerable term *melting pot* has been re-defined as a racist code-phrase.

There is nothing fundamentally wrong with words changing meanings. It has been an organic attribute of languages since…well, since languages began. English in particular has welcomed shifts in meanings to reflect shifts in society and culture, resulting in an enormous number of simple-seeming words with multiple meanings— *polysemous* words. A word as basic as *set* has, according to the *Oxford English Dictionary*, over 450 possible meanings, making the possibilities for misunderstanding even this unassuming Anglo-Saxon carry-over ever present.

Given these characteristics of English in contemporary society, it requires care and alertness on the part of speakers and writers to ensure that listeners and readers understand precisely what crucial words mean. For that reason—and because I find great pleasure in exploring words, their histories, and their permutations over time—I frequently begin essays by talking about *what* key words mean before discussing them.

This issue of *Dark Discoveries* is devoted to the *occult*. On the surface, there should be little difficulty with the word—most readers immediately recognize it as referring to alchemy, astrology, and magic, especially as such 'sciences' relate to understanding and controlling the natural and the supernatural. This has been the primary meaning of the word since the mid-seventeenth-century, when such studies began separating from what we now understand as *science* and, really for the first time, became almost universally condemned by rationalists. As the need arose for a fairly neutral word to apply to those branches of human knowledge that did not fit into the burgeoning scientific era, the word that fit best was *occult*.

But *occult* in English goes further back by a century or so, and its meanings during that hundred-year span are as interesting as its more recent one, particularly in relation to a book I would like to examine, a classic of modern horror that is *essentially* ('by its very nature') and *fundamentally* ('acting as a foundation') *occult*: F. Paul Wilson's extraordinary 1981 novel of fear and terror, *The Keep*.

Upon first reading *The Keep*, it might seem that there is little overt *occultism* in the novel, the story of the systematic but inexplicable destruction of German soldiers occupying a mysterious castle in the Carpathian Mountains of Romania—formerly Transylvania—in 1941. One by one, initially at least, they die hideously at the hands of an unseen assailant, causing the original officer in charge to send for reinforcements because, as he puts it, "something is killing my men." Not *someone. Something.*

The sole reference to *magic* occurs as a negative. When Professor Cuza suggests to the German commandant that one of his incantations the previous night had forestalled further killings, Captain Woermann realizes that "He would have laughed at this conversation last Monday. It smacked of a belief in spells and black magic." The subject of magic is raised as a means of denying it, particularly since readers know that Cuza had uttered no incantations at all; he had been talking with the vampiric Molesar.

Yet suggestions of magic of a deeper, more contemporary sort, have already entered the novel. When the Cuzas first enter their chamber in the Keep, Magda picks up a book from the table: *The Book of Eibon*. By itself, that title might mean little to most readers, but when she reads the titles of others, the implications become clearer. The stack includes Ludwig Prinn's *De Vermis Mysteriis*, the Comte d'Erlette's *Cultes de Goules*, the *Pnakotic Manuscripts*, *The Seven Cryptical Books of Hsan*, and von Juntz's *Unaussprechlichen Kulten*. Later, one more is added to the horde: the *Al Azif* by the mad Arab Abdul Alhazred, more frequently known by its alternate title, *The Necronomicon*.

One and all, Lovecraftian titles…or at least titles associated with Lovecraft's dark visions of cosmic Great Old Ones by subsequent contributors to the Cthulhu mythos.

The ancient tomes are definitively books of the occult, containing secret means of contacting—of invoking—vast, unknowable, and inimical powers in the misguided belief that such powers might be controlled. Merely reading their titles is sufficient to invoke a shudder among the "searchers after horror" to whom Lovecraft addresses his tales; the presence of such horrifying specimens of human thought in a foreboding stone Keep overseen by half-mad Nazis in the middle of a bloody world war (which, to that point, the Germans seem to be winning), fairly screams *occult*. And, readers are told, the volumes have been *hidden away*, in a hollow spot in the walls.

But, as with the entire vampire motif so intricately developed by Molesar and accepted by Professor Cuza, this suggestion of overt occultism is little more than a spot of misdirection, a literary red herring. Yes, the novel speaks of a god-like race that preceded humanity, but that race shares few characteristics with Cthulhu, Nyarlathotep, Shoggoths, or various other things fungoid, tentacled, and eldritch. Eventually, as Wilson develops his own mythology, he reveals that the ancient books of forbidden knowledge serve no function in the narrative, except as they present opportunities for Cuza to deceive the Germans. While they might contain formulae or incantations that would meet the common definition of *occult*, they cannot

explain the deaths, the increasing sense of darkness and despair, the essential mysteries of the Keep.

If one traces the meanings of *occult* backward, however, toward less common definitions, one discovers that on an etymological level, *occult* simply means 'secret' or 'covered.' It is in fact a fairly common astronomical term for what happens when one celestial body—usually the moon or an asteroid—hides a more distant one from sight—the moon, for example, might occult Saturn. There is nothing inherently magical or paranormal about such events, although *occultists* might read meaning into them.

Using *occult* in this sense, *The Keep* gradually reveals itself as an intensively occult novel. Almost everything in the novel is *hidden*—and in most cases, concealment is intentional on the part of the characters and structural on the part of the author.

To take the most obvious example: the Keep is enigmatic, cryptic. Nothing is known about it; its builder, its history, its purpose are hidden. Its size is anomalous; its condition, misleading. The 16,807 crosses embedded into its stones must have a meaning, that seems apparent to all of the characters; yet no one knows what it is or even what the crosses actually represent. In one sense, the forward thrust of the narrative is determined by the Keep; only as the Germans begin dismantling it, beginning with a stone bearing a single atypical cross—made of gold and silver rather than brass and nickel—do the murders begin. Demolishing the walls *dis*-covers the cache of ancient books Cuza uses to trick the Germans and advance his personal, secret agenda…and allows the darkness hidden within the Keep to spread.

Nearly every character hides something, and those deceptions become crucial to the story. One of the earliest examples is Private Lutz, who (rather unsuccessfully) tries to hide a streak of venality that, when discovered by Woerrman, makes the private the first victim. His initial failed attempt to pry a cross from a stone earns him night guard duty, which places him in the lower levels of the Keep and allows him to see the gleam of gold that in turn convinces him that he is on the track of a long-hidden Vatican treasure-hoard. In seeking to uncover that secret, he causes his own death.

Other secrets are more central. Captain Woermann is public but guarded about his disdain for the Nazi Party but does not dare reveal his growing fear of the Keep, a fear symbolized and made visual by his failure to discern the hanged man hidden within his sadly prophetic painting.

The ironically named Major Kaempffer ('fighter, battler') has a deeper, more incapacitating secret: he is a coward, and only the Captain knows it. The tension between the two escalates to the point that neither can function as befits a military officer, and as a result the darkness grows.

Theodore and Magda Cuza are more complex. Professor Cuza is at first motivated by an academic's interest in discovery but later becomes entrapped in his plans to—quite literally—overthrow the Third Reich and bring redemption to his people. He hides his increasing knowledge of who and what (he thinks) Molesar is; he hides his plans to destroy the Keep and release the monster; he hides his new-found relief from the scleroderma that has made his life a torture; he hides his loss of faith from all except Magda, then funnels his bitterness and frustration into overarching desires: for vengeance and for death to the bringers of death…the Germans. Magda, in turn, hides everything she knows about the red-haired stranger, Glaeken, most particularly his intrusion into her life and her growing estrangement from her father…and from the person she used to be. Between the two of them, father and daughter orchestrate much of the novel's action by withholding key information from each other and from the Germans.

Molasar and Glaeken are, of course, masters of the *occult*. Molasar presents himself as an occult figure, a creature of magic and supernatural powers, of almost infinite longevity (from a human perspective at least) and infinite power. He is all of these, of course, but not in the manner he suggests to Cuza. The truth about him is stranger—yet more rational, more easily explicable given an extended historical span—than the pseudo-history he weaves. Glaeken hides truth in the opposite direction; he presents a façade of normality, slightly tinged with superheroism in his unusual strength and agility. He fully reveals himself to none until the concluding events of the story, when he and Molesar meet. The final revelation of who and what they are, coinciding with Glaeken's 'unveiling'—of his sword and of his identity—leads to an apocalyptic struggle between good and evil, with the souls of both Cuzas at stake. (*Apocalyptic*, by the way, is an appropriate word here; it comes from the Greek *apokalýpt* (*ein*), meaning 'to uncover, disclose,' a perfect opposite to *occult*.)

The Keep, then, is a novel of the *occult*. That it bears little resemblance to contemporary tales of voodoo, demon worship and demonic possession, quasi- or pseudo-religious cults and rituals, magic black or white is at this point irrelevant. While clearly aware of the more common meaning of the word, and incorporating suggestions of traditional occultism deftly and aptly, the novel invariably turns the resulting expectations on their heads, subverting and denying them, subordinating them to explanations presented as logical, factual, and historical (within the novel's frame of reference). Instead the novel carefully remains true to an older sense of *occult*, one that provides Wilson with narrative options that would otherwise have been impossible had he committed himself to authentic vampires, for example, with all of the appurtenances that would have required. Instead, by emphasizing things that are *hidden*, he offers moment after moment of *dis*-covery, of *reveal*-ation, constantly inverting conclusions readers have reached about events, about characters, about meanings… and about the Keep.

CHARLES WILLIAMS

AND

A.E. WAITE:
A MAGICAL RELATIONSHIP

BY AARON J. FRENCH

Charles Williams, the son of a shopkeeper, was born in London in 1886 and lived until 1945. A highly intelligent individual, he received a standard grammar school education—notwithstanding that he hailed from "working-class" roots. He made it through only one year at the University of London, when his financial support ran out; nor did he serve in the military, but began work in a Methodist workroom. He later took advantage of the adult education movement, essentially attending night courses and lectures aimed at educating the working class. In 1908, he took a proofreading job with Oxford University Press, where he was so impressive that he was eventually awarded him an honorary M.A. and made him lecturer in English literature. He worked as an editor for OUP until his death (Shideler 5-7).

During the early 1940s, Williams was a member of a writing/literary group called "The Inklings," which consisted of such luminaries as C.S. Lewis, J.R.R. Tolkien, and Owen Barfield. In seeking out a magus in Williams's life, any one of The Inklings would do, particularly Owen Barfield with his connection to Rudolf Steiner and the Anthroposophical Society. However while spirituality was central to the profound discussions held at The Eagle and the Child, a pub where The Inklings met,

particularly discussions about Christianity, it seems the group functioned more as a literary group and a writing workshop.

On the other hand, as if these figures in Williams's biography are not impressive enough, turning to what might be called Williams's esoteric history we discover Arthur Edward Waite (1857-1942), British poet, mystic, esotericist, and member of the legendary Hermetic Order of the Golden Dawn (HOGD). Waite wrote voluminously on occult topics, and helped develop the popular Rider-Waite tarot deck. If there is any figure that most resembles a "magus" in Williams's life, then Waite is it. His influence on the occult and esoteric traditions, both during his time and into the present, has been vast indeed. In R. A. Gilbert's biography of the renowned occultist, *A.E. Waite: Magician of Many Parts*, the author gives this description: "Arthur Edward Waite was unique: the first—and only—scholarly student of 'rejected [occult] knowledge'[1].... It

---

1 "Rejected knowledge" is a term coined by historian James Webb.

was Waite who introduced Eliphas Levi to the English-speaking world; Waite who made the classics of alchemical literature available in English; and it was Waite who, in 1903, recreated the Hermetic Order of the Golden Dawn from the ashes of its self-destruction" (cover-jacket blurb, *A.E. Waite: Magician of Many Parts*).

Williams first met Waite in 1915, although he had begun reading the occultist's writings much earlier. Williams was particularly impressed by Waite's two books, *The Hidden Church of the Holy Graal* and *The Secret Doctrine in Israel*, which introduced him to the new and exciting concepts of the occult and esotericism. Williams had sent Waite a copy of his poetry collection *The Silver Stair* (1912) and they corresponded via the post until their initial meeting at Waite's behest. Waite had withdrawn from involvement in the HOGD, unhappy with its leadership and direction, now seeking a more mystical Christian order. Around this time (1915) he subsequently formed his own society, the Fellowship of the Rosy Cross, and consecrated the Salvator Mundi Temple. In 1917, Williams, possibly being tipped off by fellow Oxford editors Revd. A.H.E. Lee and D.H. Nicholson about Waite's order,

requested a Form of Profession from Waite, signed it, and was then initiated into the Portal Grade of the Fellowship of the Rosy Cross (Ashenden 5) (Gilbert 149) (Willard 272-273).

The first paragraph from Dr. Thomas Willard's essay on the subject describes the scenario with such immediacy that it bears reproduction:

> At 5:00 p.m. on Friday, September 21, 1917, Charles Williams went to the Imperial Hotel in Russell Square, in London, where he was to be initiated into the Salvator Mundi Temple of the Fellowship of the Rosy Cross. At 5:30, following the "Ceremonial Summons to assume the habit," the Temple was opened and the Postulant was admitted, robed in black. Before an assembly of fourteen *Fratres* and five *Sorores*, he swore that he would "keep all secrets of the Sanctuary" and received the symbolic baptism of water and fire. Thereupon, in the words of the official minutes, he was "received into the Portal Grade under the Sacramental Name of *Qui Sitit Veniat*." As he moved about the hired rooms, which were consecrated to symbolize the Temple of Jerusalem, he may have felt for a moment that he was living in a book by the occult scholar Arthur Edward Waite. For Waite

had organized the Fellowship and stood before him as now *Sacramentum Regis*, Imperator of the Rite in the Ceremony of Reception into the Grade of Neophyte (Willard 269).

From this description, the image of Waite as Williams's magus is clear. In fact, this scene closely resembles a certain scene in Williams's novel *Shadows of Ecstasy*. Williams progressed quickly through the grades and on August 26, 1919, the author was "Raised on the Cross of Tiphereth, and entered the grade of Adeptus Minor" (Ashenden 6). Eventually he reached the outer gates of some esoteric Fourth Order and later, in 1927, The Hidden Life of the Rosy Cross. But after nearly ten years of being involved in Waite's order, Williams either lost interest or left due to personal problems (namely, a midlife crisis). However, he remained an inactive member and kept in contact with Waite until the great occultist passed in 1942.

In the detailed accounts given by both Willard and Ashenden concerning Williams, the influence that Waite had on both Williams's novels and theology is substantial. But principally what the budding author inherited from Waite was a tradition of real mysticism. From Waite's books to his esoteric order, Williams picked up that "secret knowledge" said to be imparted by all the magi throughout history.

Works Cited

1. Ashenden, Gavin. *Charles Williams: Alchemy and Integration*. Kent, OH: Kent State UP, 2008.

2. Gilbert, R. A. *A.E. Waite: A Bibliography*. Wellingborough, Northamptonshire: Aquarian, 1983.

3. Willard, Thomas. "Acts of the Companions: A. E. Waite's Fellowship and the Novels of Charles Williams." Roberts, Marie Mulvey, and Hugh Ormsby-Lennon. *Secret Texts: The Literature of Secret Societies*. New York: AMS, 1995. 269-302.

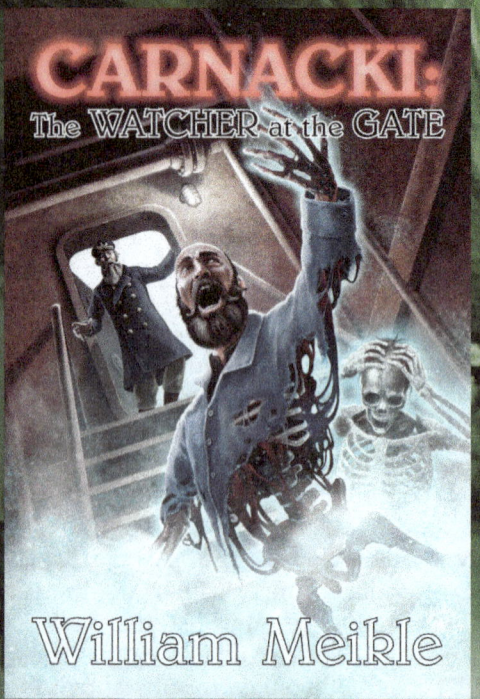

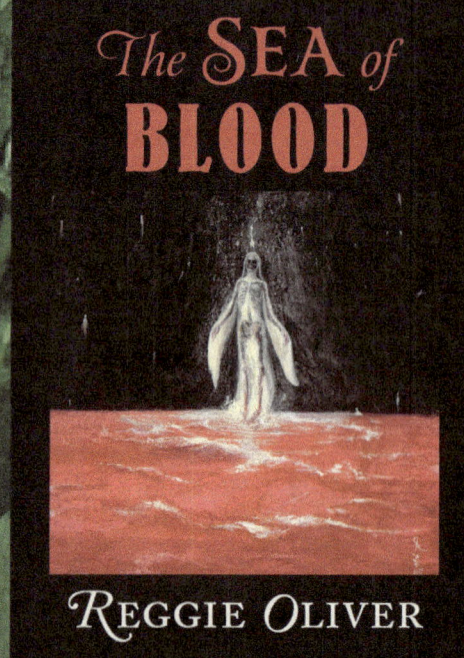

Pembroke

By Ronald Malfi

embroke's Used and Rare Books was, on the outside, a rather nondescript little enterprise tucked between a drab drinking establishment and the satellite office of a mortgage company along a brick-topped boulevard in historic Ellicott City. Its proprietor, Arthur Pembroke, had been in business at this location for the better part of three decades, yet despite the bookstore's prominence as a local fixture, few people ventured into the shop. In fact, few people even knew of its existence. This suited Pembroke just fine: a lifelong bachelor in his mid-sixties, Pembroke drew great pleasure from the quiet afternoons spent at the shop, untroubled by tourists or the occasional *curioso* who browsed the shelves but ultimately never made a purchase. His rent was cheap, his overhead low, and, with the exception of Tom DeLilly who came in on Tuesdays and Thursdays to straighten the place up, Pembroke bankrolled no staff.

What kept Pembroke afloat were the few loyal customers with whom he'd cultivated a civil yet perfunctory relationship over the years—avid collectors of rare books who visited the bookstore on occasion to make specific requests (much in the conspiratorial tones and suspicious manner of someone inquiring about an illegal enterprise) of Pembroke. So-and-so has learned of a specific book on witchcraft—could he secure a copy? So-and-so is interested in a specific Romanian book of black magic—was it possible to place such an order? So-and-so fears that his wife has been unfaithful and has heard rumor of a book that might inform him one way or the other (with no harm coming to the unfaithful wife, of course)—was this something Pembroke could locate?

He was often fulfilling such exotic requests, so when he first saw the package on the front steps of the shop that Monday morning, he assumed it was one of the orders he'd recently placed. It was indeed book-shaped—large and blocky, like a dictionary, Pembroke thought—and it was wrapped in brown butcher's paper and bound with frayed bits of twine. The packaging was a bit out of the norm, but it wasn't wholly unusual—not enough to give Pembroke pause, anyway. What *was* unusual, he noticed as he gathered the heavy package up off the stoop and carried it into the shop, was that it bore no markings, labels, addresses, or postage. Pembroke puzzled over this for several moments after he set the book on the front counter and contorted out of his tweed coat. It then occurred to him that he could stand there puzzling over that nondescript brown paper for eternity, and so, with his wiry gray eyebrows arched above the lenses of his circular glasses, Pembroke untied the twine and removed the paper.

The book was bound between two roughly textured covers, greenish-yellow in hue and networked with what appeared to be tiny threadlike fibers. There was something very plantlike about the covers, reminding Pembroke of hand-rolled cigars, of which he indulged on occasion. There was no title or author's name embossed either on the front cover or on the very wide spine. This wasn't unusual per se; what *was* unusual was the absence of author's name and book title on the title page. Moreover, there was no copyright or publishing information. The book was sizable—perhaps 800 pages or so—but as Pembroke carefully turned page after page (the intensity and fervor of his page-turning increasing with each passing second), he saw that there were no printed page numbers, no headers or footers...no printed text anywhere in the book at all.

He stood there staring down at the blank book and wondered if this was some kind of practical joke. On occasion, Tom DeLilly took great pleasure in secreting rubber spiders among the stacks or hiding the self-help books so that patrons would, ironically, have to ask for assistance in locating them. This, however, struck Pembroke as something beyond Tom's wit or capability.

Perhaps it is a journal, he surmised, *or a sketch book. That would explain the lack of title, author, and text.*

Satisfied that was the answer, he closed the book and tucked it beneath the desk. Yet at the back of his head, he wondered about its mysterious arrival. If it *was* a journal or sketchbook, he hadn't ordered it.

***

Pembroke went about his business for much of that morning, calling customers to let them know their books had arrived and answering the phone whenever it rang, inevitably, with a wrong number. At one point, during the late morning, he found himself reclining in a creaky wooden chair at the back of the shop, the strange new book splayed open in his lap. He turned from page to page, examining the paper as if willing the words to materialize before his eyes. At noon, he took the book down the block and pawed through it while he sat by himself at an outdoor cafe. However, when the young waitress arrived and looked skeptically at the blank pages at which Pembroke had been staring with studied attention, he quickly snapped the book closed and glared at the girl. Perhaps taking it out of the shop had been a mistake.

He made a mental note to ask Tom about the book tomorrow; maybe he had ordered it for some reason. But when Tuesday arrived and Tom, cheery and bright-eyed, came bustling through the bookstore's front door—*ting!* went the tiny overhead bell—Pembroke was overcome by a peculiar sense of unease.

"Good morning, Arthur!"

Pembroke nodded at Tom as the younger man scooted down the narrow aisle and tossed his jacket over a rolling cart piled high with paperbacks. Pembroke had been turning the pages of the mysterious book when Tom had entered; now, he quickly closed the book and secured it back beneath the desk. He even went as far as stacking another book on top of it, as if to hide it. Not that Tom ever went behind the counter.

"Any new orders come in today?" Tom asked as he slotted paperbacks onto a nearby shelf.

"No," said Pembroke.

"I ran into Mrs. Teatree at the Giant," Tom said. "She's still fawning over that copy of *Mystical Methods* from last month." Tom snickered affably. "Strange old bird."

Pembroke nodded but said nothing.

At around three o'clock that afternoon, as Tom was in the backroom attempting to assemble a bookshelf, a man entered the shop, his presence causing the small bell over the door to tinkle. Pembroke, who was seated behind the counter balancing the store's books in a large ledger, looked up and took inventory. The man, who stood impressively tall, wore a long ash-gray overcoat and a Humphrey Bogart fedora of the same color. Beneath the fedora, his face was long, gaunt, angular, with a chin that appeared chiseled into a perfect rectangle. He possessed the distorted nose of a prizefighter and a firm mouth that was nearly a lipless slash. His eyes were small but alert—a rodent's eyes—and they surveyed the tiny bookstore as the man stood unmoving in the entranceway.

"Good afternoon," Pembroke said, closing his ledger.

The man turned to face him, apparently startled by Pembroke's voice. His large, expressionless face creased into the approximation of a smile. Those rodent eyes twinkled like dollops of oil.

The man removed his hat, stepped toward Pembroke's desk, and said, "Good afternoon, sir. This is a lovely shop." His voice was smooth as satin.

"Thank you," said Pembroke. "Was there something I can help you find?"

"I hope so." The man's smile persisted. "I've got quite the specific request."

It was at that moment Pembroke knew what the man was looking for. A cool sweat broke out across Pembroke's forehead.

"It's a Book of No Name," said the man. "One of two, in fact. The yin and the yang, you might say." Impossibly, the man's smile widened, exposing teeth like a shark's. "The one I am seeking is quite large, and bound in a very rare organic covering."

"You'll have to be more specific," Pembroke said.

The man's smile faltered. "Will I?" he said.

"What's the author's name?" Pembroke retrieved a ream of paper from beneath the desk, on which Tom had printed (from his personal computer) their inventory in alphabetical order by author.

"There is no author," said the man. The smile had completely vanished now. "Or, to be more precise, there are *many* authors. But I think, my friend, this book isn't something you'll be able to locate on your inventory list."

Pembroke slid the stack of pages aside. From the breast pocket of his tight-fitting oxford shirt, he removed a plain white handkerchief which he used to blot his brow.

"It is my understanding," said the man, "that this particular book may have mistakenly been delivered to this address yesterday morning."

Pembroke slowly shook his head. "We received no deliveries yesterday."

Almost imperceptibly, one of the man's long, slender eyebrows arched. He cleared his throat and said, "Perhaps we've started off on the wrong foot, Mister...?"

"Pembroke," said Pembroke.

"Pembroke," the man repeated. "My name is Selwyn, Mr. Pembroke. I work for a conglomerate of well-to-do academic types who reside throughout the world and who trust me to see to their personal, ah...affairs. This book, Mr. Pembroke, was in transit from one of my clients to another. Typically, I would oversee the transfer personally, of course, but that was not how this matter was handled. Unfortunately." He added that last part with unmasked disdain, as if somehow Pembroke was responsible for the book getting lost in the mail. "It would be most unfortunate for all parties involved, Mr. Pembroke, if I am unable to locate and reclaim that book." Again, that slender eyebrow ticked toward Selwyn's hairline as he repeated, "*All* parties."

At that moment, Tom came out from the backroom carrying the bookshelf. He paused as he saw Pembroke engaged with the man, a sudden look of surprise on his face. Then Tom smiled his college-boy smile and bellowed, "Hullo! Anything I can help you with, sir?"

Selwyn's eyes never left Pembroke's. After a beat, Selwyn said, "No thank you, son. I was just leaving." Then, to Pembroke, he said, "If you happen to come across this book, here is my card. I would appreciate a speedy notification. It would be best...for everyone...if this matter was put to rest sooner than later."

Selwyn set a small white business card on the counter, then placed his fedora back on his head and moseyed out into the daylight. Pembroke looked down. The only text on the card was the name SELWYN and an 800 number printed below.

***

That evening, Pembroke could not get to sleep, his panic was so great. It was a mistake leaving the book overnight in the shop; he kept imagining that tall, gaunt stranger breaking in and stealing it. Around two in the morning, when his stress was causing his hands to shake, Pembroke dressed and slipped out onto the darkened street. At a quick clip, he covered the five blocks to the bookstore without incident, though he kept glancing over his shoulder, fearful that someone might emerge from the shadows and pursue him.

When he arrived, he went immediately behind the desk and reached for the book...but it was no longer there. Terror seized him, and he hurriedly loosened his collar so that he could breathe. Dabbing his forehead with his handkerchief, he peered into all the little shelves and nooks beneath the desk, wondering if he had misplaced the book himself, his panic rising when he still couldn't locate it. Yet the shop's door had been firmly locked and none of the windows were broken. That strange man would have had to use...other means...to have come in here and then escaped with the book.

"I'll call the police, report a break-in," he said, pacing back and forth behind the counter, swiping that folded bit of handkerchief fitfully and repeatedly across his brow. He was unaware that he was speaking aloud. "Yes, yes—a break-in. An intrusion. And I can describe that strange fellow from earlier to one of their sketch artists." But even in his desperation, he knew he couldn't make such a call. The door hadn't been jimmied, the windows hadn't been broken. And nothing else was missing from the store except the stuff Pembroke had kept underneath the counter.

And that was when it occurred to him that *everything* from beneath the counter was missing—the printed inventory list, the books on reserve for particular clients, the shop's ledger. He took a moment to consider this. Unnerved by the strange man's presence that afternoon, Pembroke had left the shop early, leaving Tom behind to close up.

Expelling a gust of sour breath, he hunkered down and peered into the shelves beneath the counter more closely. When he saw something small and dark—a spot of black within the shadow of a cubbyhole—he reached for it, plucked it out. It was one of Tom DeLilly's silly rubber spiders.

A second bout of panic took hold of him—what if *Tom* had taken the book?—but then his gaze fell upon the rolling cart, and on it was the ledger, the printout, the patrons' reserved books, and the Book of No Name.

Relief washed through him. He rushed to the cart and yanked the book free, knocking several others to the floor. Carrying it against his chest in an embrace, he went to the small reading table at the back of the shop, turned on the museum light over the desk, and opened the book.

He spent the next few hours occupied with the book— it couldn't rightly be called "reading," for there were no words, but for all intents and purposes, that was exactly what Pembroke was doing. Because there *were* words on those pages, weren't there? There were stories, at least. Even without seeing the words, he could tell they were there.

Then he noticed two very strange things, back to back, as if one had been the product of the other. The first thing he noticed was that the tops of his fingers, the palms of his hands, and the underside of his wrists had gone smudgy and gray. Having handled old books for three decades, Pembroke recognized what this was immediately, though he was perplexed to think it had come from the book splayed out in front of him: it was the smudging of ink from the text printed on a book's page. Had he been reading any other book, it would have made perfect sense. With this book, however...well, there was no text to leave smudges. Yet here they were.

The second thing he noticed was a dark brownish stain along the edge of one of the pages, near the lower right-hand corner. It was small, and may have been unnoticed by anyone other than Pembroke, who could not help but scrutinize every page and every nuance. He had, in fact, gone through every page of this book several times since he'd received it Monday morning, so he knew with certainty that the stain hadn't been there before. To Pembroke, it looked like blood.

***

The following day—Wednesday—Pembroke struggled to stay awake at the shop, having spent the previous night puzzling over that strange bloodlike stain on the book's page while trying to clean the smudgy newsprint from his fingers, hands, and wrists. The smudges did not want to come off, but only seemed to grow denser and more pronounced, almost to the point that they resembled bruises. He tried to convince himself that the smudges had come from something else, but there was no denying what he believed in his heart—that they had come from the mysterious book.

When the bell over the door tinkled, Pembroke looked up from the counter—he had been examining that bloodlike stain on the page—worried that it was the

man in the fedora again. Selwyn. But it was only Mrs. Teatree, red-faced and robust in a garish floral dress and rhinestone-studded handbag. They exchanged some pleasantries, much as they always did. Pembroke noticed the vast darkened pores in the flesh of Mrs. Teatree's face for the first time, each one glistening with its own tiny pool of perspiration. She had never repulsed him before, but now he was practically overcome by a discomfort at her proximity. It was all he could do to hand over her reserved books without touching her fat, short-fingered hands. As she waddled out of the shop, Pembroke unleashed a shuddery breath.

When the bell tinkled over the door an hour later, Pembroke looked up again. Selwyn came into the store, peering studiously at the floor-to-ceiling bookshelves much as he had done the day before, as if this was the first time he'd entered the store. When he turned and faced Pembroke, he removed his ash-colored fedora and delivered that sinister shark's smile.

"Well," Selwyn said, approaching the counter.

Pembroke had been in the process of wiping his hands with a damp rag. At Selwyn's approach, Pembroke tucked the rag under the counter, covering the Book of No Name which, thankfully, had been down there when Selwyn entered the store.

"Good afternoon," Pembroke said. His voice sounded jittery. "Mr. Selwyn, wasn't it?"

"Just Selwyn," said the man. He held his fedora in leather-gloved hands, running his long fingers around the brim. "I was hoping we might be able to approach yesterday's subject from a different angle."

"Oh?" said Pembroke. When Selwyn turned his gaze toward the smudgy marks on Pembroke's hands and wrists, Pembroke instinctively stuffed them in the pockets of his corduroys.

"You are a man who can get any book, no matter how

rare," said Selwyn. "Is this correct?"

"For the most part," Pembroke said.

Selwyn's sharp smile flashed then vanished just as quickly. "I am trying to locate a book that has gone missing from one of my clients. It went missing en route to another client, and both are very upset. They are also very wealthy.

I assure you they would pay any price if one were to locate the book and, say, sell it to them."

"I'd need an author's name and book title. Publisher's information, too, presuming they're looking for a particular edition. But of course," Pembroke added quickly, "I can't promise anything. Some books, I'm afraid to say, choose to remain elusive."

"That would be unfortunate, in this case," said Selwyn. And then Selwyn's eyes narrowed. He turned his head slightly to the left and, like a bloodhound on a scent, proceeded to sniff the air.

He smells the blood, Pembroke thought. *The blood on the page!* It was impossible, of course...but for some reason, Pembroke couldn't shake the certainty of it.

"Mr. Pembroke," said Selwyn, his voice lowering as he leaned closer over the counter. Pembroke could smell the man's cool, crisp aftershave...and was suddenly certain that the perfume was there to mask some headier, earthier smell. "We are playing a game with each other, yes? Allow me to assure you that there are other methods by which I could...obtain...what it is I am looking for. Those ways are much more difficult than a man's willingness to comply. What I mean to say, *Arthur*, is that it *is* possible for me to take the book from you by force. However, that would require certain...shall we say, 'policies'?...be violated. And my clients tend to frown on such tactics. Therefore I will leave you with this."

From within his overcoat, Selwyn procured a folded stack of paper money. He tugged several bills from the stack and placed them down flat on the counter. Ten hundred-dollar bills.

"Consider this as incentive," said Selwyn. "You will be able to name your actual price once the book is procured and turned over." Selwyn's thin lips pulled back from his teeth, and Pembroke could see without question that each tooth had elongated into a sharpened fang. There was

something patchy and reptilian about the fleshy pockets beneath Selwyn's eyes, too. As if the skin there had turned to snake scales. "Because," finished Selwyn, "we are playing a game, yes?"

"I'm afraid I don't understand..."

"You've already been tainted," Selwyn said, his gaze shifting down at Pembroke's hands, which were still stuffed into the pockets of his pants. "It still may not be too late for you."

Pembroke said nothing as Selwyn replaced the fedora atop his head and, pivoting sharply on his heels, began whistling as he headed out of the door and onto the sidewalk.

***

He planned to take the book home that evening, but instead Pembroke wound up sleeping in the store, snoring loudly in one of the uncomfortable wooden chairs at the table near the back of the bookstore, the side of his face pressed against one of the open pages of the book.

***

"Mr. Pembroke?"

It was Tom DeLilly, shaking him awake.

Pembroke snapped up in his seat, his stiff back jolting with pain, his eyes bleary and still muzzy with sleep. When he glanced down at the desktop, he was mortified to see that the mysterious book was right there, its blank pages splayed open for Tom to see. He quickly slammed the book shut.

"Did you sleep here last night?"

"I guess so, Tom." He attempted to climb out of the chair but his back screamed in protest so he remained seated.

"I brought you a coffee," Tom said, setting the cardboard cup down beside the book. Steam wafted from the tiny opening in the lid. "Looks like you could use it, if you don't mind me saying." Then Tom's eyes narrowed. He leaned closer to examine the side of Pembroke's face.

"What?" Pembroke barked, suddenly repulsed by Tom's proximity. It was an invasion of his personal space. "What is it?"

"You've got a...I guess a bruise on the side of your face, Mr. Pembroke." Tom straightened up. He looked concerned. "Did you get in a fight?"

Pembroke laughed forcibly. "A *fight*?"

"Or maybe fall down from one of the ladders again?"

"Nonsense." He touched the side of his face but felt nothing.

"Oh," Tom said. It came on the intake of air, as if Tom were suddenly prodded by something cold and pointy at the base of his spine. "Your hands."

Pembroke looked at his hands.

They were no longer covered in the smudgy bruises—or, more accurately, the smudges had coalesced to form a dense inscription of strange glyphs that appeared tattooed across the palms of his hands and circling around his wrists. They weren't so much words as symbols, but Pembroke knew, even through his horror, that words were exactly what they were. Words from some alien world, perhaps, or some alien time.

He thought of Selwyn's fangs and the snakelike skin beneath his eyes.

"Excuse me," Pembroke said, wincing as he rose from the chair. Hefting the book under one arm, he hustled through the small restroom door, which he promptly closed and latched behind him. Setting the book on the edge of the sink, Pembroke examined his reflection in the mirror. The lighting in here was so poor that, at first, he didn't notice the smudgy darkening of his skin along the left side of his face. But when he *did* see it, it was like strong, cold fingers slowly closing around his throat.

You've already been tainted, Selwyn had said. *It still may not be too late for you.*

He looked down at the book. Momentarily, its organic green-yellow cover seemed to swell then deflate, as if respiring. Pembroke convinced himself it was just an illusion of the poor lighting in the bathroom. And as much as he didn't want to touch it again, his hands went to it and he gathered it up—lovingly—from the sink.

When he came out of the bathroom, Tom was still standing there, a mixture of confusion and concern on his face. Pembroke rushed past him with a curt nod, clutching the book to his chest. Tom followed him to the front counter, where Pembroke hurriedly stashed the book underneath in one of the shelves. A bright red rubber spider bounded out of the cubbyhole and cartwheeled across the linoleum floor.

"What did you do to your hands, Mr. Pembroke?"

"It's no concern of yours, Tom."

Tom frowned. He was holding his own cup of coffee, which he set down on the counter now. "What's with that book, anyway?" he said.

Pembroke reeled on him, teeth clenched as he said, "Do not *speak* of it!"

Tom shook his head and took a step backward. But he didn't let it go. "What *is* it? There's nothing on the pages... but then, the longer I look at it, I begin to see..."

"Enough," said Pembroke. "We will not talk about the book."

"And then the other night, when I was straightening up, I went to put the book on the rolling cart when it cut me." Tom held up his right index finger, which was capped in an adhesive bandage.

"A paper cut," Pembroke marveled, recalling that odd splotch of blood on the book's page.

"Yes, of course," said Tom, "only that's not what I thought at the time. Because when it happened, Mr. Pembroke—and this is going to sound ridiculous, I know it—but when it happened, my first thought was that the book had *bit* me. I dropped it on the floor like it was some wild animal. I've gotten my share of paper cuts working here, Mr. Pembroke, as you know, but this one...this one *bled.*"

"Tom," said Pembroke, trying to keep himself calm but also speaking as firmly as he could at the moment, "I think you should go home early today."

"I want to know what—"

"Please go, Tom. I'll see you next Tuesday."

Tom wanted to protest further—Pembroke could tell just by looking at the young man—but in the end, Tom snagged his jacket from the rolling cart and, whipping it over one shoulder, he hurried out onto the sidewalk. The bell over the door chimed. Outside, Tom paused momentarily on the other side of the front window, peering in at Pembroke, before continuing down the block.

After he was sure Tom wouldn't return, Pembroke picked up the telephone. Selwyn's business card was taped to the counter beside the phone, and Pembroke was halfway through dialing the 800 number when he froze, suddenly able to decipher the glyphs spiraling around his wrist. They were images quite similar to Egyptian hieroglyphics, but for some reason, Pembroke could now read them.

—for whether it resides in the well or in the dome, in the blackness of the void or the sprockets of the earth, in the soul of mankind or the blackened heart of the devil—

Very calmly, Pembroke hung up the phone.

***

When the man who called himself Selwyn arrived at the end of the week, Pembroke was propped in his wooden chair behind the front counter, his face waxen, his pallor the color of curdled cream. In just the past week he had lost about thirteen pounds and had pretty much stopped eating. His hands shook as Selwyn approached the counter, Pembroke's eyes rolling up to meet Selwyn's ratlike gaze beneath the wide brim of his ash-colored fedora.

Pembroke had the book out on the counter in front of him. He made no attempt to hide it as Selwyn approached. As it was, his arms were bandaged and in terrible pain; he didn't think he'd even be able to lift the book now if he wanted to. The only part of his body he hadn't been able to bring himself to cut was the left side of his face, where the smudgy bruise had solidified into a series of tiny symbols, running from his temple, down his cheek, and curving around the left side of his chin.

"You are in some shape, friend," said Selwyn, peering down at Pembroke's shaking hands and bandaged wrists and forearms. Blood had seeped through the bandages and stained the gauze a ruddy copper color. There was also dried blood on the counter and fresher puddles of it along the floor. The ream of paper that was the store's inventory was soggy and bloated with blood. Atop the inventory was a straight razor. Beside the straight razor was a bright orange rubber spider.

"I tried...tried getting the words off," managed Pembroke. Even speaking took much out of him. "They cloud my head. I can't stop reading them. And when I close my eyes, they speak directly to me."

"That's because you're a fool," said Selwyn. "Are you ready to hand the book over yet?"

"Y-yes," Pembroke stuttered. He attempted to slide the book across the bloodied counter to Selwyn, but Selwyn held up one hand and shook his head. Pembroke dropped his bloodied and ruined hands in his lap.

Selwyn peeled off one of his leather gloves, liberating a hand that was as pale as a cadaver's. His fingers, hideously long, were like the pale, segmented legs of arctic crabs. Selwyn ran his palm along the top of the book. His eyes momentarily unfocused and he actually released a faint, almost orgiastic sigh. Then his face went firm again. He gathered the book off the counter and tucked it under one arm.

"My clients will be most appreciative, Mr. Pembroke."

But Pembroke hardly heard him; he was busy staring

at the small adhesive bandage at the tip of Selwyn's index finger. Selwyn followed his gaze then grinned at him like a feral dog.

"Oh, this?" said Selwyn. "Occupational hazard, I'm afraid." Then he nodded at Pembroke and headed for the door. He paused, however, halfway across the floor and turned back around to face Pembroke. "I almost forgot. Your commission. Have you decided on a price?"

"Please," Pembroke said. "Just help me. Get the words out of my head."

"I'm afraid that is beyond my ability. With any luck, you might recover. After all, it's only been a week, correct? It's not as if the exposure was unduly prolonged. Though do please remember, Mr. Pembroke—you brought this upon yourself. This was a mistake; it had nothing to do with you. You should have left well enough alone." With that, Selwyn nodded sharply, then left the store.

"Please," Pembroke shouted after him, still able to smell the man's cologne in the air like a calling card. "Please! Please!"

But there would be no salvation from that monster.

***

Pembroke's physical injuries cleared up over time. The scars left behind were terrible, ugly things, but they also served as a reminder that he had been foolish and careless and had committed himself to something that was beyond his comprehension. And after a bit more time, the voices in his head, much like the glyphs on his skin, began to fade. Soon, the only mantra he heard in his head were Selwyn's parting words: *This was a mistake; it had nothing to do with you. You should have left well enough alone.*

When Tuesdays and Thursdays passed without Tom showing up to work, Pembroke felt awful. He felt guilty the way he had left things with Tom, but he wouldn't let that guilt prevent him from making amends. Late one Thursday evening, he telephoned Tom's house. The phone rang several times before Tom answered.

"Listen, Tom, it's Arthur. I feel just terrible. I understand if you've got no interest in coming back to work here, but at least stop by and allow me to apologize and explain what happened."

"Geez, Mr. Pembroke, I really appreciate it," Tom said. "You know, I got another job, but I'd certainly like to stop by and see you in person. I don't like how we left things, either."

It delighted Pembroke that Tom was amenable to his apology, and the following Tuesday, prior to Tom's arrival, Pembroke bought a couple of coffees at the corner bakery and carried them back to the bookstore, a smile on his face.

Yet he froze midway across the street when he saw a man in an ashy-gray overcoat and matching fedora leaning against the front window of the bookstore.

Selwyn, Pembroke thought...but when the man lifted his head, he could see it was Tom's face beneath the brim of the fedora.

"Hello, Mr. Pembroke," Tom said, tipping a single bandaged finger against the brim of his hat.

Horror in a Hundred Stories

The Visitor
Catherine Bader

She opened the shower door. Drying herself off, she noticed writing on the bathroom mirror:

Don't turn around.

She felt goosebumps all over her body. That mirror was clean when she'd started her shower.
She turned around.
She heard a popping noise and found herself in a tightly confined space with a window that looked out into her bathroom. She started screaming.
Standing there, the thing on the other side raised its hand and wiggled its fingers—a wave goodbye and a wicked smile on its face as it walked out the door.

Photograph
Duncan Ralston

I'm sickened, looking at the woman across the aisle on the crowded number 6 bus, the woman without a face. Nobody's seen her. Eyes focus on shoes, on cell phones, paperbacks, cracks of cloudy morning light between crammed-in passengers.
Anywhere but her.
It?
The smooth, pale face turns toward mine. Sensing me looking, she shifts uncomfortably in her seat, smoothing her skirt.
A noise escapes the mouthless face. A sob?
I feel no pity, only anger.
She left me, not the other way around.
Out on the sidewalk, I sift through photos on my phone. Her beautiful face, forever mine.

She Fought Back
James Newman

"Why do you make me do this, girl? Ain'tcha learned yer lesson by now?"
He kicked her again. She whimpered as she slid across the floor. A photo of the two of them—taken during happier times—fell off the wall, shattered.
He brought out his belt then, the one with the metal studs.
She had suffered the belt before. No more.
She rose, on trembling legs. Leapt on him.
He screamed.
She tore out his throat with her teeth.
He fell face-first into her empty food bowl.
She barked once, weakly, before running outside to chase some squirrels.

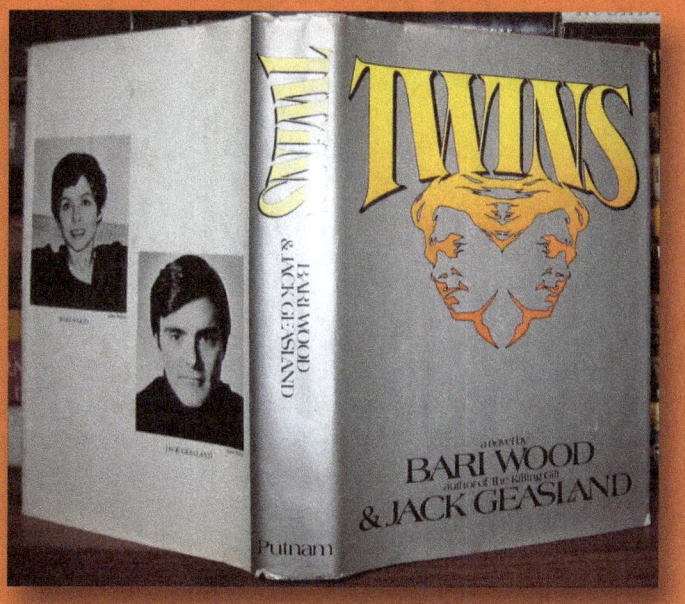

What the Hell Ever Happened to...
Bari Wood

ROBERT MORRISH

Bari Wood is that rarity of rarities, a writer who walked away from her profession while still at the top of her game, and with major publishers still interested in her work. Wood published seven novels during the 1980s and '90s, including several that made their way onto bestseller lists, and two that served as the basis for major films—David Cronenberg's *Dead Ringers* (1988), which was based on *Twins*; and Neil Jordan's *In Dreams* (1999), which was loosely based on *Doll's Eyes*.

Stephen King was a particularly big fan of Wood's, praising (for example) *The Tribe* by saying, ''The writing is sharp and lucid, the characters are wonderfully three dimensional, drawn with wit and intelligence, and that thing in the box had me nervous about going upstairs after I finished the book at two in the morning.'' Despite her success, she quit writing after the publication of her seventh novel, *The Basement*, in 1995, and has never returned to fiction.

Wood was born and raised in Illinois, growing up in and around Chicago, before attending and graduating from Northwestern University. Early odd jobs included treasurer for an off-Broadway theater, wardrobe attendant for a dinner theater in N.J., 'demonstrator' of 'Feathercombs' at a concession in Macy's, and seller of artificial Christmas trees. She moved to New York in 1967 and worked in the library of the American Cancer Society, later becoming editor of the society's publication, *CA: A Cancer Journal for Clinicians* and of the medical journal *Drug Therapy*. And she married Dr. Gilbert Congdon Wood, a biologist for the American Cancer Society.

Wood began writing fiction in the early 1970s, and her first novel, *The Killing Gift,* was published in hardcover in 1975 by Putnam. In 1981, Gilbert and Bari Wood moved to a farmhouse in Connecticut, a setting that was later employed in her final novel, *The Basement.* Several years after her husband's death in 2000, Wood married Dennis Kazee and moved to a suburb of Lansing, Michigan, where she still lives.

===================

DARK DISCOVERIES: Did you write/sell any short fiction prior to your first novel appearing?

BARI WOOD: No short fiction. *The Killing Gift* was my first effort. I had a full-time job, and wrote at night after work, after dinner, after the dishes, what have you.

DD: What led you to write thriller and horror novels? A reflection of your own reading interest, commercial reasons, or…?

BW: I'd always gotten a kick out of reading them. For a long time, they were my favorite escapist reading.

DD: How did you acquire an agent for *The Killing Gift?*

BW: My husband worked for the American Cancer Society, and was friendly with one of the writers who'd

had a lay book on cancer published; my husband asked him about his agent, and if he'd give me an intro. He did, I went to see her, or rather her assistant (the office was a couple of blocks from the office I then worked at. The assistant like/loved the book, and agreed to represent it. It was pretty much that easy. The fifth publisher she sent it to (Putnam) bought it for $3,000; $1500 up front, the rest on completion and acceptance. I couldn't believe this was really happening. The editor, also the one who wanted to buy the book, was very, very good. Basically told me what the book needed to make it work, and he was on target.

DD: How did you come to co-author your 2nd novel, *Twins,* with Jack Geasland?

BW: I'm not sure to this day. I did almost all the writing of *Twins,* the co-author acted mostly as super-editor, and keeping me, as much as he could, on track.

DD: A marketing blurb for your third book, *The Tribe,* describes it as "What *The Exorcist* was to Catholicism, *The Tribe* is to Judaism." Is that what you had in mind when you were writing the book?

BW: No. It was just a good story, I thought. And many years before I had worked for (as treasurer, basically ticket seller) an off-Broadway production of 'The Golem,' and was fascinated with it.

DD: For *The Tribe,* you changed publishers from Putnam's to NAL—how and why did that change come about?

BW: They offered a great deal more money than Putnam. Not sure to this day why, and in retrospect, I'm sorry the money dictated my decision. Putnam had been good to me. I should've shown more loyalty.

DD: Your fourth novel, *Lightsource,* seems like more of a straight-ahead thriller novel, without any supernatural or macabre overtones, unlike your other books. Is that a fair description and, if so, what led you to take a different approach with that book?

BW: I don't know. I really have no answer. Just must've liked the idea.

DD: Whereas *The Killing Gift* focused on an adult woman with a unique power, *Amy Girl,* your fifth book, features an 8-year-old girl with unique abilities… in your mind, is there any connection between those two books, and those characters?

BW: None that I'm aware of.

DD: After those first five novels, it was seven years until your next book, *Doll's Eyes,* was published, and it came out from a different publisher, William Morrow. What led to that long span, and to the new publisher?

BW: It had been so long between books for many reasons. Some I can't define. And no one was really very interested as I recall, except Bantam, and Morrow. I went with Morrow because they were willing to do a hardcover edition, Bantam was not. I think Bantam was right, I'd have been better off with the book as a paperback original. Plus I was much more simpatico with the Bantam editor. Hindsight!

DD: Your last published novel, *The Basement,* seems like more of an old-fashioned horror novel than your other books… do you think that's a fair assessment, and if so, what led you to go a more traditional route with this book?

BW: I had lost my way with writing, I think. I didn't like *The Basement,* but couldn't seem to make it better no matter how hard I tried.

DD: What happened after *The Basement?* To put it another way, why haven't we seen any additional books from you? Have you written additional, unpublished novels?

BW: A number of personal reversals, involving death, and sickness, and by the time they were resolved, or rather in the past, I was out of the habit of writing, and have not been able to get it back.

DD: In 2013, Centipede Press reprinted your novel *The Tribe* in a lush limited edition. Any chance that Centipede will be reprinting any more of your books?

BW: Not that I know of.

DD: As far as I can tell, none of your backlist is available in ebook format… are you interested in seeing your books published in that format?

BW: Sure, I guess. And I should investigate doing so. The Author's Guild has a 'back in print' program that I probably should try to take advantage of. But so far…

DD: Did you ever dabble at all in other forms of media—for example, screenwriting?

BW: I tried to do a screenplay of *The Tribe*. It was a mess… Never tried again.

DD: What did you think of the two films that were made based on your novels—*Dead Ringers* (based on *Twins*) and *In Dreams* (very loosely based on *Doll's Eyes*)?

BW: It's hard to say. *Dead Ringers* I guess is a good movie. A lot of people have told me so, anyway. But it was so different from any vision I had, it was hard for me to like it. I never saw *In Dreams.* I'd read the screenplay and it was so different, and so (I thought) lousy, I never wanted to sit through it. I saw the titles once on TV, saw my name, and got a kick out of that, then changed channels. I thought *Doll's Eyes* was a pretty decent story, and would've made a pretty decent movie if anyone had tried it.

DD: Do you actively read in the horror genre? If so, any favorite works you can cite from recent years?

BW: Not so much anymore. I think I sort of overdosed on them, even before I stopped writing them. Though one I've been working on and off, is like *Doll's Eyes*.

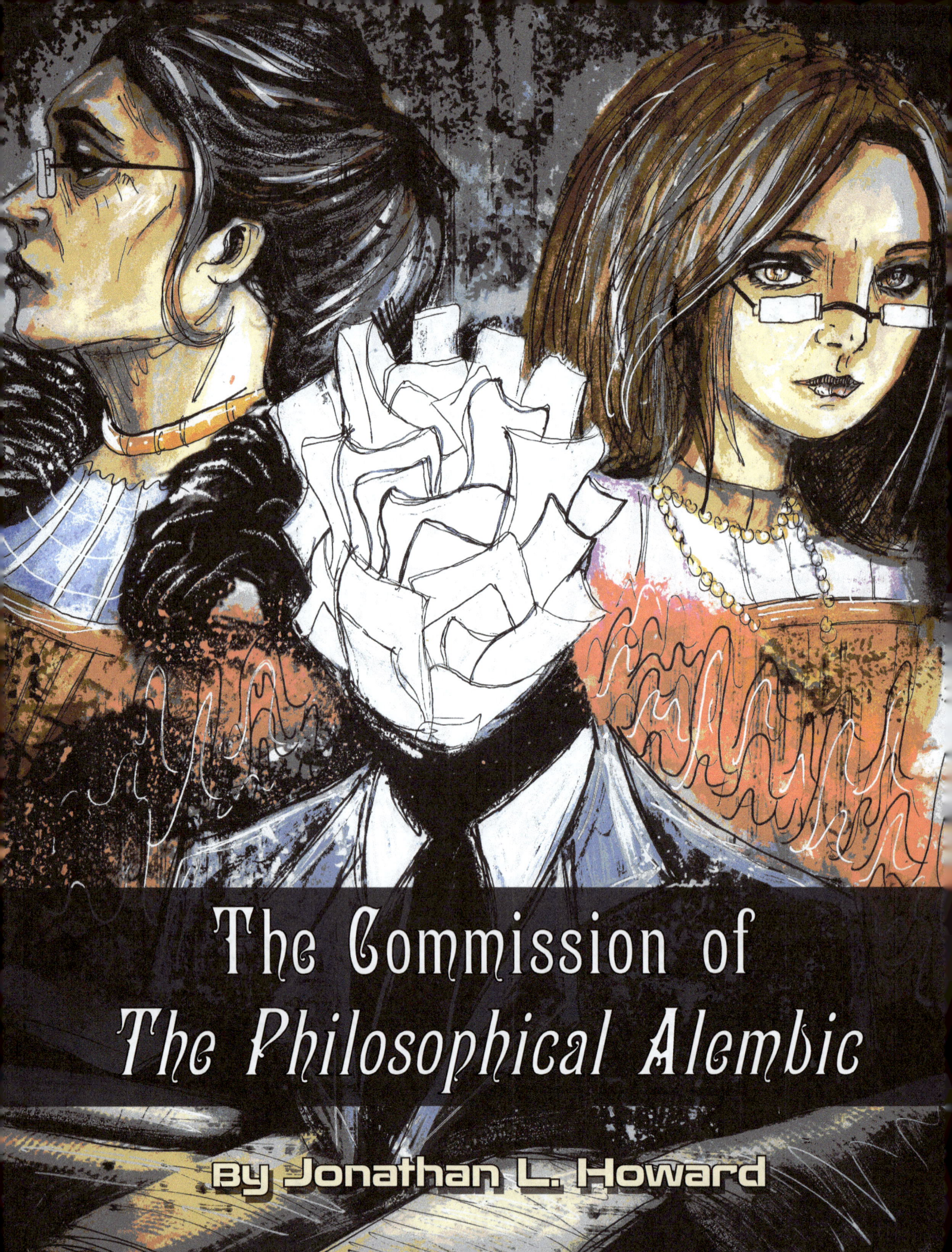

The Commission of
The Philosophical Alembic

By Jonathan L. Howard

A dirty little backstreet in London, bordered upon the east by Tottenham Court Road and upon the south by Oxford Street. A dirty little backstreet, shadowed and unfashionable, the walls darkened with unattended soot, the windows blinded with grime. It was home to the backs of restaurants on one side and the rears of glittering retail emporia upon the other, and little else but for a couple of residences, a pawnbroker, and a bookshop.

The sign over the window read "Vesperine & Daughter. Dealers in Rare & Antique Books" and, while this was true, it was also somewhere short of the whole truth.

But attend; a customer approaches.

He was in his middle years, prosperous and sedate, a bowler hat upon his head, a wing collar of decreasing fashionableness about his neck, and an expression of bland benevolence upon his face. He was likely an office manager of a respectable company, and to him all things were equitable. Alas, his equilibrium would perforce suffer, for he paused before the shop's front, read the sign with the mildest curiosity, peered at the grimy window seeing nothing but grime and his own shadow, and thence passed within.

The interior of the shop was understandably dark, but only towards the front. The area of the floor, some fifteen feet wide by twenty five deep, was divided by a counter that put two thirds of the shop behind it. Before it was a place of dour shelves of dark wood containing books calculated to be of interest to casual browsers, illuminated by the dim light of the street through the filthy panes of the shop's front window feebly assisted by gas mantels. The counter, in contrast, was of light elm, and the area behind it was well served by a large array of casements—in which the glass sparkled—and that was further lit by electrical lights. The shop, therefore, gave an ineffable sense of being some manner of border facility between light and darkness not merely in a gross, sensual form, but even philosophically. This sense was not wholly fanciful.

Certainly the middle manager to whom we were earlier acquainted had a distinct sense of eccentricity about the establishment. He paused two steps past the threshold and looked about him. He saw the badly illuminated bookshelves, the titles of the books they bore all but illegible in the gloom, he saw the flickering gas lights, one sporting a cracked and smoking mantel that could hardly have been doing the books any good, and he saw the counter behind which a handsome woman in her late fifties or perhaps even her early sixties waited, regarding him with a patient smile. He hurried to her, as a pilgrim hurries from perdition toward a better place.

"Good afternoon," he began. The woman said nothing, but continued to smile. He had a tiny tingling frisson of a sense that her smile was not merely patient, but perhaps slightly amused. "Good afternoon," he began again. "I am travelling tomorrow… upon the railway… and I anticipate longueurs along the way. To ameliorate this anticipated tedium, I thought I might buy a book."

He looked at her. She looked at him. She said nothing. "To read," he finished.

"Did," she began, and then paused. Her eyes slid to one side as if listening. The man listened, too, and made out the sound of soft bumps on the floor above. Shortly these resolved themselves into footfalls that travelled from over their heads and then—judging by cadence and variation—descended stairs towards the door in the far corner of the area behind the counter. Presently, the door opened and a woman with a distinct familial similarity to the first woman entered. She was in her early twenties and pretty enough to set up base camp in the foothills of "beautiful." It was clearly a path the elder had once walked, for despite her years she was still—*vide supra*—handsome, which is to say, striking.

The elder woman's eyes slid back to regard the office manager. "…you have anything particular in mind? A particular author? A particular novel?"

"I was thinking, perhaps, of Trollope." He said it as if making a claim to be a literary renegade.

"Trollope." The woman repeated it slowly. Behind her, the younger women gave a small sigh and went to the well-lit shelves that filled the domain of the proprietors. "Trollope."

Her calm smile now held elements of what, to the startlement of the office manager, seemed to be mockery. He must be mistaken, he told himself. So, he persisted. "The Chronicles of Barsetshire, madam. You must have—"

"Hist!" The woman hushed him into silence, a finger raised in admonition. When she was sure he would say no more, she looked off into space, seeking inspiration. "Trollope…"

"Madam, he is a famous author!"

This stirred her from her reverie. "He is? You seek a first edition, then?"

"I do not. Merely some reading matter for my railway journey on the morrow. I am travelling to the north," he added this last datum in a lowered tone, to impress upon her the necessity of carrying culture with him.

"Ah." Her smile now became purely supercilious. "Then we have been speaking at cross purposes. I naturally assumed that you were seeking a volume that was rare or at least antique. What you require, sir, is W.H. Smiths. I believe most railway stations have branches upon their platforms."

He looked at her, both thunderstruck and insulted. "You do not wish my custom?"

"I do, but only as it pertains to our stock in trade. Not desultory tales of clerical life written by a Postmaster General. Do you wish to bless your library with incunabula? To delve into esoterica? To collect literary arcana? No, no, and no? Then I fear we have little to offer you at this time. Good day to you, sir. Good hunting at Smiths."

The office manager went to the door in a fug of astonishment and outrage. There he paused and glared at the elder woman. "A moment! You *knew* Trollope was a Postmaster General? You know who he is, then?"

"Of course, sir," said the woman, smiling pleasantly. "It *is* a bookshop, you know."

The man vanished through the door, muttering. "Please tell all your friends about us," said the woman in a mild undertone as it closed with a slam that set the bell dancing.

"Passing trade, Mother. Passing trade." The young woman replaced several volumes of Trollope she had just taken from the shelves before the office manager's huffish exit had forestalled her intention to offer them. "Money is always nice."

Elodie Vesperine wrinkled her nose, and slouched against the counter in an indecorous manner, the better to surveil her daughter. Then again, she was possessed of an highly indecorous past, so at least she was practised. "But he was *awful*. Such a horrid little man, coming in here and pawing at the stock."

"The stock in the front section is there to be pawed. I chose it myself. There is nothing of any great value, just things for casual browsers." Elodie made a dismissive noise, and her daughter—Aurelia—looked hard upon her with lowered brow. "Rare creatures though they are when you're in the shop."

Any further remonstration was interrupted by the jolly jingle of the bell. Less jolly was the new customer who slid through the door into the gloomy front section and, if anything, thereby deepened the gloom therein. He was tall and pale, perhaps thirty years of age, and the hair that showed beneath the hat in the Müller style he wore was blond. His wardrobe was a study in realised monochromia, a black suit, shoes, waistcoat, gloves, and cravat, his shirt white, the Müller black, his gloves black. The only spark of colour was the pair of blue glass spectacles, and even the baffles they sported at their sides were black. He was a spectre in flesh, a man to make undertakers seem frivolous.

Elodie Vesperine was delighted. "At last! A real customer. Mr C, it is a tonic to see you."

The man doffed his hat and half-bowed courteously. "You are always kind, Madam Vesperine." His accent betrayed a certain Teutonic heritage.

"And how may we help you this fine day?" She smiled and gestured toward the rear windows, where the first drops of a heavy downfall were starting to collect.

"There is a book…"

"Good."

"A *rare* book…"

"Excellent."

"It is entitled *The Philosophical Crucible*. I very much require it for my researches to continue."

"Perfect. And why do you not procure this book yourself, may I ask?"

The man lowered his spectacles sufficiently to fix her with an inquisitorial glare. She was entirely unabashed by this. Indeed, her smile deepened.

"Please, Mr C, your reputation precedes you. You have shown yourself perfectly capable of acquiring 'rare books required for your researches' on many previous occasions. Why do you come to *Vesperine & Daughter* on this?"

The man regarded her stonily for a moment. Finally, he removed his spectacles and stowed them in his breast pocket. He went to the door, flipped the sign to show "Closed," and shot home the bolt. When he was satisfied that the shop was reasonably secure, he said, "Three reasons, Madam Vesperine. Firstly, I do not have the time. Secondly, I am not entirely certain of the book's location or even if it is still extant. Thirdly, if it *does* still exist, it is likely to be in the hands of a rival with a passion for security. I do not know if I possess the skills to extract it."

"A moment," said Elodie. "Are you suggesting that you would like to hire us to *steal* this book?"

The man considered for a moment. "Yes, madam. I am."

Elodie turned to Aurelia, glowing with happiness. "You see, darling? A *real* customer."

***

"You are a terrible mother," said Aurelia Vesperine, but she said it entirely without rancour, otherwise distracted by opening the secret compartments in their steamer trunk.

"I am a *wonderful* mother," replied Elodie Vesperine, entirely without reproach. She was busily spreading out an Ordnance Survey map of the area on the table of the room they had secured at a country hotel most used to passing travellers and hikers. She weighted the corners and quickly cast an eye upon the lay of the land as presented at six inches to the mile. "Why, wasn't I always here for you, even after your dear papa's tragic death?"

Aurelia removed a brace of revolvers from their concealments and placed them on the carpet. "You killed papa before I was even born."

"Yes. You know the story well enough. He passed away about twenty minutes or so after your conception, in fact. A fine man. Handsome, intelligent, ruthless, a paragon of self-interest after my own heart. But, alas for him, not very adept with a throwing knife." She paused, remembering. "Not as good as me, at any rate." She returned her attention to the map.

"And will it be necessary for me to murder the father of my child, too, Mother?"

Elodie seemed stung. "Hardly murder, darling. He got the first throw. And, no. I would just rather you didn't marry. That isn't our way, and nor has it been for five generations. You wouldn't want to upset a family tradition, would you?"

"What if I have a boy?"

Elodie laughed at such an absurd notion. "You have the strangest ideas. Positively perverse. Now, did you remember the explosives?"

"Eight sticks of dynamite, fast and slow fuses. Really, Mother, *I'm* not the absentminded one." She withdrew a stick from its hiding place in the trunk and sat regarding it perhaps a little ruefully. "Are you quite sure this is how one runs a bookshop? It's not the impression I got before we started the business at all."

"I can't talk for bookshops as a whole, of course, only for ours. And in our particular area of the literary market, we lead the field. Now, then. Where's the ammunition?"

***

Their client had furnished them with a list of likely hands in which the book—*The Philosophical Alembic*—might be found, and they had spent some time winnowing the list down to one very likely pair of hands indeed, those belonging to one Cornelius Merrow.

Merrow was, ostensibly at least, a successful mill owner in a moderately-sized town in the regions, a local councillor, a philanthropist, and a collector of political works, memoirs, and theses. These he would show visitors to his relatively modest manse at the end of a wooded close on the outskirts of the town, demonstrating his interest in politics and the development of economics.

Far more rarely he might show interested parties to his second, confidential library, and here they might pore over unique manuscripts and codices whose names were rarely even whispered. It would be something to explain that Merrow was, in reality, a dark and terrible magician or even a necromancer, but that would be an exaggeration. He dabbled a little, it is true, but rarely with any measurable results. He was successful in business because he was an effective and shrewd businessman, not because he depended on the patronage of otherworldly entities. Merrow's main interest in the occult was that it was perversely transgressive, and permitted him a degree of temporal power exerted upon those intimidated by such things. Thus, within this special circle he made a point of maintaining his "studies," in reality a honing of a weapon more psychological than supernatural.

This had the side-effect of advertising his purchases, albeit quietly; the Vesperines were long practised at hearing such subtle echoes. So, it was a small matter to find a usefully placed hotel in the same outskirt as the Merrow house under the pretence of a few days spent painting watercolours. Indeed, the watercolours were already painted in case friendly inquiries were made as to progress, generic studies of subjects that might reasonably be found anywhere in the British countryside: a tree; a quantity of water bearing weed and a duck; a different tree.

Some casual inquiries confirmed what other sources had already revealed; that Merrow had one servant, a butler called Belker, who subcontracted other staff as and when they were required, but otherwise was the only soul in the building apart from his master. No extraneous persons and no dogs.

The main library was upon the ground floor, and a perusal of some floor plans culled from a gazetteer published some decades previously indicated a second study on the topmost storey that fitted the hearsay pertaining to Merrow's "secret" library of local legend. A brief reconnoitre on the morning after the arrival of the Vesperines showed this room had no external window, a change in the pattern of bricks in the external wall showing where it had been sealed.

"This all seems very straightforward," commented Elodie as they promenaded together across an adjacent meadow, parasols upon their shoulders. "I shall make the acquaintance of Mr Merrow, prevail upon him to invite me to afternoon tea in the garden on this pleasant day, and then proceed to run the legs off his butler with specious requests."

"And I…?" asked Aurelia, although she was already of a certainty as to her role.

"You will enter the house unseen and attain the first floor using any moments of solitude that I can provide for you through the medium of unreasonable demands. There you will enter Mr Merrow's second library, locate *The Philosophical Crucible* and any other small volumes that take your fancy, abstract them, and then yourself from the building with an alacrity that is not devoid of caution."

"So, while you drink tea and eat cucumber sandwiches, I commit all manner of felonies and risk gaol?"

"Of course. Well, really, you can't expect me to run around like a doe when I am, I fear, in my autumn years. Besides, it is hardly the case that I have not earned a little rest."

This was true; in her youth Elodie had been a trusted agent for some of the greatest criminal masterminds the world had ever known, as well as at least one slightly underwhelming one. She had more than earned her spurs by any lights. It had been an interesting sort of professional life, unburdened as it was by legality or morality. Aurelia had learned not to press her mother too hard on recounting tales from those days; all too often they caused her to go pale and have to excuse herself.

Her mother looked at her seriously. "If you are uncomfortable with the endeavour, I shall evolve some other stratagem by which I shall relieve Mr Merrow of his property. I shall not hold it against you. Not everyone is cut of the same cloth."

Aurelia said nothing, but her expression was unhappy as she twirled her parasol and watched a pair of magpies on a nearby fence. "I shall do it, Mother. I am not afraid—"

"I did not accuse you of a lack of intestinal fortitude, dear. You suffer something more pernicious, I fear." She smiled a little sadly. "Moral rectitude."

Aurelia lowered her head. "I'm sorry, Mama. I *do* try."

"I know, I know." Elodie drew her daughter to her and kissed her lightly on the cheek. "It truly isn't your fault. These things… they can just happen. Poor unfortunate people are born with imperfections, or grow into them. Just assure me on one point; that you shall never become a policewoman."

Aurelia laughed. "I never shall."

Elodie smiled and took her daughter on her arm. They walked together until the house was left behind.

***

Mrs Elsa Carmichael, a widow holidaying in the area for a rest cure and a little watercolour painting—primarily of trees—made the acquaintance of Mr Cornelius Merrow, mill owner, entrepreneur and philanthropist via the offices of the small hotel where she was staying. Mr Merrow, a confirmed bachelor, was pleased to invite Mrs Carmichael for afternoon tea. He extended the invitation to Mrs Carmichael's daughter Emilia who had accompanied her mother, but—*hélas*—she was unable to accept, having already accepted another invitation that would keep her away for the afternoon. Thus it was that, at precisely 2:45 on a pleasant Wednesday afternoon, Mrs Carmichael made her way up the gravel drive of the Merrow house and drew on the bell pull.

She heard, quietly but distinctly, the sound of a jingling bell somewhere beyond the door, presumably in the butler's pantry. Satisfied that she would soon be greeted, she took a moment to step back and examine the house once more.

The building displeased her and, she was dismayed to realise, disquieted her. She had thought the client had overstated matters when he had deferred the book's collection to her on the grounds of—amongst other things—the level of security under which it lay. Their preliminary investigations had indicated nothing of the sort. She hesitated to liken any endeavour to "taking sweets from a baby" as both an indecorous phrase and one betokening a complacency that could only result in disaster at some point. This particular commission, however, certainly had enjoyed aspects comparable to depriving an infant of confectionary.

Now, however, she began to wonder.

She had not lived as long as she had, surviving any number of perilous encounters and problematical situations along the way, without a certain sense of trepidation troubling her at times when trepidation was called for despite outward appearances of normality and safety. This sense was currently trilling in her breast like an excitable canary. The house, pleasant enough at a distance, seemed now to lower over her like a fragile mountainside or a stuffed grizzly reared upon too small a dais. The sense that it might fall upon her at too heavy a breath dimmed the day and depressed her spirit.

A humble enough mansion of three and a half storeys, one entirely covered at the front of the building but exposed to the rear where the landscaped garden fell away down the hillside, it had seemed nothing so very extraordinary when Elodie and her daughter pored over its plans in their sitting room. Up beneath the ridge of the roof lay a central landing flanked by two rooms, each graced by a single ovoid window in the gable ends. One of these windows was, as earlier stated, now blocked with brickwork. After considering and dispensing with the idea of Aurelia practising her climbing skills to penetrate the other window and thence make her way across to the second library as unnecessarily perilous and fraught with all manner of potential exigencies, a simpler infiltration of the house had seemed much preferable. Close to, the house seeped an indefinable psychic menace. Perhaps their client had been wiser than they had thought in employing them himself rather than taking the matter into his own hands.

Menace it may well have exuded, but immediate attention it did not. Despite her misgivings, Elodie rang the bell again, waited again, and went unattended again. She checked her pendant watch; she was undeniably on time and certainly expected. She glanced up toward the neighbouring meadow for a moment. She saw no one, but nor did she expect to; Aurelia was far too good at concealment to be detected by a single glance. Aurelia would, however, see that glance and know that it was meant for her—an indication that all was not well. The signal sent, Elodie went around the side of the house to see if there was anyone in the garden awaiting her.

There was not. No host, nor butler, nor table, tea, and sandwiches. The quietness of the place now troubled her. The grass of the lawn trembled beneath a sudden breeze, the rose bushes shook, but there was barely a sound at all. She was considering going around to the servants' entrance to see if she might find the butler there when she saw the French windows overlooking the lawn were gaping wide. These she knew to open onto Merrow's study. Perhaps she would find him there?

She entered cautiously. "Mr Merrow?" she called for propriety's sake and to afford her a rock upon which to base a defence against claims of trespass should that prove

necessary. "Mr Merrow, are you there? You invited me to tea? This is Mrs Carmichael. Have I come on the wrong day?"

The study was empty of persons, but not entirely of interest. Elodie Vesperine's eye quickly took in the open inkwell, the discarded pen, the record book carelessly left upon the blotter and the slip of paper protruding from it. From what she knew of Merrow's personality, this was tantamount to a mare's nest of disorganisation. She went to the door, listened at it, and—hearing nothing—quietly opened it and looked out into the hallway. The place was static but for dust in the air, and there was nothing to hear except the steady ticking of the grandfather clock on the first landing. She slipped back into the study, closing the door silently behind her.

The pen and inkwell were witnesses to sudden haste and disruption of Merrow's routine. Perhaps the record book might provide the cause of it. It opened easily to the last notated page, bookmarked with a telegram. She glanced first at the book entry and was dismayed to see it was a handwritten catalogue of acquired books. The most recent entry was *The Philosophical Alembic*.

Lips pursed with growing professional dismay, she now turned her attention to the telegram and let slip a small sigh of exasperation. The initialled signature was little clue to the message's provenance, but its import was clear enough; Merrow had made enquiries as to the *bona fides* of Mrs Elsa Carmichael, and they had been found wanting. Elodie muttered something hardly genteel under her breath. A fine state of affairs it was when a gentleman didn't simply accept a lady's word. In other circumstances she would have worked harder to create a more resilient alias, but she had assumed it unnecessary in this case. It had been foolish of her she now realised, but Vesperines are not inclined to cry over spilt milk. Taking a moment to check the toy-like .25 semi-automatic in her reticule and the fierce twin barrelled Derringer in her fox fur muff, she went to explore.

First, she went to the front door and went out to perform a small pantomime of looking along the drive as if expecting Mr Merrow to appear there. During this act she blew her nose, a signal to her watching daughter that all was not well. Then she went back in, leaving the door on the latch. Aurelia was more than capable of extemporising as the situation demanded, she knew; she only hoped this didn't all become terribly messy and strident. That was her usual experience when securing books on the Continent, and she would be unhappy if it were repeated in the more sober land of her birth.

As her alias was already worthless it seemed pointless to try and maintain it, and so she did not call again. Instead she moved from room to room with a grace and silence born of decades of wandering around other people's homes without permission. She noted knick-knacks and gee-gaws of moderate taste and worth, paintings of the same sort, and Merrow's primary library, which heaved with worthiness and little else for the inquisitive, acquisitive, and illicit visitor.

The kitchen was next, and proved home to a plate of small sandwiches under a clean tea towel to keep them moist, and a stand of cakes within a fine mesh cage to keep the flies off them.

It also featured the corpse of Belker the butler, which was a surprise even to a seasoned adventuress. Indeed, she stood shocked for very nearly two seconds before going to examine him.

It had not been an easy death by the look of things, but nor had it been drawn out, to judge by the great pool of blood around the hapless man. Elodie took a moment to examine the edge of the pool and noted that there was no sign of coagulation; this had happened very recently. As for the method used, it showed a peculiar admixture of viciousness and perfunction. It seemed the unhappy Belker had been caught in his shirt sleeves whilst working on the household accounts. With sufficient rapidity to give him no chance of rising from his chair, his assailant had laid into him with a razor, delivering a multitude of wounds that were equally remarkable for their cleanness, their depth, and their length. It must be quite a razor blade, she concluded—at least a foot long and capable of cutting bone as effortlessly and neatly as the skin. Elodie recovered some matting from the boot room and laid them into the pool, hitching up her skirts to cross the impromptu bridge to the body so formed. The sheer ubiquity of gore on and about Belker made observation of the wounds difficult but not impossible, and a little prodding with a wooden spoon from the table showed that, somehow, the wounds extended even to the rear of the dead man's upper thighs and across his buttocks. This while, presumably, he was sitting.

Elodie retired from the blood pool to consider matters. This put a very different complexion on…

She looked cautiously around the kitchen and listened intently. Nothing.

…matters. She was coming to the conclusion that she had quoted an insufficient remuneration to the client for taking on the commission. Potential legal entanglements she had anticipated, perhaps even some physical contretemps, but this? Ah, well. Live and learn. With any luck.

She withdrew the Derringer from the muff and instead secreted it within a pocket sewn into the inside cuff of her coat's left sleeve for precisely such eventualities. Once it was secure she took the .25 "Baby Browning" pistol from her reticule, disengaged its safety catch and led with it back into the hallway. All seemed quiet there, so she dropped her bag by the door to facilitate subsequent recovery (likely in a hurry) before making her way upstairs.

Up past the first landing upon which the grandfather clock ticked sonorously, the heartbeat of the house. She noted the time and paused there while the minute hand clicked to twelve, the hour hand moved to three and the chimes sang the hour.

As the sound died away, she was moving slowly and stealthily up to the first floor. If she had been intent on searching the whole house, she would have gone down to the lower ground floor. She was not, however. Her driving concern was to gain the desired book, possibly a handful of others if opportunity presented, and then exit the house, the grounds, and the county in rapid succession, leaving the identities of Mrs and Miss Carmichael blowing tattered in the breeze behind them. Towards this end, she did not care greatly about the state of affairs on the first floor beyond a cursory search to ensure that it was vacant and her retreat would not be cut off there.

She found no one, but she did not find nothing. Or, at least, she suspected she hadn't. Twice she was startled upon entering a room by a figure in the corner of her eye. Twice she swung her gun to bear upon it. Twice she found herself threatening nothing. While human perception is a long way from perfect and even the sharpest eye can occasionally be fooled, what perturbed her most was that there was nothing on which to blame the illusion. She did not find herself aiming at a suit hung from a wardrobe door for example, or upon a long mirror in which she herself was reflected. There was nothing there at all, merely some shelves bearing curios in one case, and an entirely blank wall in another. It was not impossible that her ageing senses were proving less reliable these days, but she had experienced no such illusions before. Why should they trouble her now?

She examined her impressions and found them largely consistent; a man standing motionless, a pale-faced man in a dark suit, *sans* hat. No, not simply pale, but white as snow. He had vanished as she had swung her head, taking him from the edge of her perception to its centre. No, this also wasn't entirely accurate. The figure had not vanished in the blink of an eye, it had done something more involved, though still within the space of a blink. It had diminished, becoming less in some fashion until it wasn't there anymore. Not shrunken away, but lessened, diluted, reduced as something to be seen, yet not actually fading away. Elodie was reminded of mice scampering out of view.

She regarded her pistol with an acid eye; she was regretting the practicality that had forced such a small weapon upon her. She permitted herself a momentary pang of envy for the Webley .577 she knew her client preferred. Such a pistol would have done wonders for her confidence at that juncture.

The topmost landing was small, sandwiched in between the "secret" second library and what seemed to be a box room. Elodie tried the latter first, silently opening the door and glancing briefly inside to confirm that its only occupants were tea chests and suitcases. She left the door open; the only light otherwise was through a small skylight over the stairwell. The illumination afforded by the box room's unsealed and uncovered window was much appreciated.

She turned her attention to the door's mate. Assuming Merrow was actually somewhere on his own land and wasn't dead or lurking on the lower ground floor, then here he must be. She considered concealing the pistol, but then remembered the telegram and decided that where guile had failed, threat would just have to prevail.

She moved closer to the door and listened. Beyond the mellowed oak, she could just make out fast breathing, almost panting, intermitted with small wavering groans. It was a sound she had heard before; the sound of somebody in mortal fear of their life.

Curioser and curioser. Depending on circumstances, this could be an advantageous thing, or a very unfortunate thing. Only one course of action could define it.

Elodie Vesperine pushed down upon the door handle and, finding the door unlocked, opened it.

Cornelius Merrow was an impressive man by reputation, less so when observed curled in a tight ball, whimpering. Elodie took in the room before entering; all the walls were covered in shelving, and all the shelves were heavy with a wide variety of tomes, including some she instinctively noted to be rarities. Many of the books, however, had been ill-treated and recently; they lay scattered on the floor or open on the table, rudely stacked upon one another. There was a small fireplace by the end wall, offset due presumably to the window that once took up the centre of that wall, a table, and two comfortable chairs. An electric light depended from the ceiling, and another stood upon the table. Both were lit. Of any other presence, however, the room was clear. She noticed with a small glow of pleasure that, lying on the thick, rich carpet by Merrow was a demi volume bound in maroon leather. Even from where she stood, she could make out enough of the silvered title upon the spine to identify it as the elusive *Philosophical Alembic*. The sensible thing would simply be to take it, bid Mr Merrow a good afternoon, and leave him to his delirium.

"What ails you, Mr Merrow?" she said instead, curiosity outweighing prudence not even for the first time. Then she added as an afterthought, "Your man Belker's dead, by the way."

She did not say it cruelly, it must be emphasised: merely informatively.

For his reply, Merrow reached in a curious reflexive, spastic manner and flicked the book further away from him with the back of his fingertips, as if the thing were hot.

"Take it!" he cried. "Take the damnable thing! Take it away! Take it and its..." and here he paused, and gazed fretfully up at his not-entirely-invited guest.

"Its *what*, pray?" Elodie smiled charmingly as she said it. "What troubles you so, Mr Merrow? What visited such a terrible fate upon your servant?"

"You wanted it." Merrow flicked the book another three inches closer to her. "You may have it! With my best wishes! With my blessings! Just... take it!"

"I may be able to help you with that, or I may not. In the first instance, however, I would—" A creak on the stairs below distracted her. She leaned out through the open doorway and looked down the stairwell. For a moment she thought she saw someone, but then there was a flickering in the light and the well stood vacant. She frowned. Definitely not an optical illusion. She had just seen a man—hatless, in a black suit and as pale as paper—vanish.

"Who is your guest, Mr Merrow?" she said with rising urgency. "The man who isn't there? Who or what is he?"

"This is your doing!" he said frantically, pushing himself away from the door with his heels although his back was already hard against the shelves. "Your fault!"

"Mine?" Elodie admitted to some mild surprise. "I have been responsible and, indeed, guilty of many things in my life, but I doubt that entity may be counted amongst my crimes, moral or judicial."

"You wanted *that book*!" Here Merrow glared at *The Philosophical Alembic*. "It was new to my collection and I had not the leisure to examine it previously. When I discovered you were not who you pretended, I guessed you were after some artefact or book in my possession, and *that* seemed most likely."

"And so, out of curiosity as to why I should be so interested in it, you read it?"

Merrow nodded miserably. "Only the first few words. That was all it took. The book is guarded. Ensorcelled. There is a thing that watches over it. Its true owner would know never to read that first page. That damnable first page..." Merrow here became quite unmanned, and sobbed miserably at an unkind fate.

Another creak upon the stairs. Elodie Vesperine did what she did best, which was to weigh options, consider stratagems, and evolve imperatives. "I have a little experience of such guardians," she told Merrow. "They are neither infallible nor unavoidable, believe me. They invariably have a weakness."

"They do?" He looked up at her with sudden uncritical hope. "You can help me?"

"Quickly, tell me how it is that this creature is unable to attack you? I would have thought its entire *raison d'être* would have been to do you to death as soon as possible."

"I know a little of the occult," he said, waving at his library. "When it manifested, I ran from this room and managed to shake off its pursuit, albeit briefly. You're right; it is not infallible! Hoping to find some method of defeating it, I returned here and was able to create a protective ward. Then, my prospects dwindled. I could think of nothing that might defeat it, could find nothing. Nothing! I was trapped. I rang for Belker, but he never came. Dead, you say? Poor Belker. Poor, poor Belker."

Poor, poor Belker, indeed. And poor Madam Vesperine if she failed to solve this little conundrum. So, to consider the parts of the problem, she had the book, the paper tiger of a magician who was naught but a *poseur*, a slapdash sort of ward, and a frustrated guardian that was more than happy to dispose of anybody else in the environs. She very much hoped that Aurelia was showing enough sense to stay in her covey and not come gallivanting to the rescue. Even with the far more combative .38 revolver that her daughter was carrying, she would stand little chance against this curious creature of the book, the snow-faced man of glimpses and flickers.

Still, even the possibility of it served to crystallise Elodie's thoughts admirably, and it took her only a moment to conceive a plan, and only a moment more to put it into action. She walked to Merrow and took up the book. "This volume is the author of your misfortune? Then our course is clear. This is the focus of the entity that slew your butler. It is therefore the key to the solution."

Merrow seemed troubled. "You will destroy it? I considered it, but—"

"Great heavens, no." She chided him like a slow child. "If it is destroyed, the creature's servitude is dissolved. What, then, is to prevent it wandering as it sees fit, killing at random?"

She failed to add that nor would she get paid if the book were burned.

"Well..." Merrow could see advantage in that, shameful though it was. "...as long as it leaves the house."

"No." She said it firmly, and hoped it gave the impression of a greater morality than his own. It would be an inaccurate impression, but she couldn't help that. "We shall not be responsible for such a horror. Imagine! A hapless maiden waylaid upon the lane! A child slaughtered upon the meadow! A…" Inspiration deserted her for a moment. "…puppy. Killed. No, we have the creature's leash here, and we may use it to bring the beast to heel."

So saying, she stepped smartly out onto the landing, taking the book beyond the line of Merrow's unexpectedly efficacious ward. His gasp of dismay was joined by Elodie's own as she turned and saw the figure upon the intermediate landing.

This time it did not fold out of sight but stood and watched her, the construct of a printer's nightmares, man-sized in woodcut. It gave the impression of a man one moment, and of a figure constructed from criss-crossed pieces of printed card the next. Its features were as planar as any upon a page, and it seemed to draw from every illustration that had ever felt the touch of an inking roller. No detail stayed the same for one moment to the next, but riffled and altered before the confused eye of the observer, and where the parts of its form were presented edgeways on, they disappeared. Now she understood its nature and its *modus operandi*; it was a creature of three dimensions but wrought from two, and every surface was infinitely thin and therefore infinitely sharp. This was how Belker had died; opened and emptied by a storm of paper cuts.

"Well." She spoke as much to herself as to the protean facsimile of a man. "This is a new meaning to a 'printer's devil,' isn't it?" She turned her head far enough to address the occupant of the second library, but her eyes never left the devil. "Mr Merrow, it is as I surmised. Used properly, the book controls the guardian. We are safe."

"We are?" Merrow's voice was thin and tremulous. "Are you sure?"

She forced herself to smile. "I yet live, do I not? But my control is insufficient to return it to the book. You summoned it, you must dispel it. Please come here so that we may finish the matter."

One short flight of stairs below her, the devil's face flickered through a thousand different countenances as a child's flick book. There was expression there—curiosity, rapacity, and hatred.

Slowly and with the utmost reluctance, Merrow came out of his sanctum, hesitating for long seconds before Madam Vesperine's impatient imprecations could cajole him from safety. When at last he stood by her, looking fearfully down at the killing thing, she passed him the slim, maroon demi volume. "There," she whispered encouragingly, "show it who's boss."

If Merrow knew one thing, it was showing all and sundry who was boss. He stood at the head of the stairs and raised the empowering book high. "You see this?" he demanded of the devil. "This means that I…" He happened to look up at this point, and beneath the better illumination of the skylight, was able to see the book properly. "This isn't the right book," he said in wonderment.

A lesser person than Elodie Vesperine might have chosen that moment to say something pithy and moderately amusing at his expense. But, she was in a hurry so she just got straight down to business and pushed Merrow down the stairs.

It wasn't far, and he would certainly have survived the fall had he not met a triumphant entity at the end of the trajectory that was dedicated to the destruction of whomsoever might be foolish enough to summon it. In this, Madam Vesperine had been nothing but honest; Merrow had summoned it, and so it fell to him to dispel it. She had merely neglected to mention that this would be at the cost of his life.

As for her, she stepped smartly into the second library even as Merrow was still tumbling, all the better to avoid the inevitable arterial spray. Blood is the very devil to get out of lace.

***

Subsequent events unfolded quickly, largely for purposes of avoiding the forces of law and order. Certainly Madam Elodie Vesperine in the company of a baffled Miss Aurelia Vesperine were on the train away from town and heading by degrees—in a deliberately circumspect manner—towards London. In this journey, they were slightly burdened by an extra suitcase borrowed from Merrow's box room, laden with books and trinkets that he was never going to miss given his present circumstances. Finally they regained the safety and anonymity of the great metropolis, and sent a letter to an assumed name at a *poste restante* address.

The following day they were blessed by the reappearance of the saturnine Mr C.

"Excellent, excellent," he said as he accepted the book in return for an envelope containing a decent bundle of bank notes. "I knew you would be able to find and secure it for me if anyone could. I am in your debt, ladies." He made to open the book where it lay on the counter.

He was frustrated by the tip of Elodie's finger coming down firmly on the cover, holding it shut. "No, *mein Herr*. We have been recompensed for our expense and trouble in gaining this book for you. You are not in our debt. But, if you wish to live for any length of time subsequent to opening that book…" she smiled the most charming of her many charming smiles, "…you are about to be."

Photo courtesy of Jeff Howard

To the casual observer, video games are awash in the occult. Spooky mysteries, unlockable secrets, and ancient tomes abound, to the point where the occult has become, for lack of a better word, prominent. From the hidden world of the *Dark Souls* franchise to the ancient mysteries of *Destiny*, the occult has become a key part of games, both in their worldbuilding and in their practical design.

But in many cases, the definition of "occult" remains fuzzy or misunderstood. Seeking to clear up that misunderstanding, and to give game designers a better tool set for grappling with the occult in their creations, is designer and professor Jeff Howard. The author of *Game Magic: A Game Designer's Guide to Constructing Magic Systems*, Jeff deals with both the practical and theoretical ends of the equation. He was kind enough to sit down with us to discuss how game controllers are occult devices, what to do about "old and spooky," and the benefits of making your game more occult.

Dark Discoveries: In popular culture, "occult" tends to get used simply to mean "old and spooky." How would you define the term, particularly within the context of games?

JEFF HOWARD: I define the occult as a set of esoteric imaginative and spiritual traditions comprised of systems and mythologies representing the supernatural and metaphysical forces of the cosmos that can be communed with and controlled through magic. The word "occult" literally means "hidden."

DD: But that still leaves us with that popular definition, which feels much broader but less interesting than yours.

In certain ways, it's almost become a marketing term.

JH: Rather than contesting the definition of occult as "magical" and "spooky," I am extending this definition by exploring the underlying structure of magic and the origins of spooky atmosphere. Magic and spookiness come only partly from a set of surface or aesthetic tropes (pentagrams, goats' heads, skulls), and these symbols were originally meant to point toward deep underlying metaphysical forces and ideas, such as the sublime and the divine (sometimes expressed through its contrary, the infernal). Putting the magic back into magic systems means recovering the experience of the sublime: that which challenges our ability to represent or put into words. The symbols of religion and mythology were meant to operate as springboards that allow us to take a leap toward the sublime. Finding a glowing pentagram is cool, but summoning a secret spirit by placing a dragonglass candle at the pentagram's top right point while chanting "hekas hekas este bebeloi" is sublime. Both are occult, but one is purely a matter of surface and the other is intimately embedded in systems of gameplay and narrative.

DD: How would you fit your notion of the occult into a more formal game context?

JH: In terms of game systems, I would define the occult as any system that is deliberately opaque, obscure, and hidden beneath the surface: requiring complex and seemingly arbitrary actions that actually obey a deep and rigorous symbolic logic. If magic is the alteration of reality through the will, then game magic is the alteration of a simulated and virtual world through symbolic operations. At the heart of the occult is a deep reverence for the combinatorial power of symbols, for the permutations and depth of symbolic expression and interpretation as found, for example, in Kabballah, Tarot, and the angelic Enochian language of John Dee.

DD: What's the benefit of adding literally "hidden" systems and information to games?

JH: In games, the occult can provide

a) Mysterious, resonant symbols (spirits, gods, planes, artifacts) and combinatorial principles for generating rich, deep, and systemic lore out of these elements. This lore consists of esoteric explanatory frameworks for the hidden forces that govern a given universe or plane of the multiverse.

b) These hidden forces and esoteric logics then provide inspiration for systems of gameplay that correspond to the lore of a particular world. The fictive metaphysical rules of a particular simulated world can help to generate coherent yet mysterious rules for playing within this world.

c) A sense of mystery and foreboding associated with metaphysical depth.

d) Freedom and transgression associated with the inversion but also deepening of many of the religious structures that shape Western society and storytelling. Alternative and openly heretical ways of envisioning or re-visioning ideas about God, the gods, the sacred, and the profane.

DD: That's a significant contribution. As you've described it, it seems to lean more heavily towards worldbuilding and less towards the actual mechanics of play. How would you describe "occult gameplay?"

JH: Some game magic systems, starting with the 1980's CRPG *Dungeon Master* and extending forward into the tabletop game *Ars Magica* and the GameCube horror title *Eternal Darkness*, feature language-based magic systems in which players combine runes and words through grammatical rules to form spells. These grammar-based magical game mechanics resemble actual occult systems and also the equally arcane craft of programming used to make computer games and other software. Programmers write incantations in obscure symbolic languages governed by hidden logic that, when precisely and correctly arranged, can orchestrate rich multimedia experiences.

DD: One could conclude that any form of modern video gameplay is, in a sense, occult because you're using the representational language and symbology of the controller and the game UI to produce desired results in a world.

JH: I would definitely agree that any act of gameplay is inherently occult because of the use of symbols in order to interact with and control a simulated world. One could extend this argument further to suggest that all acts of programming and therefore software/game development are also occult, since lines of code are incantations that,

when uttered correctly according to a prescribed ritual, control computational processes. This line of logic leads to the famous Arthur C. Clarke statement that "any sufficiently advanced technology is indistinguishable from magic."

DD: So that understanding of gameplay as intrinsically occult is what inspired *Game Magic*?

JH: I wrote *Game Magic* to help game designers, developers, writers, and programmers put the magic back into magic systems, re-enchanting systems that have often degenerated into repeatedly mashing a button on a row

of icons in order to fire a combat spell. *Game Magic* is a game design grimoire, a cookbook of recipes (including computer code and pseudo-code) for making richer, deeper, and more immersive magic in games. I triangulate magic between three nodes: game magic, fictive magic (from the literature of the fantastic), and occult magic (historical human sorcerous beliefs and practices). The magic of games can be enriched by weaving inspirational ley-lines between all three types of magic.

DD: What's the biggest failing in the way games attempt to integrate the occult?

JH: Most games that purport to simulate or represent magic and the occult have a narrow vocabulary, simplistic grammar, and neglect of the multimodal performative aspect of language (i.e. the way that colors, gestures, artifacts, and musical sounds can communicate alongside and in conjunction with words). Spells like "throw fireball" imply a world with a shallow ontology (structure and order of being) that is physical and mechanistic rather than metaphysical and mysterious. Far too many games treat spells as magical artillery.

DD: What advice would you give a designer looking to incorporate occult elements into their game?

QUESTS
Design, Theory, and History in Games and Narratives

Jeff Howard

JH: Designers should strive toward an orthogonal relationship between the things in a world and the magical symbols used to affect these things: for every word a thing, for every thing a word, in perfect symmetry. However, in keeping with the definition of occult as hidden, it is equally important that the richness of a given gameworld be obscured, secret, and not always visible. The occult manifests in lore, which refers to narrative through mythos and backstory rather than story understood narrowly as plot. Lore depends on secret connections and ambiguous, multivalent symbols.

DD: One of the big pushes in games today is towards

accessibility—making games as easy as possible to play for players of all experience and skill levels. How do you reconcile that with a sense of the occult, which by definition has to be hidden and not immediately apparent?

JH: I reconcile accessibility with occultism through the idea of depth. The mantra "easy to learn, hard to master" springs to mind. In a game with depth in the form of hidden secrets, it is often perfectly possible to play the game at a surface level and enjoy it. A sense of awe sometimes comes from discovering that depth and complexity were hiding in plain sight, lurking like the sailboat in a magic eye poster or a fearsome face in a "when you see it" meme. I formulated this idea as "Howard's Law of Occult Game Design" in the book *100 Game Design Principles* (Ed. Wendy Despain). To quote, "Secret Significance is Directly Proportional to Seeming Innocence × Completeness." In other words, the power of secret significance is directly proportional to the apparent innocence and completeness of the surface game.

DD: What are you working on now?

JH: The *Arcana Ritual Toolset* is the most recent, ongoing iteration of my long-term transmedia project, called *Arcana*. The *Ritual Toolset* has two parts: 1) a game about performing rituals 2) an editor for building one's own rituals for other players to explore. Players perform symbolic actions, such as lighting candles, burning incense, chanting, and tracing sigils in order to invoke extraplanar entities and/or travel to their planes. Behind the scenes, these symbolic actions nudge the player (and/or the summoned entity) along various vectors in an n-dimensional concept space or metaverse. In its furthest extension, *Arcana* is intended as a set of open-source tools, assets, and resources for occult game design: a shared world of game lore in which a community of players and developers can create any desired form of magic (whether historical, fantastic, or purely invented).

DD: Sort of a Lego of magic for game designers?

JH: I sometimes use the phrase "the *Minecraft* of magic systems" to describe *Arcana*. Instead of making worlds out of cubes, players and users of *Arcana* make rituals out of symbols. One of the exciting aspects of *Minecraft* is that it blurs the lines between playing and developing games, since the true interest of *Minecraft* is building in creative mode. This creative gameplay is possible because *Minecraft* consists of a relatively small number of interesting building-blocks (types of cubes) and a dizzying number of possible combinations of these elements. In *Arcana*, I am attempting to leverage the combinatorial explosion of occult symbols in order to create emergent magical gameplay.

◇◇◇◇◇◇◆◇◇◇◇◇◇

BUYZOMBIE
THE UNDEAD ARE ONLINE

HORROR
WORLD

HELLNOTES

THE HORROR
REVIEW

HORROR, SCIENCE FICTION
& FANTASY REVIEWS

FICTION, MOVIES, AND ART
DEDICATED TO THE HORROR GENRE

JOURNALSTONE
YOUR LINK TO ARTISTIC TALENT

We Are Monsters
Brian Kirk
Samhain Publishing
July 7, 2015
Reviewed by Tim Potter

Brian Kirk's new Samhain release, *We Are Monsters*, employees the tried and true horror setting of the mental health asylum to ask some provocative questions: What does it mean to heal the mentally ill? Who really needs healing? and Who are the real monsters? The employees and patients of the Sugar Hill state hospital become involved in a reality bending conspiracy to use experimental treatments to cure schizophrenia and the results are horrific. The story has strong characters and starts very strong before slowing down some in the hallucinatory third act.

The novel starts off strong with the main character, Dr. Alex Drexler, administering an unapproved trial drug to a restrained patient. After just a matter of moments it becomes clear that things have gone very wrong and that Drexler will have to take extreme measures to see his experiment through to its conclusion. His desire to complete his work soon becomes central to the goings on at his main place of employment, Sugar Hill hospital. Drexler has to navigate the maze of employees from his boss, Eli Alpert, who knows nothing of the experiment, to board member and chief supporter of the experiment, Mr. Bearman, who pushes Drexler to use his new procedure on Crosby Nelson. Nelson is the famous Apocalypse Killer, a clearly paranoid schizophrenic man who appears to be a perfect test subject, but will end up being the downfall of all involved.

The plot starts off strong, establishing a cast of believable and relatable characters and a realistic setting in the Georgia state hospital, Sugar Hill. In the first act, the doctors, counselors, orderlies and patients have a rich a thoroughly developed backstories, and in establishing this the story never becomes bogged down in exposition but keeps plowing ahead. Dr. Drexler's need to prove his experiment a success leads him to try it on his mentally ill brother. The experiment with his brother ends in tragedy for his family and the hospital. The second act follows the hospital through changes in the wake of the events with Alex's brother. Dr. Drexler is forced into even more drastic actions when his entire professional life is put at risk.

The third act is, in concept, a fascinating idea. It forces mental health professionals into a situation where they must deal with hallucinatory mental states themselves, effectively putting them into the position their patients have always had to deal with. While the concept works, the execution is lacking. There are three parallel narratives at this point and only the one focusing on Dr. Drexler fully works. The threads about Angela, the counselor, and Dr. Alpert, the boss, seem extraneous to the greater plot, as did shorter passages about them earlier in the work. The backgrounds of these characters is filled in here, and some readers may appreciate that, but it takes a while to get there.

The end of the story is satisfying and worth the digressions of the third act, especially considering the strength of the majority of the novel. *We Are Monsters* is a solid horror novel and an entertaining read, but it is the discussion of mental health and its attendant issues that makes it really worth the read. Author Brian Kirk manages to strike the delicate balance of discussing pressing social issues without ever resorting to preaching to the reader.

<><><><><><><><><><><><><><><><><><><><><><><><>

Dawn of the Dead
George A. Romero and Susanna Sparrow
Gallery Books
2015
Reviewed by David T. Wilbanks

With a short introduction by actor Simon Pegg, what we have here is a reprint of the 1978 novelization of the classic zombie movie *Dawn of the Dead*, brought to us by legendary director George A. Romero–who is, as we all know, the godfather of the post-voodoo apocalyptic zombie tale–with writing assistance from Susanna Sparrow.

So why would you want a reprint of an old book of an old movie? For one thing, it's an attractive trade paperback–even if it does feature the obligatory dead man's hand on the cover, with outstretched fingers reaching toward an orange sky. For another, it would make the perfect gift for any rabid reader of undead literature, a collectable companion to the classic movie.

But what does the book offer that the movie does not? Why read it when you can watch the film any time you get the urge? Here's why: this is a novel, not a script; at time, a character's motivation may be unclear in the movie, but it is not so in the novel, because you are privy to each character's inner thoughts and motivation–something you don't get from the movie. In all other ways, the book follows the movie except for a few minor differences (for example, there's a puppy in the novel that didn't make it to the big screen).

If for some reason you have not seen the movie, but decide you want to read the book anyway, what you'll get is a workmanlike zombie story that seems rather mundane because you've seen this sort of thing all before a hundred times. But you must remember, before the original *Dawn of the Dead* movie, there had been nothing like this (unless you count *Night of the Living Dead*, of course). This movie was the inspiration for nearly every other zombie story that followed, in books and on screen. At the time, it was unique.

So what we have here is an important piece of horror cinema history, and it's a great thing that a publisher made it available again for the swelling hordes of zombie fans.

◇◇

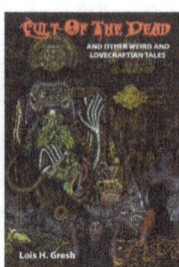

Cult of the Dead and Other Weird and Lovecraftian Tales
Lois H. Gresh
Hippocampus Press
August 2015
Reviewed by David Goudsward

New York Times bestselling author Lois H. Gresh is a triple threat as a writer. She writes nonfiction guides such topics as *The Science of Superheroes*, and companions to everything from *Twilight* and *The Hunger Games* to *The Mortal Instruments* and *The Spiderwick Chronicles*. She also writes science fiction such as *Blood and Ice* with hibernating alien vampires in Antartica. And she writes horror. Her first horror collection, *Eldritch Evolution* was released by Chaosium in 2011.

Hippocampus has wisely chose to issue a new collection, *Cult of the Dead*. Her companion guides and her science fiction demonstrate her comfortableness with technology and science. In her short horror, Gresh integrates science into her supernatural in a variety of ways that seamlessly add to the building tension. In the titular story, the ossuary catacombs beneath Lima's San Francisco monastery are the background to both a tale of death cults that are quite dead and social inequity. There are no happy endings in Peru, but there is a satisfactory denouement.

And having considered the morbid side of archaeology, Gresh launches into tales of the aftermath of nanotechnology run amok, A tale of the Wild West, Lovecraft style, foot fetishes gone bad, regretful angels of death, swords and sorcery, and several tales of dystopic futures where technology has created a new form of normal that is beyond disquieting. Underlying all the tales is also an underlying theme that family, biological, acquired, or evolved, is the best defense against evil, even if it's only a delaying tactic or motivation to fight.

If there is one shortcoming in the collection, and it is minor at best, is the inclusion of fairly new stories, including from her previous collection, and one from Joshi's *Searchers After Horror*, an anthology published barely a year ago. I would have much preferred to see the space utilized for less recent tales from Gresh's prolific library of tales available. Still over all, it is an outstanding collection of work from one of the justifiably popular horror writers currently in the field.

◇◇

A Debt To Be Paid
Patrick Lacey
Samhain Publishing
September 1, 2015
Reviewed by Tim Potter

Patrick Lacey's new novella *A Debt To Be Paid* is a compelling page-turner that manages to be a thrilling horror story and interesting exploration of mental illness. The story follows Meg Foster, a woman who was kidnapped by her schizophrenic mother when she was young, and exposed to the terrifying effects of profound mental illness. As Meg ages out of her teens and college years she is forced to face the fact that she may have the same illness as her mother, or that there could be something even more sinister happening.

Meg Foster is estranged from her mother and has a relationship that is distant at best with her father. She's moved to a new town and taken a new job in an attempt to distance herself from the past, but can't entirely forget it thanks to a scar on her forehead she always rubs in times of stress. It's a stark reminder of the night her mother's mental illness came to a terrifying climax and resulted in her unintentional wounding. As she nears the age her mother was when her mental illness became overwhelming, Meg begins to notice things that scare her. Things that remind her of what her mother believed she saw and heard as her health deteriorated.

Meg is a complex character, balancing the demands of her average life as a bank teller with too many bills and impending student loan payments. In her attempt to forge a life of her own away from her parents she relocates to a small town where she has no history and doesn't know anyone. A random night drinking cheap beer at a bar leads her to meet Brian Peterson, a lifelong local. Meg unloads on Brian and thinks she has alienated him, but when fear and fate drives her, coincidentally, to the door of his bookstore, she discovers that they have a connection.

With Brian at her side, Meg must confront the possibility that she is following in her mother's footsteps down the road of schizophrenia. She also must answer the seemingly impossible question of what she saw when she was a child, during her mother's break from reality, and what it means if she's seeing these things again. Is it possible that schizophrenia is not the root cause of the problems of mother and daughter.

As someone who has experience of working with individuals diagnosed with schizophrenia I found Lacey's depiction of the illness and those living with it and around it to be not only accurate, but sympathetic and humane. He does an admirable job of balancing the serious nature of the disease with the task of telling a great horror story. *A Debt To Be Paid* is a great work of fiction that leaves the reader with only one objection: that it had to end.

◇◇

Mutt
Shane McKenzie
Rothco Press
May 4, 2015
Reviewed by Marvin P. Vernon

In Shane McKenzie's tense and different novella *Mutt*, Patrick, a young white/Korean male who is often mistaken as Mexican, lives with his mother, works at a boxing gym cleaning up and basically stays out of trouble. That is until he meets a Mexican girl who mistakes him as being the same as her. Pat is too smitten with desire to correct her and finds himself taken to a party by the local gang Los Reyes Locos. When he discovers he has been "drafted" into joining, it is too late and he is neck deep in a lifestyle he doesn't want with a girl he cannot resist. He must fight his way out to save himself and his family.

McKenzie's writing is very visceral. As in his previous work, *Muerte Con Carne*, there is plenty of action and violence. Yet while *Muerte Con Carne* is clearly a horror tale, *Mutt* is closer to a suspense and crime tale, and throws in a lot of human drama into its characters' development and emotions. Patrick is mixed race but is frequently mistaken as Mexican. Patrick is based on the author's own situation and speaks of his own dilemma as being judged as someone he is not. While the author is taking his queues from his own life, I am fairly certain the actual plot is not auto-biographical or at least I hope not! The fictional Patrick's situation is extreme but it works as an illustration of one of our own inescapable issues in our American life: being judged on appearance and race rather than for who we really are. *Mutt* is just as much a coming-of-age tale about growing up in race and class torn America as it is an edge of your seat thriller about gangs and violence.

That is why this book and the main character of Patrick moved me so much. Patrick is a normal kid who wants to be accepted and wants the girl. He is tricked into a lifestyle he does not want for a girl who may have other plans for him. In the midst of this plot we have great writing that brings Patrick and the gang of Los Reyes Locos to life. There is no sugar coating. Patrick is sleeping with cobras and he knows it. The scenes of violence are intense but fit squarely into the story and we see Patrick's own terror and bewilderment as he experiences it.

It is that part of McKenzie's writing that senses the horror of life choices when it collides with the human-created horrors of society that makes me come back to his stories.

Whether it is cannibal families as in *Muerte Con Carne* or homicidal gangs as in *Mutt*, the author goes deeper than the suspense and visceral thrills inherent in the tale and digs into the existential dread that one will find themselves in. I hope the author continues this exploration of the human side of dark social and racial themes in future stories. Even if he decides to just thrill and terrorize us I will be pleased. He does it so well. But he has the gift of social observation that does not ignore the individual psyche and I hope he uses it again.

◇◇

The Gods of Laki: A Thriller
Chris Angus
Yucca Publishing
2015
Reviewed by Michael R. Collings

Chris Angus's *The Gods of Laki* is one of those fascinating and deeply satisfying novels that are ultimately impossible to classify.

It is, as the subtitle claims, a thriller. Set primarily in—and often underneath—Iceland, it details multi-national political, religious, and economic intrigues that place its protagonists in constant danger of death by assassination, by suffocation, by incineration in lava flows, by nuclear blast, by drowning, and by absorption (but to discover by what or whom, I leave you to read the story). It includes among its characters:

Tenth-century quasi-immortal Vikings;
Nazi scientists developing a heinous plan to win World War II and gain global domination;
Iranian terrorists determined to manipulate and control the price of oil;
A cabal of Catholic cardinals privy to a decades-old secret that could shatter the foundations of religion;
The Majority Leader of the Senate, the President's science advisor, and the President himself;
A potentially god-like entity unlike anything the characters can imagine;
And scientists, linguists, volcanologists, and half dozen others whose specialized talents blend seamlessly with a complex, coherent narrative.

It depends upon level after level of secret plans and machinations, each deadlier than the last, that must be unraveled and understood.

It is horror as well, at least as far as featuring tentacle-encrusted human chrysalides animated by a fearsome power as unknowable and, perhaps, as indifferent to human life as any of H.P. Lovecraft's Great Old Ones helps define that genre. It incorporates gruesome death and eldritch creatures from the depths…although in this case, not the depths of the sea but of the unfathomable and constantly changing world of sub-volcanic caverns and passageways. It is science fiction in that at the core of the problems that develop as a result of human tampering with Laki, a volcano on the southern coast of Iceland, such things as strangelets, the Higgs boson/God particle, the Large Hadron Collider, black holes, and alternate universes become crucial to explaining events. Or do they?

Along the way—but certainly not peripherally—it deals with religion and reason and questions of ultimate existence, of the purposefulness or futility of humanity. It deals with appearance and reality; with illusion and fact and the often tenuous interface between them; with life, death, the prospect of immortality and the unanticipated consequences of obsession with longevity; with ambition and greed and pride and virtually everything else that makes life interesting. It deals with gods and devils, believers and atheists, and the differences and similarities linking them.

And it does so by telling a compelling story of two central characters—ex-Secret Service agent now expert in geothermal energy Ryan Baldwin; and Samantha Graham, daughter of a powerful senator, seeking to understand the mysteries of Laki. The progress of their relationship—which gives the novel a light touch of romance—parallels the gradual revelation that Laki is more than just a volcano…and that penetrating the enigmas surrounding it will forever change perceptions of reality.

A thoroughly enjoyable read on multiple levels, well-written, fast paced, and intriguing in its suggestions and possibilities.

Darkness Rising
Brian Moreland
Samhain Publishing
September 1, 2015
Reviewed by Tim Potter

The latest release from the prolific and talented horror author Brian Moreland, *Darkness Rising* is a compelling novella. It deals with complex themes like the power of the written word, expressions of darkness in art and trying to break away from one's own past. The story has an incredibly high body count that is balanced out by poetry and a tender love story.

After a brutal opening scene, in which three animal mask-clad killers dispatch two people on the shores of a deserted lake, the author introduces the book's hero Marty Weaver. A janitor at St. Germaine College in the Pacific Northwest, Marty tries to juggle work, a girl he's crazy about, his poetry and a horrific past while longing for love and the chance to attend St. Germaine himself. The romance between Marty and Jennifer, a student he helps with Shakespeare and poetry homework, is well realized and full of youthful longing.

Using poetry as his emotional outlet, Marty regularly visits a local lake at night and reads his work to the water. After an eventful meeting with Jennifer, Marty heads out to the lake, where he is overheard reading by a trio of sadistic killers. The violence begins not against Marty's person, but against his most prized possession: his journal. It was a gift given to him by his long ago murdered mother and

the rage and sorrow he feels at its destruction is palpable. Marty's pain becomes the reader's pain as he embarks on a mission of vengeance.

Marty becomes a young man held together by his poetry and the love and other emotion therein. Maybe even literally. What follows is a tale of revenge, redemption, love and facing the demons of the past. Is what Marty experiences something fantastic and supernatural, as it would seem, or is it something more real and more terrifying? Could Marty be following in the footsteps of his father, a man whose depravity went beyond the pale?

Darkness Rising is not just an entertaining exercise in extreme horror. It's a great character study and, if the reader is interested in finding it, a meditation on the nature and power of art. Either way it is a great read that's well worth the price of admission.

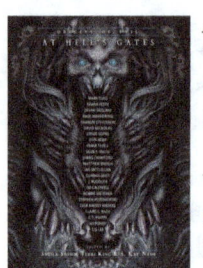

At Hell's Gates: Origins of Evil
Various Authors
February 1, 2015
Reviewed by Matthew Scott Baker

When I first read the blurb about *At Hell's Gates: Origins of Evil,* I thought to myself, "What a perfect title for an anthology!"

Hell is always an interesting backdrop for horror stories, and the gates of hell make for a more specific setting for terror to unfurl. I am excited to promote this anthology, but not just because of the title. The tales within this collection are all excellent for various reasons, and the authors who wrote them are all talented. But this book is also being used to promote a worthy cause. Thus, this anthology is a win-win, all the way around.

If you are not familiar with *At Hell's Gates: Origins of Evil,* here is the plot synopsis courtesy of amazon.com:

Welcome back to Hell's Gates! The palpable sense of dread may seem familiar, but this time things are a bit…different. Fresher. Newer. As though just recently born… See that squealing baby over there? He could grow up to be a lifesaving doctor (or perhaps the antichrist.) What about that scientist burning the midnight oil? He could be working on a bug zapper (or a doomsday device.) Did you catch that comet out of the corner of your eye? It might bring good luck (or an apocalyptic plague.) Yes, every darkness has a source, every monster has a birthplace, and every evil has an origin. In the second volume of the #1 Bestselling AT HELL'S GATES series, twenty-three of the finest dark fiction authors working today will force you to witness the ORIGINS OF EVIL. Each unique tale of terror traces an unspeakable horror back to its very beginning. All proceeds from this horror anthology series go to the Intrepid Fallen Heroes Fund, a charity benefiting military veterans suffering from Post-Traumatic Stress Disorder and Traumatic Brain Injury. The authors and editors of this series are pleased to donate their time and effort to a truly worthy cause. So sit back, relax, support a fine charity, and enjoy twenty-three tales of dawning calamity from some of horror fiction's leading lights.

I am a huge supporter of our armed forces and any

cause that works to support them. As such, organizations like The Wounded Warrior Project and The Intrepid Fallen Heroes Fund are certainly to be commended in my eyes. One of the coolest aspects of this book is that proceeds from the sales of this anthology are donated to The Intrepid Fallen Heroes Fund. So not only is it entertaining, but it is being used to do some good.

As I mentioned, every story in *At Hell's Gates: Origins of Evil* is written well and flows smoothly. A couple take a bit to get going, but this is a minor detraction and takes nothing away from the collection as a whole. The authors showcased here are very talented, and I would wager many (if not all) will have long, successful careers in the industry.

I particularly like how broad the usage of the subject matter is. Some stories utilize the concept of the book's title literally, while others use it metaphorically. This diversity is nice and works well to satisfy the collection's overall theme.

One of my favorite stories in *At Hell's Gates: Origins of Evil* is "Operation Devil Walk" by David Mickolas. This tale is set in World War II and chronicles a British Commando Team who is sent to infiltrate a secret Nazi sect. In addition to great fight scenes, the story combines a heightened sense of tension with some truly horrific imagery. This might be my favorite story in the whole book.

At Hell's Gates: Origins of Evil is a major win for me, and I highly recommend it. Fans of horror will want to eat this up, and those interested in quirky literature will want to give this a look as well. But if you're wanting a unique way to support our troops and their families, this will satisfy that as well. The book is available now in a variety of formats.

<><><><><><><><><><><><><><><><><><><><><><><><><><>

The Hitchhiking Effect
Gene O'Neill
Dark Renaissance Books
2015
Reviewed by Michael R. Collings

It is rare when a collection of stories and novellas spanning some thirty years leaves me with a single, overwhelming emotional impression. In the case of Gene O'Neill's *The Hitchhiking Effect*, there is an additional sense of the unusual in that his compilation of ten stories—most dealing with the physically, mentally, and emotionally debilitating effects of war on those most closely connected with it, whether serving or supporting—contains its share of realistically portrayed grief and loss, of violence and bloodshed, of death and disruption, yet when I finished the final story, "Firebug," what I felt was a highly paradoxical sense of gentleness and peace.

In "The Burden of Indigo," for example, the earliest of the stories, O'Neill introduces readers to a world in which criminals are punished by being stained, a specific color representing a specific crime. The main character is known simply as "the indigo man" and is a deep, rich purple-blue from head to foot, including his hair and clothing. Such Colored People are ostracized from the domed communities where humanity now lives and are doomed to wander the empty stretches between. The story deals with his increasing belief that his indigo is fading—that he is perhaps gaining some kind of exoneration, a cure, for his unnamed (but implied) crime of two decades before. Yet even as he feels a nascent hope, he must deal with the fears and prejudices of normals he encounters, until his final meeting with a strange, almost mystical figure, who in the most unusual way, alleviates his suffering. In the final novelette, "Firebug" (first published here), a neophyte arson investigator is assigned to a series of fires in abandoned warehouses, the most recent of which killed a homeless person. As clues accumulate, he is forced to include among his prime suspects his own father. While that story progresses, however, readers enter the mind of the firebug through journal entries, following an all-too-familiar progression from abused childhood, to traumatic loss of parents, to infatuation with violence and destruction…in this case, a developing pyromania. Oh, and along the way, O'Neill reveals that the pyromaniac is not technically the Firebug—there is an actual (?) fire-bug inside the flame of a cigarette lighter that, when released, causes the conflagrations. The story ends, as it should, in the discovery of the perpetrator and the resolution of unsolved cases, but again, as with "The Burden of Indigo," there is a powerful sense of rightness, of peacefulness and gentleness and ultimate reconciliation.

I've chosen to write at length about the first and the last, but other of the stories could have demonstrated my point. "Graffiti Sonata" concentrates on a man's harrowing loss and his discovery of images chalked onto an overpass… that seem to move and that eventually bring him to understanding, acceptance, and peace. In "Balance," a Force Recon vet, recently released from a VA hospital, commits outright murder but does so for the purest, most humanitarian of motives, only to have the stakes suddenly reversed. "Dance of the Blue Lady" allows a boy-man who abruptly has no place in the community to find peace and solace. A longer piece, "The Confessions of St. Zach" breaks the pattern slightly in its depiction of a United States devastated by atomic bombs. In the aftermath, Jacob Zachary, his wife, and his seventeen-year-old son initially find shelter among a small group of survivors, only to discover that safety is relative and that what is at risk is not only their lives but their humanity. In spite of the grimness and horror of the story, however, the final paragraph—indeed, the last three words—transforms and elevates it beyond its overt content.

"The Hungry Skull: A Love Story" and "Rusting Chickens" approach the power of love and loss from different directions. The first is a science-fictional story set in the same world of Cal Wild as "The Burden of Indigo" and centers on a jump-ship pilot—half human, half machine—who seems oddly entranced by a death-play at a histro-bistro, in which the actors performing in The Gunfight at the O.K. Corral literally shoot to kill. In the second, Force Recon veteran Rob McKenna becomes convinced, first that the metal chickens ornamenting the yard are moving of their own volition, and then that his wife is somehow betraying him. Both stories are tightly told and devastating in their implications for the characters—and for the readers' conceptions of love and loss and sacrifice—yet when the end comes to each, there also comes the realization that what happens is perfectly imagined and perfectly accomplished.

I've not said much about the intensity with which O'Neill confronts the realities of warfare in story after story—that becomes obvious as readers explore his worlds. War destroys…even its survivors. The point is not the number of the enemy killed or the amount of territory captured or even the points of belief justified but the lasting damage warfare does to individuals and the extraordinary, often supernal, effort it takes to overcome it.

◇◇

Alien vs Predator: Fire and Stone
Written by Christopher Sebela
Illustrated by Ariel Olivetti
Dark Horse Books
June 23, 2015
Reviewed by Jess Landry

The *Alien vs Predator* universe sure is one crowded house. There's a whole bunch of awesome movies (and a couple not-so-awesome ones), some badass video games, there's action figures and now, there are some brand-spanking new comic books.

There are currently four different comic series set in the Fire and Stone storyline: *Prometheus: Fire and Stone, Aliens: Fire and Stone, Predator: Fire and Stone,* and this one, *AvP: Fire and Stone*. Each series is four issues long and every series shares an interconnected story. The upcoming June 23rd release of *AvP: Fire and Stone* collects issues 1 through 4 of the same name comic, previously released throughout 2014 by Dark Horse Books.

AvP: Fire and Stone picks up after the events of *Prometheus: Fire and Stone*. Elden, a synthetic (think Bishop from *Aliens* or David from *Prometheus*) who has mutated and is currently self-evolving into some sort of alien-robot-human thing, is on the hunt for his creator, Francis. Elden finds Francis aboard the Geryon, a ship initially sent on a rescue mission to the planet LV-223, where the events of *Prometheus* transpired. The ship is now on the trip home to Earth, seemingly unaware that Elden is on his way to seek answers (and maybe get a little vengeance) on his creator.

The Predators show up…because…well, this is an AvP installment after all. I'm assuming it's because the Preds love a good hunt, and hey, what better game than the ever-transforming, ever-unstoppable Elden? Either way, once Elden, the Predators and the Aliens are onboard the same ship, there's a whole lot of blood, guts and metamorphosis going on.

The storyline is very Mary Shelley's Frankenstein. Elden struggles with his identity and his *raison* d'etre as he becomes more and more self-aware. His quest to find Francis, his creator, isn't so much to kill him, but simply

to find out why Francis made him the way he is. Elden is a sympathetic character; he's the robot-alien on the verge of self-discovery. The story, penned by Christopher Sebela, has enough action and keeps the pace of the story moving along well enough that boredom isn't an option.

Artwork wise, there are a lot of gorgeous things happening here. First and foremost is the beautiful cover art by E.M. Gist. Also included is a variant cover by *Hellboy* creator Mike Mignola. The interior art by Ariel Olivetti is amazing. Every decapitation, every instance of acidic green blood, every mutation and evolution, it's all lovely. It's the kind of stuff that you want to hang on your walls and stare at all day.

Based on the artwork alone, this compilation of the *AvP: Fire and Stone* series is worth getting your hands on. It's the best way to get your fix of the *Alien* and *Predator* universes until the next adventure in the franchises comes out.

◇◇

White Knuckle
Eric Red
Samhain
June 2, 2015
Reviewed by Marvin P. Vernon

Eric Red's *White Knuckle* is as high octane a horror thriller as they come. It is a cross between *Silence of the Lambs* and Richard Matheson's *Duel*. It also bears a very slight resemblance to the 80s film *The Hitcher*, which was written by Eric Red himself, as well as was one of my favorite vampire movies, *Near Dark*. Those two movies and this novel have something in common and that is they show that Red knows how to write dark and evil characters that jump out at you. If his psycho villains come out a little too super-human sometimes, it just revs up the suspense and gives us a little more worry and need to cheer on the hero or, in this case, the heroine.

Our heroine is FBI agent Sharon Ormsby who is assigned to the FBI's Highway Serial Killing Initiative which tracks and hunts down murders on interstates and highways. She comes across a pair of bodies that appear to be linked but, if so, it means that the killer has been active for over 30 years. In the meantime through alternating scenes, the reader discovers quickly that this is a trucker who uses the CB handle White Knuckle. He is abducting women and imprisoning them in his own torture chamber on wheels.

White Knuckle has the right amount of action, crime know-how, suspense, and terror to appeal to a number of genre readers. The FBI/CSI enthusiasts will get a lot of crime-fighter stuff. The author certainly know a lot about the trucking industry too. The suspense/thriller reader will not be disappointed with the tense writing and many taut action scenes. And the horror fans will find lots of scares, both psychological and physical. But it is the cat-and–mouse relationship between Sharon and White Knuckle that kept my interest. The character of White Knuckle is a larger than life serial killer. He's obsessed, he thinks he is smarter than everyone else and just may be, and highly misogynistic. His killing of women is described by the author in a way that hides no facts about his villainy and frankly may be too much for some readers. Yet when Sharon, who is undercover and on the road with a veteran truck driver she had partnered up with, comes into contact with him we can feel the killer being both threatened and challenged by this woman. This is handled well by the author and only adds to the tension as Sharon builds her case and White Knuckle prepares for what he sees to be his final triumph. The final climatic scene is one of the best written action segments I have ever read on paper.

But it isn't all perfect. That best action scene on paper sometimes comes across too well and feels like a send-up for a film. This is not necessarily a big problem but there are a number of times that some scenes felt too cinematic or too pat. Like the hitcher in the aforementioned film of the same name, the character of White Knuckle is often too "there" when he should be. Also, considering how detailed his descriptions of both FBI and truck driving is, there are some moments that stretch believability. For instance, it is hard to think that an agent that develops a sudden major disability would be kept in the field for such an important and dangerous manhunt. That almost lost me, to be blunt.

Yet overall, I have to admit that *White Knuckle* ends up as one of the most visceral and on-the-edge-of-your-seat reading I have done in a long while. It never lets up. Red has an affinity not just for villains but for the victims, which adds a lot of poignancy in the writing. Sharon Ormsby is a great protagonist with enough nerve and back story to make her easily likable. If this isn't one of the best literary horror/action thrill rides of all time then it still easily goes to the top of the list for best action thrillers in 2015.

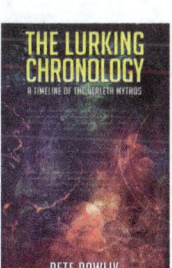

The Lurking Chronology: A Timeline of the Derleth Mythos
By Pete Rawlik
Lovecraft eZine Press
August 15, 2015
Reviewed by David Goudsward

For those unfamiliar with the work of Pete Rawlik, let it suffice to say he writes tales set in the Lovecraft mythos, with a twist. Rawlik's characters interact with the mythos characters and events, both of Lovecraft and his devotees. And he does this interaction within the confines of a chronology of the stories, weaving his stories around this self-imposed canonical timeline, inspired in no small part on the work of Peter Cannon in his 1986 chapbook *The Chronology out of Time*. Rawlik's short stories and novels are based on the premise that Lovecraft's stories are not stand-alone tales, but rather that all of his works take place in a shared universe.

The problem with this approach, as with so many other things Lovecraftian, is August Derleth. Derleth's stories are based on Lovecraft's work literarily and figuratively; a number of them are posthumous collaborations. But they often contradict the established events, change the dates, and just muddy the waters.

Rawlik's solution to these Derleth tales, instead of ignoring or glossing over them, is the *Lurking Chronology*, creating a separate timeline of the Derleth version of the Mythos. In other words, Derleth's mythos is an alternative universe to Lovecraft's fictional world, separate but equal.

For the casual reader, this is not an issue, but to fans of the Mythos, it is a helpful tool in keep track of events in lesser read tales. And to a *Call of Cthulhu* role-player building a game, it offers twists to confuse the doomed adventurers before their inevitable slide into madness and death.

It's a small book, a chapbook really, with 40 pages of text and reasonably priced. But for a little book, it's a valuable reference tool, and a fun reminder that Derleth's much maligned pastiches still have entertainment value.

Blood Sushi
Edited by Jinx Strange and Angela Meadon
Dirge Publications
August 3, 2015
Reviewed by Eden Royce

The editors of Dirge magazine have put out a sample anthology of dark and twisted stories that reflect their tastes in horror. I hadn't heard of Dirge Magazine before reading this anthology, but you better believe I'm going to check them out now.

In 63 pages, this anthology puts you through some of the most disturbing horror I've read in a while. But it does so with clever wordsmithing, which can sometimes be a rarity in this genre. I don't often say, 'Wow." upon finishing a story and I did so more than once with this all-too-brief collection. It's all the more impressive that there are only eight stories in the anthology.

A bit about a few of the stories that stood out to me:

In "Happy Sunshine Music" by S.C. Hayden, a record collector thinks he's discovered the find of a lifetime in a shop. But then he places the needle on the record. (Put the needle on the record when the drumbeat goes like this! Sorry… 80's hip-hop moment there.) He realizes he's found something altogether different, something all too willing to destroy anyone in earshot. Hayden's descriptions of the sounds coming out of that record made my skin crawl and I was glad I was sitting in bed reading it as I felt somewhat more secure. A good duvet will do that for you.

A short story that is essentially the killer giving a soliloquy. I'll admit I thought it was going to be a bit like O.J. Simpson writing the book, *If I Did It: Confessions of the Killer*. But Richard Lee Byers makes the first person POV work in "Honor Killing". Although we only hear the voice of the shape-shifting bounty hunter, I could almost feel the emotions of the cop he's speaking to. A huge part of the horror of this story for me as a woman was reading about the world in which a girl can be killed for not agreeing to her arranged marriage and trying to leave the city.

I loved Kat Dalziel's "Remember This" for its descriptions of the protagonist's visceral emotions: fear, isolation, confusion, and ultimate realization. So well done, I can hardly believe it's her first published piece. It won't be her last. It had better not be. *Shakes fist* I also appreciated that Dalziel didn't attempt to answer all of the questions the reader is inevitably left with ("Why is this happening?"), instead choosing to leave us with the feelings of her protagonist.

A good detective story always gets my vote, and "A Splash of Blue" by Richard Dansky delivers a cool, clever detective who gets paid in emotions. Part Harry Dresden and part Phillip Marlowe, he discovers that the Blood can be a Gift or a curse. Mostly, I enjoyed that the detective was gumshoeing it around, interviewing people, going places to hunt down clues, not typing things into a search engine for a path to follow.

The final story is K.L. Grady's "Her Mother's Daughter," in some ways the most unsettling of the bunch. A young girl approaching her sexual maturity struggles to keep her family happy by following the rules her late mother set out for her. But in this post-apocalyptic world, is she better off with or without her father?

I don't know if *Blood Sushi* is just that—a beautifully wrapped appetizer for those unfamiliar with the Dirge Magazine publication. Maybe a little amuse bouche to garner a larger, more diverse readership? If so, it's worked on me. (I've now signed up for their newsletter.) If Dirge plans to publish more stories like these—strong voices, clever twists, and inventive storytelling—I'll be on the lookout for their books.

Strongly recommended.

◇◇

Stealing Propeller Hats From the Dead
David James Keaton
Perpetual Motion Machine Publishing
October 1, 2015
Reviewed by Tim Potter

David James Keaton follows up his first two impressive novels with a collection of zombie tales from Perpetual Motion Machine Publishing. *Stealing Propeller Hats From the Dead* is a work that finds success on multiple levels. It is a great set of entertaining genre stories that any zombie fan dive into and enjoy one bite at a time, but it is also a deep, well thought out commentary on the history of the subgenre. The individual stories all work and, even though a few are rather forgettable, comprise a great book with a few of the finest zombie tales of recent years. The book opens with a foreword by David Tallerman, in which he coins a phrase that well describes the stories that the reader is about plunge into as "Keatonesque pulp-literary goodness."

We've all skipped introductions to books and then lied about having done so. Don't skip "Introduction: Scare Quotes and Coffin Rides" as Keaton uses a true story of his involvement with zombies as a launching pad for the fiction to follow. Keaton describes visiting the Monroeville Mall where the original *Dawn of the Dead* was filmed and the backroom pseudo-museum dedicated to the film as a way of celebrating the sale of his novella, "Zee Bee & Bee (a.k.a. propeller hats for the dead)." It's just one episode in what must have been, as the content of the book proves, a life full of zombie education.

"Greenhorns" is the first piece of fiction in the book and takes zombies in a very different direction. New recruits begin working on the famous crab fishing vessel *Gone Fission* from the *Crab Monsters* television program, a show long since cancelled. *Gone Fission* is the only craft to survive the finale of the show's last season. The story is terrifically suspenseful as it tells the true history of the boat from the middle out. While the reader learns about Jake and his current and future on the ship, they learn the root of the disaster that wiped out so many ships and resulted in the show's cancellation. Jake's ultimate fate is directly related to the beginning of the problems for *Crab Masters*. "Greenhorns" is a skillfully crafted and entirely entertaining story.

The second story in the book is "… And I'll Scratch Yours (or the one who had none)," a tale of genetic engineering and how to properly care for one's severed arm backscratcher. The story has a few callbacks to "Greenhorns," which actually makes "Greenhorns" a better story after the fact. There is something of a parallel to this story and the classic film *Gremlins* that I was fully prepared to discuss here, but Keaton goes ahead and discusses it within the story itself. There's no need to include more of that here except to say that *Gremlins* fans will likely quite enjoy this one.

"Do the Munster Mash" and "The Doppelganger Radar" do not follow each other in order in the book but are certainly related. Between the two tales there are a rash of dog bites that may or may not be dog bites and a discussion of how people tend to look so much like their pets. These stories are best read in the order in which they appear, but reading them a second time back-to-back is recommended for a more complete reading experience.

For an extended riff on dead baby jokes and other repellant and honestly funny comedy, "What's Worst?" is for you. "The Ball Pit" tells the story of how humankind faced a possible extinction event because of a rogue medication that causes priapism. It's likely the first time a fictional boner has threatened the future of the world. "The World's Second Shortest Zombie Story" is fascinating and leaves the reader wondering if they know what really just happened.

"Three Ways Without Water" is a story set in the same fictional world as Keaton's novel *Pig Iron*. The story was written some time before the novel and presents an interesting challenge in describing how the two works are related. "Three Ways Without Water" includes elements that are scattered throughout the entire novel, which is about 175 to 200 pages longer. It could be considered a prequel, but that doesn't quite fit that definition correctly. The best explanation of the story is that it's an early version of a story that would evolve into something much larger and more complex. It's a great stand-alone short story and a rare glimpse into the creative process.

The main course of the book is served up in "Zee Bee & Bee (a.k.a. propeller hats for the dead)." It is a novella of good length that serves as an homage to, and a complete deconstruction of, the zombie story. With copious references to just about every significant zombie film ever made, this is the zombie story against which all should be judged going forward. Actors have created a combination bed and breakfast dinner theater-like experience that allows couples to spend a weekend in a rural house fighting off the zombie hordes. If you can have an honestly serious conversation about the Nazi zombie film *Shock Waves* or argue the spelling and chronology of Lucio Fulci's *Zombi 2*, or *Zombie*, you will swallow up this piece in one sitting. There is also a great twist that takes the story to an ending that it's unlikely readers will see coming. "Zee Bee & Bee (a.k.a. propeller hats for the dead)" is a crown jewel to this collection of stellar fiction.

Readers new to Keaton will find *Stealing Propeller Hats From the Dead* a smart and fun entry point to the author's work. *Pig Iron* and *The Last Projector* are both excellent novels, but are both very challenging reads. Challenging in the best way, as they experiment with the most basic elements of narrative storytelling, taking old ideas in very new directions. Keaton does not shy away from the bizarre, nonlinear and, most notably, the unapologetically anarchistic in his novels. He does the same, to a lesser extent, here. These stories are easier to understand than his previous books, but they do introduce the author's unique style and do not pander to the reader.

The collection ends with the rules to a great zombie movie drinking game that you must absolutely never, ever consider playing.

<hr />

Wolf Hunt 2
Jeff Strand
Dark Regions Press
October 2014
Reviewed by Michael R. Collings

George Orton and Lou Flynn are having another bad day with werewolves.

Their first encounter with the creatures—detailed in *Wolf Hunt* (2011, 2014)—consisted of taking a contract to transport one on the orders of a shady but powerful underworld boss. It wasn't entirely their fault that Ivan Spinner broke loose and led them on a bloody, not-so-merry chase through the woods. In their defense, neither George nor Lou, like any rational thugs, actually believed werewolves existed until the man locked in the cage in the back of their van reached out with an extremely long, extremely hirsute arm. Eventually, after a number of hair-raising escapes and escapades, they killed him. And took off for foreign parts to lay low. (For a review, click here.)

Quick cut to some months later: a one-room hut in Costa Rica, where George and Lou are sweltering, sipping margaritas, and watching a telenovela. They are attacked by Mr. Dewey's men. They kill Mr. Dewey's men.

Another quick cut, this time to Northern Ontario: George and Lou are wrapped in blankets to avoid freezing to death and arguing about the efficacies of various tortures. They are attacked by Mr. Dewey's men and Mr. Dewey. They do not kill M. Dewey or his men. This time, they are captured. And thus (in seven pages of mayhem and witticisms) Wolf Hunt 2 begins. George and Lou are taken to winter-bound Minnesota…in a cage in the back of a van. This time their assignment is not merely to transport a werewolf but to kidnap one—a fourteen-year-old school girl named Ally. Like Ivan, she looks nothing like a werewolf. Like Ivan would have, had he had a chance, she protests at being kidnapped. Protests vehemently.

And transforms, heading for the nearby woods.

Against all of their better instincts, wishes, and judgments (and though they are professional thugs, they are not stupid thugs) George and Lou must capture Ally before she tears anyone apart, and, at the same time, avoid harming her. Low-lifes they may be, and occasional finger-breakers and knee-shatterers, but they are determined not to injure a girl, even though in her werewolf state she is eminently capable of damaging them.

What neither George, Lou, nor Ally know is that a number of others are invested in capturing Ally. On a sliding scale of Goodness, George and Lou are, it must be admitted, well over the median line onto the side of Bad. But they do have standards and try to maintain to them. Ally's position is ambivalent—as a human she is an innocent and therefore good; as a werewolf….

Mr. Dewey is venal and self-serving; he wants a brain transplant from a possibly immortal (or at least self-healing) creature and will go to any expense to get one. His colleague, an old man named Reith, craves revenge against any and all werewolves. Their hired minions will do anything for money. None of the men have any visible scruples. As a result, their positions on the scale lie well beyond George's and Lou's: they are Depraved.

None of these, however, are aware that Ally has an extended family…of sorts: her father, Shane; his girlfriend, Robyn; and his best friend, for reasons best explained by the text called Crabs. They are all werewolves. In their human forms they are (with the signal exception of Crabs) mild-mannered office workers. When they transform, they are rapacious, single-minded, gluttonous, sex-obsessed, bloody-minded murder-machines with few principles and no consciences. And they want Ally back. No matter who has to die.

Actually, the more people that have to die, the better the trio will like it. On the sliding scale, they are pure Evil (pronounced in the villain-accepted way, E-vil).

And then there is Eugene—but readers deserve to discover him for themselves.

As in his other comic-horror novels Strand establishes his plots early and then masterfully moves characters through incident after incident, each more outrageous than the last. In Wolf Hunt, there was a werewolf in a cage in a van; in Wolf Hunt 2, a werewolf, several humans, and one indeterminate, all in the same cage at the same time. One scene includes a life-or-death version of "urban surfing" from the film Teen Wolf; another describes, in great, gruesome, and gory detail, one of the most ingenious and ridiculous ways yet of killing a werewolf—all that is needed is an aluminum baseball bat; a score or so bits of silver goth jewelry, the sharper the better; super-glue; and a children's slide.

There is blood-letting aplenty, some purposefully repulsive, some necessary. The bad guys lose in appropriate ways; but the good guys (relatively speaking) are not immune to harm. By the end, rough justice has been served, Ally is safe (perhaps), and the stage—as noted in "About the Author"—may or may not be set for Wolf Hunt 3, Wolf Hunt 4, Wolf Hunt 5, Wolf Hunt 6, or Wolf Hunt: All-Vampire Edition.

Any of which would be welcome.

The next real stand out for me was Morgan's "The Humming." I think just the idea of a giant hummingbird is both awesome and terrifying all at the same time.

Braun's "Bring Back the Hound" is up there with "Juggernaut" as one of my favorites as we see as an escaped Cerberus being returned to Hades.

DJ Tyler's "Avanc" deals with the classic monsters brought up in the traditional sense that *Godzilla* was created—nuclear power! This one was a fun one as well.

Now I'll preface Kerry Lipp's tale of "Blood Run" by saying that he's a strange guy so it should be no surprise that he's including a tale about giant giraffes of all things.

As someone who greatly welcomes the return of behemoths who dwarf mankind I say that if you share the love of giant monsters that you'll want to grab up a copy of this one!

Stomping Grounds: Short Sharp Shocks Volume 2
Edited by Neil Baker
April Moon Books
December 24th, 2014
Reviewed by Stuart Conover

In the second volume of *Short Sharp Shocks* we have Neil Baker giving us the 'Stomping Grounds' of giant monsters! If you grew up loving giant creature features as much as I did than you're probably gobbling up as much as you can these days with how much new blood *Pacific Rim* and *Godzilla* tossed into the literary realm. With the Kaiju flooding the markets you might be wondering if it is too much but each of the new tales and collections have been a pleasure to read—*Stomping Grounds* is no different.

A truly fun collection of seventeen stories that range from demons to Lovecraftian influences to giant monsters, Baker has been able to run the gambit with the variety of tales found within.

You'll find work from CJ Henderson, Aaron Smith, Patrick Loveland, Christine Morgan, Konstantine Paradias, Doug Blakeslee, David Bernard, Edward Martin III, Martha Bacon, R. Allen Leider, Amy Braun, DJ Tyrer, Kerry G.S. Lipp, Michael Thomas-Knight, D.G. Sutter, Pete Mesling, and David Longshore.

While none of the tales in the anthology were bad, the following six are the ones I felt truly stood out in the terms of both quality and creativity. If you enjoy a fun take on a classic giant creature feature these are the ones which will most likely grab your attention.

Personally I feel that this anthology starts off with a bang as CJ Henderson's "Juggernaut" is a special kind of Lovecraftian inspired piece that I found to be highly entertaining.

Smith's tale about a frog from Hell didn't quite live up to it but was still quite a bit of fun.

Horror Library: The Best of Volumes 1-5
Edited by R.J. Cavender
Cutting Block Books
April 30, 2015
Reviewed by Jess Landry

How do you pick thirty-three of nearly one-hundred and fifty awesome stories spanning over five volumes for one bad-ass Best Of collection? Pick names out of a hat? Quickly flip through the past volumes and plop your finger down wherever it feels right? Whatever the method, the thirty-three stories collected for the *Horror Library: The Best of Volumes 1-5* really are something to write home about.

What sets this Best Of collection apart from other anthologies is the sheer variety of genres, subgenres and wild plots. Sure, there's the usual stuff like ghosts and monsters and zombies but because of the calibre one comes to expect from the *Horror Library*, it's a guarantee these aren't run-of-the-mill stories. There are even stories about exterminators, puppets, children made from meat chunks and magical dildos. Yeah.

In a collection of entertaining stories, a few that stood out for me include "The Exterminators" by Sara Joan Berniker. It's a short but not-so-sweet tale that could also serve as a warning to read something before you sign it. And "The Apocalypse Ain't So Bad" by Jeff Strand, which is a snarky little take on a post-apocalyptic world overrun with zombies (or mutants). Any respectable smart-ass will get a kick out of it.

As far as notable names goes, this collection has tales penned by Bentley Little, John F.D. Taff and Colleen Anderson, just to name a few. There were some new names in there for me and after reading the collection, it's safe to say I've added a few more authors to my must-read list.

Not only is the content great, but the cover artwork suits the collection to a T. Just looking at the creepy family portrait (appropriately titled "Freak Family" by William Smyers) is enough to set the tone for what's ahead.

So do yourself a favour, pick up *Horror Library: The Best*

of Volumes 1-5. And while you're at it, you might as well pick up volumes 1 through 5 and see what you're missing.

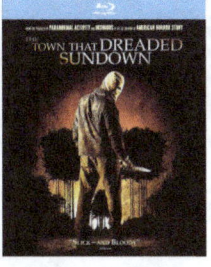

The Town that Dreaded Sundown
Director: Alfonso Gomez-Rejon
Cast: Addison Timlin, Veronica Cartwright, Anthony Anderson
Reviewed by Brian M. Sammons

Back in 1976 there was a little movie called *The Town that Dreaded Sundown*, about the real life rash of murders that terrorized the small town of Texarkana in 1946. It was a very…odd movie. It had a sort of documentary feel to it, and yet several major points were changed from the real case for the sake of the movie. Then there was the completely out of place attempts at "wacky" (yes, those are ironic finger quotation marks) humor. A very uneven movie to be sure, the film nonetheless garnered a small but loyal cult following. So when I heard about this movie, I thought it was a very odd choice for the remake treatment, and I stand by that. But this, this new movie with the same name isn't exactly a remake.

Surprise, surprise, in this day of everything getting remade, what we have here is a sequel of sorts, but a sequel to what, that is the question. To the original murders? Well unless someone else went on a new murder spree in Texarkana, which thankfully hasn't happened, that's can't be it. So it's a sequel to the movie based on real life events? Well, sort of, as in the world this movie is set in, the original 1976 film also exists as a film. It's kind of like *Book of Shadows: Blair Witch 2* in that regard, but is it better than that? Well come with me and let's find out, but if you see a guy in a white hood watching you, run.

What this *Town that Dreaded Sundown* does so well is blend fact and fiction until it's hard to tell the two apart. Things start off here at the annual showing of the old 1976 movie to the residents of Texarkana, which is a real

tradition. But when a couple leaves the drive-in early they are attacked by the infamous sack-masked killer who murders the boyfriend, but allows the girl to escape. From then on, this new faceless killer makes a special connection with the girl, calling her and taunting the police through her, all the while continuing to kill locals in gruesome and violent ways.

This *TtDS* is far more slasher than the original, but also far more a mystery, as it has a central protagonist who actively does the Nancy Drew bit and stats to look into the case she's been dragged into. It is also much better made, as director Alfonso Gomez-Rejon shows real skill and I look forward to seeing what he does next. The kills are nice and bloody, so gore hounds will be happy, and it has plenty us suspense, so horror fans into more than gore will dig it too.

The one part of this movie that falls flat is the ending. It is so "been there, seen that" that it's a real letdown when compared to just how good the entire movie was before it. I had heard through various sources that the ended suffered from some studio meddling, as I would like to think that the filmmakers of this movie would know better than to use this ending unless it was forced on them, but I don't know. I was hoping that maybe this would be explained somehow in the specials on this Blu-ray. It was not. In fact, let's get to this "specials," shall we?

As good as this movie is, you would think that this new disc from Image Entertainment must come loaded with extras and special features, right? Well if you think a single, solitary, trailer is "loaded" then you would be right. Sadly, this is a bare bones as Blu-rays get, and that's pretty inexcusable. Come on, no extras could be done for this? Bah.

This new version/sequel of *The Town that Dreaded Sundown* is still a strong enough movie to overcome the weak ending and even weaker Blu-ray release. It is well made, beautifully shot, bloody, scary, and just plain good. So for those reasons I give this a recommendation.

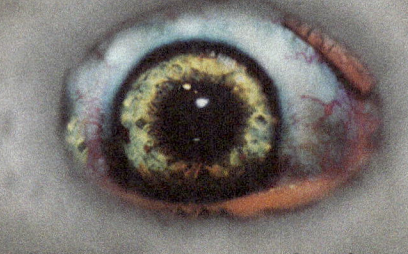
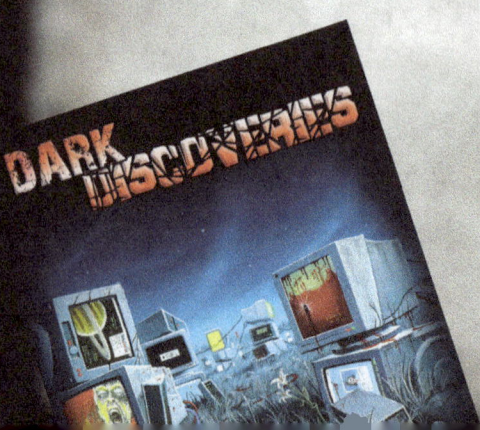